The Island At The End Of The World

To Michele,

Enjoy!.

Colin.

ISBN - 978-1-909832-15-2
Published by Pictish Beast Publications, Glasgow, UK.
Printed in the United Kingdom
First Printing: 2015. First Edition.

www.ForThoseInPeril.net

Cover Image: Copyright C.M. Drysdale, 2015.

Preface

This is the third book in the *For Those In Peril* series. Originally intended as a single, stand-alone novel (*For Those In Peril On The Sea*), it has now expanded into a trilogy of separate, but interconnected stories set in the same post-apocalyptic world. In this book, I again draw heavily on my own experiences of working amongst the islands of Scotland's west coast, and in particular, on a visit I made to the remote and uninhabited island of Mingulay in the mid-1990s. I fell in love with Mingulay the moment I first set foot on it, and, to me, it is one of the most beautiful and magical places in the world. However, while it is amazing to visit, I can imagine that living on it would be a much more daunting prospect.

While I've tried to be as true as possible to the actual landscape of the island, those who are familiar with Mingulay will see that I've used some artistic licence, and tweaked things here and there to fit in better with the flow of the story. This includes adding a non-existent rocky beach on the south-eastern corner of the island (near Skipisdale), and making the bay on the east side, by the main settlement, sufficiently sheltered to be able to act as a suitable anchorage for boats, even in the worst of weather (which, visitors beware, is far from the truth). I've also re-established flocks of grazing sheep on the island, something which no longer happens, although it did until recently, and ignored the fact that there is a lot more still standing of the old schoolhouse than simply ruins. Similarly, I've ignored the fact that there's a lighthouse on the neighbouring island of

Berneray (the Barra Head lighthouse) which, for those who are interested in such things, would make a much better base for anyone wishing to survive a zombie apocalypse, and I have pretended that it doesn't exist in the world in which this book is set. Finally, while seabird research is conducted on Mingulay, the hut which features in this book is purely fictitious, and I don't know how similar it is to any real seabird research facilities which are on the island. However, I would hope that they are less basic than the one I have invented in this book (which is an amalgamation of various marine biology research facilities where I've lived and worked over the years – some of which were much less salubrious than others).

In addition to drawing on my own experiences of Mingulay, I also drew on a series of events that have become part of sailing folklore, but, unusually for such things, the true stories behind them more than live up to the myths that have grown up around them. These events are those that took place during the Golden Globe race to be the first to sail single-handedly and non-stop around the world. In the late 1960s, while America was preparing to put a man on the moon, this feat of endurance had yet to be achieved, and towards the end of 1968, a series of vessels set out to do what some considered beyond the realms of human capability.

It might have been called a 'race', but winning it was less about being the fastest, and more about being the first to manage to keep their boat, and their sanity, intact long enough to make it across the finishing line. Amongst the tales of survival at sea, and unknown to anyone at the time, something more bizarre was going on alongside the race itself. One of the competitors, for reasons which remain unclear to this day, started faking his position, giving the false impression that he was sailing faster and further than he actually was. With radio being their only point of contact (as was the case in the 1960s), he managed to keep up this subterfuge for many months, never venturing out of the Atlantic, into the dangers of the Southern Ocean, before finally succumbing to the pressure that he'd be found out. His boat was eventually discovered abandoned and drifting, with a diary on board which tracked his apparent descent into insanity and presumably suicide. This then, provided the inspiration for some of the events which unfold in this book.

As always, there are many people to thank for the help, inspiration and encouragement they provided during the writing of this book. They include Stephen Burges, Andrea Airns, Chris Parsons (thanks especially for the suggestion about the 'red-neck hot tub'), Anna MacLeod, Barry Nichols, Emily Lambert, Lilian Leiber and Liz Small. Thanks, as always, also goes to Gale Winskill of Winskill Editorial (*www.winskilleditorial.co.uk*), for her help and advice.

Finally, the biggest thanks of all must go to Sarah: for her patience as I developed the basic plot for this book; for her editing advice (which, I've learned over the years, is always better than my own); and for her support throughout the writing process, and throughout my life. If there were ever a zombie apocalypse, you'd be the one I'd move Heaven and Earth to save (and the guinea pigs!).

The real-world locations where the fictional events of *The Island At The End Of The World* take place.

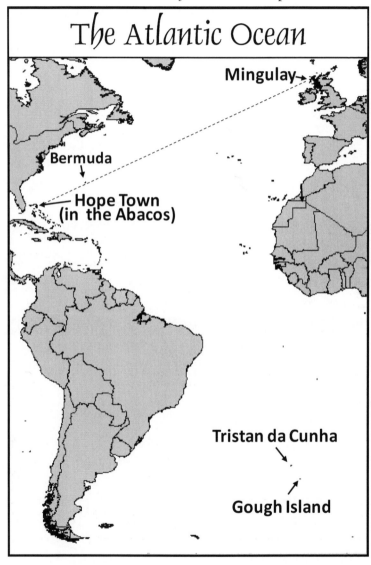

The Atlantic Ocean

Mingulay

Bermuda

Hope Town
(in the Abacos)

Tristan da Cunha

Gough Island

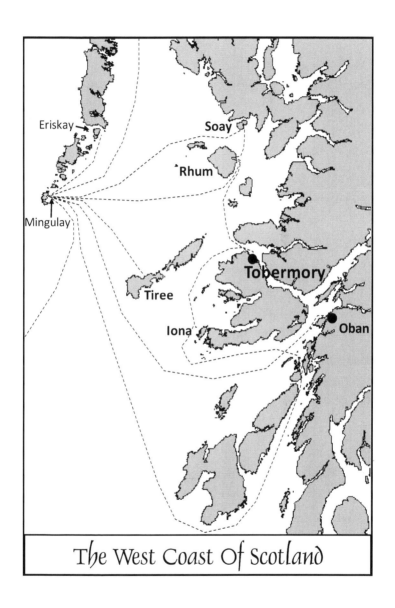

Eriskay

Soay

Rhum

Mingulay

Tiree

Tobermory

Iona

Oban

The West Coast Of Scotland

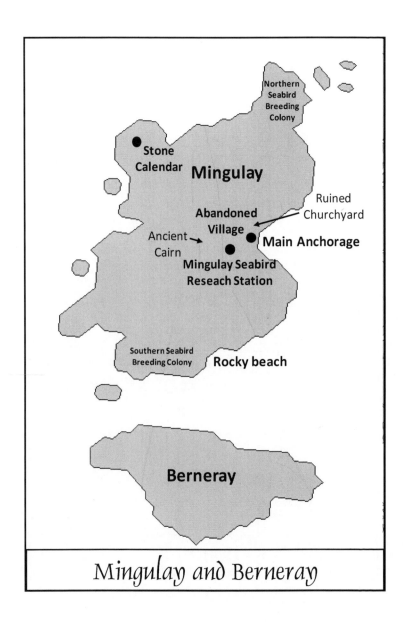

Mingulay and Berneray

One by one the lights around us blinked and went out, until ours was the only one left. Our candle flickered and guttered, and we wondered how long before we, too, would be swallowed up by the ever-encroaching darkness that was the end of the world.

Prologue

'Hey, Jack, what's that?' Andrew pointed over the older man's shoulder. The two of them had been sitting in the cockpit of Jack's large sport-fishing boat since before the sun went down, drinking rum and coconut water. It was the first drink either of them had had in many months, but for the first time in what seemed like a very long time, it felt like they had something to celebrate. Around them, four sailboats that, like Jack's boat, had clearly seen better days, rode at anchor, while further off, the shorelines of low-lying islands were just visible in the darkness.

A chart lay on the table in front of the two men, a series of small crosses marked on it, each with a date pencilled alongside in Jack's neat, but spidery handwriting. Rob and his crew had been gone for almost two weeks, and today, they'd reached the point of no return; they were now closer to their journey's end than to its beginning. If everything carried on as well as it had until that point, they'd reach their destination in another couple of weeks, and that would be when they'd finally find out if it had all been worth it; they'd find out if Mingulay was still the paradise that Rob remembered, or whether it was as infested with infected as the islands which lay all around the shallow channel, in a remote corner of the northern Bahamas, where Jack's boat was currently anchored.

Jack turned to look where Andrew was pointing and saw a bright light burning high in the sky. It was moving fast towards the western horizon, but before it got there, it seemed to hit something they couldn't see and explode. Glowing fragments radiated out in all directions, colliding with other invisible objects and causing further explosions.

Soon, it seemed like half the sky was filled with glowing, burning balls of fire that spun through the heavens. They were bright enough to mask the stars, and the night was now so filled with light that Jack could clearly see the people on the decks of the nearby boats as they gazed upwards in awe and fear. These five boats — six if you counted the one that had departed two weeks before — with a total of twenty-seven people on board, were all that was left of the once much larger Hope Town community.

'I don't know, Andrew.' Jack placed his glass carefully on the table in front of him. He'd heard people talk about this type of thing back before the world changed. Then, it had been little more than idle speculation, but now it seemed like it was becoming reality. The Earth's orbit was crammed with defunct satellites, old booster rockets and other pieces of abandoned junk, left there by what had, until not so long ago, been a thriving space industry. This meant there was always a risk that one of the active satellites would be hit by a piece of trash zooming around, high above the Earth, at unimaginable speeds. If this happened, the satellite could be thrown out of its assigned position and into the path of another one, damaging both of them. Once started, this could happen again and again, destroying satellite after satellite, until there was nothing left: it was an unstoppable chain reaction, called by those in the know 'the Kessler syndrome'.

In the past, space agencies had to constantly manoeuvre their space craft to prevent this from happening. Now, with no one left to monitor the risks and order the appropriate actions to be taken, it seemed like it had finally come to pass. It was a measure of just how badly humans had screwed up their planet that in a little over half a century since they'd first ventured into the space which surrounded it, they'd made even that uninhabitable.

Jack frowned. 'Andrew, turn on the GPS.'

Andrew eyed Jack curiously. 'Why? We already know where we are.'

'I just want to check something,' Jack answered in his soft, southern American accent.

For a moment, Andrew hesitated, but the note of concern in Jack's voice made him obey without further questioning. Leaning backwards, Andrew pressed the power button on the GPS set into the bulkhead behind where he was sitting. He watched as the screen lit up and it started to search for the signals it used to work out where they were. Soon it had picked up the required four satellites and had provided a position.

Jack nodded towards the machine. 'Go to the receiver page.'

Andrew pressed the appropriate buttons and the screen changed. Now, it showed a plot of all the satellites the GPS was picking up signals from, and their positions relative to the boat.

'Shouldn't there be more than that?' Andrew was staring intently at the screen when one of the dots on it vanished. 'Hey, where did that one go?'

Jack walked over and stood behind Andrew. Just as he got there, another satellite blinked out, then another.

Jack's forehead furrowed. 'This isn't good.'

Andrew glanced at him. 'What d'you mean? What's happening?'

For a man in his sixties, Jack still had a surprisingly large amount of hair, but like his beard, it was as white as snow. As the wind ruffled through it, he reached up and did his best to flatten it down again. 'It's the satellites, Andrew. Something must have gone wrong with one of them. They're crashing into each other. If this goes on much longer there won't be any left.'

They both stared at the screen, watching the signals vanish one by one. Soon, a message flashed up, telling them that there were no longer enough for the GPS to calculate a position. A few minutes after that and the last satellite disappeared.

'Christ!' Andrew's attention was drawn back to the chart and the line of crosses that snaked out into the middle of the Atlantic. 'How's Rob going to know where they are? How're they going to get there safely?'

Jack gazed up at the still-burning objects racing through the sky far above them. 'They've got a sextant. Jon told me once.'

Andrew was much younger than Jack, and unlike the older man, he was local, having lived almost his entire life on the nearby islands. Or at least that was where he'd lived until the infected came and drove him, and the other survivors, from them. He shifted nervously on his seat. 'Do any of them know how to use it?'

'I don't know.' Jack hesitated momentarily and then carried on more quietly. 'I hope so.'

Suddenly, the peacefulness of the night was shattered by a single roar, followed by another, then another. Jack's eyes shifted from the sky to the nearest island. There, he saw infected emerging from the remnants of buildings and out of the bushes. They were staring up into the night sky, reaching out towards the brightness. They didn't know what it was, but they assumed it meant their favourite prey was near, and for them, that was humans. They milled around, howling and moaning in frustration, unable to find anything worth attacking.

Jack took his binoculars and examined them. It was the first time he'd seen infected in such numbers since the night the hurricane had ripped their community apart, killing many who'd survived the infected's initial onslaught. Most of them were thinner and more emaciated than ever, yet still the urge to attack, to rip, to kill, burned deep within their hearts. Here and there, amongst these skeletal figures, Jack spotted ones that were different: some had bellies bulging from their otherwise withered frames, while others seemed to have suffered little or no hunger at all. These infected had clearly been eating recently and regularly, and Jack wondered how they were sustaining themselves. Surely there could be little left for them to feed on? All the stray dogs, the feral cats and the rats must have been consumed by now. And yet, while most looked close to death, some of the infected were clearly not just surviving, they were thriving. There must be some resource they were consuming that others were not. Did this mean the infected were doing something different now? Or had these individuals always been there, and were only now visible as the others thinned? Jack wondered what this might mean for their ability to survive. They'd always assumed the infected would eventually starve to death, but did this mean that maybe they wouldn't? Or at least, that *some* of them wouldn't? Maybe they'd always be there, lurking in the shadows, waiting to attack the moment they tried to return to the land.

Jack lowered his binoculars and picked up his drink again before draining it. As he did so, a creeping sense of despair started to work its way into his mind. Every time the situation worsened, they'd adapted to it, but just as it seemed like they were about to get back on top, something else happened and it would worsen some more. The hurricane had shown them they couldn't hope to survive in the Abacos in the long term, not with the infected on the nearby islands, the drifters in the surrounding sea, and the ever-present risk of more storms. Yet, Rob had come up with a plan that might just save them all, and he and his crew were now halfway across the Atlantic to check it out.

If it turned out to be a viable option, the other boats in the community would all need to be able to follow in Rob's path, but with the loss of the GPS satellites, this would be much more difficult than they'd originally anticipated. Indeed, without a working GPS, Rob might not even make it to Mingulay in the first place. If that happened, the rest of them, those that made up what was left of the Hope Town community, would have no other option but to stay in the Abacos, and then their only chance would be if the infected died off sooner rather than later. And now it looked like some of the infected were able to survive, even though there were no humans, or seemingly any other animals, left on the land for them to feed on. If Rob's plan failed, one way or another, Jack couldn't help but think that it would signal the end. It might be long and drawn-out; it might take years; but still, looking back, they'd see that Rob's failure to find a safe haven where they could rebuild their shattered community marked the point where the end had begun.

Chapter One

Ahead of us, silhouetted against the rising sun, was the first land we'd seen in almost two months. It was little more than an isolated rock rising above the ocean, but it was land nonetheless. More importantly, it was the first landmark we'd seen since the night we'd lost the GPS satellites, and with them, our ability to know exactly where we were. We'd all taken our turn trying to use the sextant and make the required calculations, but while Rob was the best at it the resulting positions were still too erratic for us to have any idea of where we really were. This meant that since the satellites went down, we'd been navigating by dead-reckoning and little else. Rob had told us to try to steer due east at all times, meaning that, based on our last accurate position, we should reach land somewhere around northern France. Yet, the ocean currents we were sailing with were strong, and they'd been pushing our catamaran northwards with every passing mile. How far off course they'd pushed us, we didn't know, and this meant the land we'd now spotted could be anywhere between Cornwall and the Faroe Islands.

'Hey, CJ, is that a lighthouse?' Jeff was shielding his eyes from the early morning sun and squinting towards the horizon.

I screwed up my eyes, trying to get a better look at the island, and the object that I could just make out perched on its summit. 'I think it is.'

Jimmy picked up the binoculars and started to raise them up to get a closer look when Mike batted his arms down.

'What d'you do that for?' Jimmy sounded hurt. Mike rarely treated him as roughly as that.

'Jimmy, you'd be looking straight at the sunrise.' Mike sounded exasperated. 'You'd burn your eyes out.'

'Oh,' Jimmy replied sheepishly, 'I hadn't thought of that.' Then, after a brief pause, 'Thanks.'

Mike ruffled his younger brother's hair. 'Not to worry, that's what I'm here for.'

I watched the scene play out in front of me: it seemed so normal, and yet the world we now found ourselves in was anything but. At nineteen, I was only a few years older than Mike, but while Mike played the role of older brother, more often than not, as the only woman on board, I ended up playing the role of mother to all three boys. I didn't mind it most of the time, but every now and then, it would cause friction between us, and I sometimes wished that Rob, as the only other adult on board, would act more like a parent and not just as the captain of our little crew.

Rob and I had been sailing across the Atlantic when everything changed, and when we had finally reached the other side, we'd found the world we'd known before was gone, all because of a disease. It sounded so unlikely, but this was no normal disease. Humans had lived alongside the rabies virus for as long as they'd been on the planet: an uneasy truce meaning that while the disease killed people, it did so slowly and they rarely passed it onto others before they died. Then someone decided that humans should strike back. They created a vaccine in an attempt to wipe out the virus, but that wasn't what had happened. Instead, the vaccine caused it to mutate. Suddenly, it became more virulent, but less deadly. People were now overwhelmed in hours or minutes, rather than weeks or months, and it no longer killed them; it just took over their brains, turning them into violent killing machines that attacked anyone close to them, thus passing on the disease. Spurred on by its increased contagion, the mutated strain of rabies spread like wild fire, bringing down country after country, taking over the land mile by mile, until all that was left of humanity were a few scattered groups, clinging on in remote outposts, where they could somehow avoid the disease, and the infected it created.

There had been four of us on the boat originally: Bill, Rob, Jon and me. Bill had been our captain and Rob his second-in-command, while Jon, just a few years older than me, came next in the onboard pecking order, and I, as youngest and least experienced, came last. I was born Camilla Jamieson, but everyone's called me CJ since before I can remember. Everyone, except my mother when I was in trouble and Jon, who, when we'd first met, insisted on calling me 'Cammie', just because he knew how much it annoyed me. Rob and I were both British, while Jon and Bill were American, and together, the four of us had made up a barely functional crew. At least, that was how it was in the beginning. Then we'd discovered that in our absence, the world had changed beyond all recognition, and we'd realised we'd need to learn to work together if we were to have any hope of surviving.

Our numbers grew to six when we rescued Mike and his younger brother, Jimmy, just off the coast of what was left of Miami. By then, they'd survived a week on their own, and I doubted they'd have been able to keep going much longer if we hadn't found them when we did. We dropped to five when we lost Bill, but then we'd found the Hope Town community, nestled in a sheltered anchorage in the northern Bahamas. Jeff came on board after his family were killed, making us six again. Then we lost Jon and were back down to five. I still thought about Jon a lot, cried over his loss and why it had happened. I hadn't known him long, and at first, I'd despised him, but as the situation had worsened, he stopped acting like a spoiled brat and started acting like the grown man he was. That was the Jon I'd fallen in love with, and that was the Jon I'd lost. I wasn't alone in having lost someone: everyone who'd survived as long as we had had lost people they loved, but knowing this didn't make my pain any less.

Hope Town had been an oasis in a world fallen apart; a little piece of normality that we hoped would allow us not just to survive, but to live, despite all that had happened … only it didn't last. The second hurricane had been unexpected and brutal, and only six of the twenty-seven boats in the community made it through intact. The storm had shown us that Hope Town wasn't a place where we could survive forever, and it was Rob who'd come up with an alternative plan. There was a remote, uninhabited island he'd once visited, which he thought would allow us to regain a toe-hold on the land and give us a better chance of rebuilding our lives, far from the threat of the disease. The only problem was that it meant we'd have to cross the Atlantic to get to it, and the others in the community were unwilling to take the gamble of leaving Hope Town and crossing an ocean, without knowing exactly what they were heading for. After all, it seemed like the virus was everywhere, and how was anyone to know whether Rob's remembrance of an island was any safer than where they were now?

To solve this problem, Rob had offered to sail ahead, so that he could report back on the situation using our shortwave radio. Then the others would have all the information they'd need to decide if they wanted to follow, or not. By then, Hope Town was just a reminder of what had happened to Jon, and I was more than willing to go with Rob. Jeff was keen to go with us too, for similar reasons, plus we'd become like a family by then and we didn't want to be split up. Mike and Jimmy felt the same, so the five of us had set off, the three boys seeing it as an opportunity for adventure after having been cooped up in the anchorage in Hope Town for so long.

The first part of the voyage went like clockwork, and we'd reached the halfway mark within a couple of weeks. Then, as suddenly as if someone had flipped a switch, it all started to go wrong. First, we lost the GPS satellites, meaning we no longer knew exactly where we were. Then the storms started: one after another, they rolled over us in what seemed like an endless procession, slowing our progress to a snail's pace, sapping our morale, and even threatening to sink us at times. With the storms, we lost the opportunity to fish for fresh food and, instead, we had to survive on the rapidly dwindling supplies we'd brought with us from Hope Town. For Mike and Jimmy, this didn't matter too much because the seasickness that came with the storms meant they could barely keep anything down for more than a few minutes after having eaten. From then on, for the most part, they remained in their bunks or hunkered down in a corner of the cockpit, staring off into the distance, looking grey and gaunt.

The storms meant Rob and I needed all the help we could get to keep the boat moving forward, but the seasickness meant the two brothers were in no condition to help, and at thirteen, Jeff wasn't able to take on much in the heavy weather. This left just the two of us, and I was hardly experienced enough to remain alone on deck in such strong winds. The result was that Rob had barely slept for more than a few minutes at a time for I don't know how many days. I could tell this was wearing him down, taking a heavy toll on him both physically and mentally. Rob wasn't a natural leader and he'd only took on the role when we'd lost Bill. While he'd grown somewhat used to being in charge on board when we were still in Hope Town, he'd always had Jack and Andrew to talk things over with and to share responsibilities. Out on the ocean crossing, we were on our own again, and I could see his old insecurities pushing their way back to the surface, especially after the radio antenna had been damaged and we'd lost contact with those who remained in Hope Town.

At first, Rob talked to me about how he was feeling and the pressure he felt he was under. He was regretting bringing the boys, and now thought he should've left them behind, taking others with more sailing experience instead. He worried about whether we'd be able to find our way to our destination without the help of the GPS satellites to tell us which way to go. He was concerned that the whole trip might fail; that Mingulay wouldn't prove to be the answer to our problems that he hoped it would be ... and what that might mean for those we'd left behind.

As the storms continued, day after day, week after week, I noticed Rob was starting to talk less and less, both to me and to the others, and when he did speak, it was only to bark orders. Before my eyes, he was sinking into himself, just as he had after Bill's death, and this worried me deeply. I needed Rob to keep it together because, without him, there was little chance the rest of us would survive. Yet, I couldn't tell him this because it would just add to the pressure he was already piling on himself, and so make the situation even worse.

Eventually, the storms eased and Rob could finally get some rest, but no sooner had he gone below than the island appeared over the horizon to our south-west. By my reckoning, it would be several hours before we got anywhere near it, and this left me torn between letting Rob catch up on some much-needed sleep and calling him out on deck so he could see that we might finally be close to reaching our destination. After a couple of minutes deliberating, I came to a decision. 'Jeff, take the wheel. I'm going inside.'

Jeff jumped to his feet and was over at the helm in an instant, eager as always to help. His had been a sailing family and he'd grown up around boats, so despite the fact that, at thirteen, he was the youngest of the three boys, he was generally the one Rob and I turned to first when we needed an extra set of hands. Jimmy was a few months older than Jeff, but he'd never been on a yacht of any kind before we'd rescued him and his brother as they fled from the disease. At sixteen, Mike was the oldest of the three boys, and he'd been gradually building his sailing skills, soaking up everything Rob taught him, but then came the storms and the seasickness, and he'd barely been able to stand much of the time, let alone assist us with running the boat. Looking at him now, I could see he'd lost a worrying amount of weight over the past few weeks and was little more than skin and bone. I made a mental note that we'd need to do something about that as soon as we were able, but before we could, we'd need to rebuild our stores because there was little food of any kind left on board.

As I approached the glass door of the cabin, I noticed my reflection and saw that Mike wasn't the only one who'd lost weight. I'd never been particularly fat, but now my cheeks looked sunken and hollow. Some of the girls I'd gone to school with, back before everything changed, would've given anything to be this thin and would've said I looked amazing, but to me, after all that had happened, I just looked tired and ill. I took a step closer and examined my reflection in more detail. I couldn't remember the last time I'd looked at myself so closely, and was shocked by the face that stared back. Before all this, I'd been the type of person who'd always had perfect hair and make-up, and a tan to die for. Now, my hair hung dull and lifeless, caked in salt and tied back in a functional ponytail to keep it out of the way. My face was weather-beaten and my skin was flaking away on my cheeks and nose. For the first time, I noticed wrinkles around the corners of my tired-looking eyes and dark bags beneath them, while my lips were blistered and peeling. It was mid-way between my nineteenth and twentieth birthdays, but I looked so much older and more haggard. I shrugged to myself: there was nothing I could do about it and given all the other problems we now faced, my appearance barely registered as something to worry about. Maybe if Jon had still been here, I'd have cared more, but with him gone, there seemed little point.

I slid the door open and stepped inside, seeing Rob curled up on one of the seats, using his waterproof jacket as a makeshift blanket. I left him sleeping for the time being and walked as quietly as possible across to the chart table, to see if I could work out the name of the island we were now approaching, and therefore, where we were. We had a chart laid out on which we'd marked any positions we'd calculated using the sextant, but rather than forming a neat line indicating our route, they were scattered all across the ocean, some of them hundreds of miles apart, even though they were meant to mark positions on successive days. I looked at the one I'd calculated the day before, and tried to work out which island was closest, but the map was not detailed enough, showing as it did, the whole of the North Atlantic.

'What're you doing in here? Who's looking after the

boat? What's happened?' I turned to see Rob struggling to his feet. I wasn't the only one who was looking worse for wear. Rob had the same dark bags under his eyes that I did, and both his hair and beard were unkempt and uncared for. There were flecks of grey in them which I was sure hadn't been there before and, like me, he was starting to resemble someone much older than his actual age of forty.

I did my best to calm him down. 'Don't worry. Nothing's happened. Jeff's got the wheel and it's calm enough now for him to be able to handle it.'

Rob yawned and stretched. 'So how come you're in here?' He was clearly on edge, fretting about what might be going on outside. He'd been like this for weeks and I was worried that if the pressure he was putting on himself didn't let up soon, it might send him over the edge.

I felt my lips crack as I tried to give him a reassuring smile. 'I was just coming to wake you, actually.'

Rob frowned. 'So something *has* happened?'

I shook my head. 'No. It's just that there's an island out there. I think we might've made it.'

'An island?' Rob turned, weaving his head back and forth as he tried to see it out of the windows at the front of the cabin. 'What island?'

'I was just trying to work that out. It's got a lighthouse …' I ran my eyes over the chart, trying to see if there were any lighthouses marked on it, but there were none.

Rob scooped up his jacket. 'What does it look like?'

The question confused me. 'The island?'

'No,' Rob moved towards the cabin door, 'the lighthouse.'

I replayed the image of the tall, narrow building in my mind. 'Like the one in Hope Town, but all white.'

Rob nodded. 'That sounds promising!'

Before I could ask why, Rob had pulled on his raincoat and stepped out into the cockpit. I took one last look at the chart, then followed after him. Outside, Rob was already on the foredeck, binoculars raised, taking care not to look too close to the rising sun as he stared at the slowly approaching island. I went forward and stood beside him. He must have felt my presence because he lowered the binoculars and smiled for the first time in weeks. 'I think it's Flannan … or North Rona. Either way, it's Scotland somewhere.'

I scrunched up my eyes, trying to get a better look at the distant island, but it didn't work. 'How can you tell?'

He held the binoculars out to me. 'Because of the shape of the lighthouse and how it's built.'

I took the binoculars and examined the tower, but I couldn't see anything distinctive. 'It doesn't look that much different from the ones in the Bahamas.'

Rob grinned. 'Exactly! It means they're British. The lighthouses in the Bahamas were designed by the same people who built the ones in Britain: they all have the same basic layout. And if they're British, then there are really only two that are this far out.' He took the binoculars back and lifted them again, this time scanning the horizon to the left and right of the island. 'I can't see any other islands, so I'm guessing it's North Rona. Even if I'm wrong, it doesn't matter, it still means we've made it.' He turned and strode back towards the cockpit, calling back to me as he did. 'Come on. Let's see if we can find something we can have as a celebration.'

I watched him walk away, noticing a spring in his step that I hadn't seen in a very long time. I smiled to myself, knowing that with Rob's spirits back up, we were in a much better position than we had been when he was weighed down by the responsibilities of leadership.

Chapter Two

'What d'you think?' I glanced at Rob nervously.

He shifted uncomfortably from one foot to the other and back again. 'I don't know, CJ. It wasn't there last time I was here.'

We were anchored in the sparkling turquoise waters of a sheltered bay, fringed with golden-white sand, on the east side of a small island. Off to either side, the island rose in height, rearing up to form towering cliffs that no infected could ever hope to scale. On the shore, lit by the light of the low autumn sun, I could see the crumbling ruins of small stone buildings scattered amongst tussocks of grass. Here and there, sheep grazed peacefully, while seabirds wheeled overhead. Up to the left, a wooden hut stood silhouetted against the background, its well-maintained appearance contrasting sharply with the ramshackle remains of all the other buildings I could see.

The sail from North Rona to Mingulay had, thankfully, been short and uneventful, and now we were here, we were keen to get ashore to see what we could find. Mike, Jimmy and Jeff were already eyeing up the sheep and talking about cooking up as many lamb chops as they could consume without making themselves sick, but Rob and I were more cautious. The hut looked relatively new and in good condition, suggesting there might've been people living on the island when everything changed. If there had been, would they still be there? And would the virus be there with them?

Rob's mood had improved dramatically since we'd finally reached the other side of the Atlantic, and he was almost back to his former, more confident self. It also helped that we'd been able to fish as we made our way south from North Rona, catching more than our fair share of mackerel, cod and fish that Rob called 'coalies' which I'd never eaten before, but that tasted great. The result of this was that we were all now well enough fed to start putting back on some of the weight we'd lost on the voyage over. The unexpected presence of the hut, however, threatened to set Rob back, and I could see he was starting to fret once again that he'd dragged us all this way for nothing. I knew it wasn't just us he worried about; it was also those we'd left behind. He knew there was a lot riding on our voyage for everyone who was part of the Hope Town community, and our success or failure would pretty much determine the success or failure of the community as a whole. We hadn't been able to communicate with those back in the Abacos since the radio antenna had come down, and I knew they'd be worrying about what had happened to us and whether we'd been lost.

As we'd sailed down from North Rona, Rob had talked eagerly about taking the shortwave radio ashore and setting it up on the island. This would give it a greater range, and make it more likely we'd be able to contact Jack and the others again, but that was before we'd arrived and found the hut. Now, before we could even start thinking about doing anything like that, we'd have to make sure the island was, indeed, uninhabited and free of the infection.

On our arrival, we'd sailed around the island twice, past the impregnable cliffs that formed the northern and southern ends, and the entire west side, past a rocky beach at the south-eastern corner, which was the only other place where you could hope to land, and past a natural arch that reminded me of the one at Hole-in-the-Wall, where we'd had our first inkling that something bad had happened to the world all those months ago. Mingulay was just under three miles long, and about a mile and a half across at its widest point, meaning it was small, but it seemed to offer us all that we might need: a sheltered place to anchor boats; few places where drifters could come ashore unnoticed in the night; and I could make out what looked like several small streams making their way down to the shore close to the middle of the bay, suggesting a reliable source of fresh water.

A second smaller island lay not far from its southern limit, but this seemed to offer few of the advantages of Mingulay, beyond the fact that it, too, was surrounded by imposing cliffs. For this reason, we focussed our attention on the larger one, and during our circumnavigations, we'd kept a keep close eye on the shore; but apart from the hut and the occasional sheep, it looked as deserted as Rob remembered. The hut, therefore, remained the big unknown: who, or what, might be lying in wait inside?

'D'you think someone's been living here?' Mike was standing next to Rob and me as we gazed towards the island, while Jimmy and Jeff lounged on seats in the cockpit. I picked up the binoculars and examined the hut more closely. It was the size of a small cottage, but it didn't have the appearance of a home. Instead, it looked more basic and functional. 'I don't think it's a house. It looks more like a glorified shed or something like that.'

I passed the binoculars to Rob, and he examined it too. 'Yeah, it's not exactly homely, is it? But that doesn't mean there aren't infected inside. Someone's clearly been doing something here, and they could've brought the disease with them. They could be in there right now, just waiting for someone to be stupid enough to open the door and let them out.'

Jeff sat up, worried by what Rob had just said. 'How're

we going to find out?'

Jimmy sat up, too. 'Find out what?'

'We've come all this way, haven't we? We can't just turn back because there might be infected in there, can we?' Jeff got to his feet and padded over to where the rest of us were standing. 'I mean, it could just as easily be empty,' he looked round. 'Couldn't it?'

I ruffled Jeff's hair. 'That's very true.' I was impressed with how Jeff was coming along. When we'd taken him in, he'd been little more than a child, but now he was starting to develop into an adult, willing to take on responsibilities and take part in discussions about what we were going to do next. I still heard him crying in the night from time to time, but, given what he'd been through, that was only to be expected, and I knew I did the same. Jimmy was growing up too, and while it would have been nice for both of them to have been able to enjoy their childhoods a little longer, in the world we now lived, they had no choice, but to grow up fast. Mike was maturing, too, and becoming a quiet, but sensible young man. As the older brother, he felt responsible for Jimmy, and keeping him alive and safe was his number-one priority. With Jon gone, I knew that Rob and I would have to start relying on him more and more, especially now that it would be just the five of us until the others made the trip across the ocean to join us. And, depending on what was in the hut, that might not happen.

Rob leant forward on the guard rail that ran along the side of the catamaran. 'I guess one of us is going to have to go ashore and check it out.' He turned to face the three youngsters. 'Any volunteers?'

Surprise and shock shot across their faces; much as they tried to act tough, they were still terrified by the merest possibility of encountering any infected, and I couldn't blame them. The infected had to be seen to be believed: their speed; the anger burning deep in their eyes; the unrelenting violence of their actions as they attacked anyone they could grab hold of, tearing into them, ripping them apart. They showed no mercy, driven, as they were by a virus which had taken over their brains and erased all that had once been human. Now, they were little more than machines; machines the virus used to ensure it was spread as far, and as fast, as possible.

Seeing the looks on the boys' faces, Rob laughed. 'Don't worry, I was only joking. I'll be the one going ashore.'

I felt my eyes narrow as I replied, 'No, you won't; it's too risky and you're too important. I'll go.'

Jeff stepped forward. 'I'll go with you.'

He was trying to sound strong, but the tremor in his voice gave away his true feelings; yet, still he'd volunteered. I glanced at him: he was still growing into his lanky teenage body, and this left his movements clumsier than usual. While I appreciated his offer, I knew I'd be better off on my own. I also knew I'd be able to move faster and react quicker if I didn't have to worry about Jeff's safety as well as my own. While I wasn't *that* much older than him, I'd become like a mother to him and because of this, I felt he was my responsibility in a way I didn't necessarily feel for Jimmy and Mike. It wasn't that I didn't care about what happened to them — I did, deeply — but it was different from how I felt about Jeff. Our shared pain at how, and why, we'd lost those closest to us had created a bond between us that went well beyond how I connected with the others, even Rob, who I'd known the longest. 'Thanks for the offer, Jeff, but I'll go on my own.'

Rob let go of the guard rail and straightened up. 'No,

you won't. I couldn't ask you do to anything that's potentially so dangerous. It'll be me that's going.'

I scowled at him. 'Rob, I know you're the captain, and that means you get the last say, but you've got to act like one. You can't go risking your own life just because you don't want me risking mine. And besides, you're not asking me to go; I'm volunteering.'

Rob folded his arms and said nothing.

'Rob, think about when Bill died. Look at how devastating that was for us. We nearly didn't make it through that.' I didn't like bringing up the subject of Bill's death, but I felt I needed to make my point. 'If we lost you, it would be the same situation all over again, and I'm not so sure we'd make it through a second time.'

Rob stared down at the deck, avoiding my eyes. I knew he still blamed himself for Bill's death, but I also knew this was the best way to get through to him. After a minute, he looked up. 'You're right.' He sighed and sank down onto one of the seats, shaking his head slowly from side to side. 'When did you become so bloody brave, CJ? I remember when I first met you: you were such a quiet young girl, you'd barely say boo to a goose. Now look at you, and what you're offering to do.'

'I'm only doing what I have to.' I smiled at him, knowing that this was his way of saying sorry for arguing with me. 'And besides, I've had some pretty good teachers.'

Whenever I think about how I was before, it always makes me laugh, but sometimes it makes me cry, too, especially when it reminds me of all those I'll never see again. I was completely different back then, but then again, so was the world. When I first met Rob, I was still just a child. I'd thought I was so grown-up, but with hindsight I could see that I'd been far from it. My upbringing had been sheltered and privileged, so before going on to university, I'd decided to take a gap year and see how the other half lived. In a bar in Cape Town, I'd got chatting to a man old enough to be my father: Bill. It was because of him I'd ended up on the catamaran that was now my home, as part of a crew delivering the newly built catamaran from South Africa to its owners in Miami. And it was almost certainly the only reason I was still alive.

The trip itself had been a nightmare. Jon was a pompous prick back then, and Rob kept himself to himself as much as he possibly could. Only Bill had treated me well, teaching me about life at sea and giving me my first lessons in how to sail a boat. However, while I'd been learning a lot, the longer the experience went on, the more I had been looking forward to arriving in Miami and getting back to my real life in London. Yet, when we reached land again, several weeks after a sudden squall had wiped out all our electrical equipment, civilisation was gone, and with it, everything we'd known before: on the land, humanity had been replaced by the infected, and we had no choice but to remain at sea.

It was only when we rescued Mike and Jimmy that we found out about the disease and what it did to people. While the rest of us fell apart, each in our own way, Bill kept us going, and together we worked out a plan. We'd headed east to the Bahamas to see if we could find any others who, like us, had survived the onslaught of the disease. That was how we'd ended up in Hope Town, although we lost Bill along the way. His loss had been devastating, but after some initial wavering, Rob had replace him as captain. I watched how the others changed and knew that I had to leave behind the

24

stroppy teenager who'd boarded the catamaran in Cape Town, and do a bit of growing up myself. Jack had helped with that: he was the one in charge of Hope Town, although all decisions were made by the community as a whole, and I had learned a lot from him about how to handle other people, and how to survive.

As we both matured, the animosity between Jon and me evaporated and we started to realise that, underneath the facades we used to protect ourselves from the world, we were actually pretty similar. It would be easy to say that we'd just got caught up in the situation, but it was more than that. I'd never believed in the existence of soulmates until Jon — the real, grown-up Jon — and then he was taken away from me. It was Rob who'd killed him, but by then he was no longer the Jon I'd grow to love: the disease had seen to that.

Now here I was, sitting off another remote island on the other side of the Atlantic, offering to go ashore and check a hut for infected. I'd never have been this brave before, and if Jon had still been here, I probably wouldn't have been able to do it. But now, with Jon gone, I knew I couldn't let him down; I knew I had to step up, just as he had. And with no one else around who could do it — not without putting the survival of our little group, and indeed the remnants of the community which remained in Hope Town, in greater danger — what else could I do?

The rubber dinghy bumped against the sandy shore, and for the first time in more than two months, I stepped onto land. I felt the ground move beneath my feet, but I knew it was just an illusion caused by spending so much time floating around on the ever-moving surface of the sea. The hand-held radio tucked into my back pocket crackled and I pulled it out.

I pressed the transmit button. 'What did you say, Rob?'

I let the button go and waited. It was a second before it crackled again. 'I said, how's it looking from your end?'

I swept my eyes across the beach and back again before replying. 'Everything seems quiet, but I'm nowhere near the hut yet.' I glanced up at it. 'How do things look from where you are?'

I heard Rob key the microphone. 'Nothing's moving, CJ, at least not that we can see.'

'Roger that.' I tucked the radio back into my pocket and looked out towards the catamaran, the cabin's superstructure stretched between its twin hulls and its mast stuck high into the air. The once-white paintwork was now dull, grey and peeling, and I could see long strands of seaweed growing along the waterline. It had been brand-new and sparkling clean when I'd first boarded it in Cape Town, but now, just over six months later, it was a battered and weather-worn shadow of its former self. Given all it had been through, this was no surprise, and I wondered how much more it could take. No boat would last forever, and this was one of the reasons we had to find somewhere where we could live on the land once more; somewhere which was both free of the disease, and where the infected couldn't reach us.

The others were crowded on to the roof of the cabin, binoculars trained on the island, ready to warn me the moment they saw anything which might suggest trouble coming my way. We'd done this type of thing before and we all knew the drill, but there was one difference: last time, Rob had been armed with a hunting rifle, ready to shoot any infected that got too close. It wasn't that we didn't still have the rifle, we did, but we were out of bullets, so it was pretty much useless until we found some more, and I had no idea when that might happen.

I took a deep breath and started walking slowly up the sandy beach towards where the hut stood on the hill high above it. My eyes moved constantly, searching for anything which might indicate infected were coming, but everything remained still. I worried that the sound of the blood rushing through my ears might stop me hearing something important, but try as I might, I couldn't get my heart rate down; the fear and adrenaline surging through my body meant I could do nothing to stop it pounding away like a freight train.

At the top of the beach, I stopped and glanced back. There was about fifty feet of loose sand between myself and the dinghy, and I wondered how fast I could race across it if I had to. My legs were still wobbly and I was walking unsteadily. I guessed I wouldn't be able to run at full speed without tumbling to the ground, and in an emergency, that could be the difference between life and death. I pulled out my radio. 'You got anything I need to worry about?'

For a moment, there was silence. I continued to watch those back on the boat and I could see Rob scanning the island with the binoculars. Mike was beside him, pointing at something and my heart leapt into my mouth. I considered running, just in case, but I stood my ground, hoping I was misreading the signals. Finally, the radio came alive again, but it was Jeff's voice, not Rob's, and I could hear laughter in the background. 'Mike thought he saw something, but it turned out it was just a sheep!'

I breathed a sigh of relief and turned my attention back to the hut. It was a couple of hundred yards from where I stood, and the ground between me and it was covered in uneven tussocks of grass. Between these, narrow trails wove, which, judging by the small piles of dung along them, had been made by sheep and not humans. In fact, other than the hut, there was no trace that anyone had spent more than a few hours on the island in years. Here and there, in amongst the grass, I could see the remains of long-abandoned buildings: some were little more than heaps of stones; others were more recognisable, with fireplaces and chimney stacks still discernable. I wondered how long it would take until all of what had once been civilisation, for places where I'd once lived, to look like this: abandoned, decaying and overrun by nature. I felt an urge to explore them, but I knew I had to keep my attention focussed on the hut, and on finding out what was inside, before I could do anything else.

I crept forward, placing each foot carefully on the ground, trying to make as little noise as possible. I could hear the cries of seagulls off in the distance as they wheeled and circled above the island, and occasionally the soft bleating of an unseen sheep. Grass brushed against my legs, feeling alien and strange after so long on the boat. I remembered the joy of running, carefree, through long grass as a little girl, chasing others on warm summer days, but that world was long gone. Now, I wondered what might be lurking, unseen, in amongst the long stems, waiting to pounce on me. I did my best to push these thoughts from my mind as I carried on, the hut growing larger and nearer with each and every step.

Before I knew it, I was there, the closed door staring back at me; now was the moment of truth. I reached out my hand and then withdrew it, not sure of what to do next. While the day was sunny, the air blowing in off the sea was chilly, but despite this, I could feel beads of sweat running down the sides of my face. I pulled out the radio. 'Anything?'

Rob's voice came back. 'Nothing.'

I kept the radio in my hand as I tiptoed around the hut, looking for any signs that might indicate what was inside, but I found nothing. There were windows, but they were shuttered, and much as I tried, I couldn't get them to move. I returned to the door and knocked on it tentatively, half expecting to hear the unmistakable sound of an infected echoing back, but there was only silence.

I lifted the radio and spoke into it. 'I think it's clear.'

'Are you sure, CJ?' Rob sounded concerned.

'No,' I readied myself for what I knew I had to do next, 'but I'm going in anyway.'

'Just be careful,' Rob shot back.

I didn't respond. I banged on the door again, this time more forcibly, but still there was no reply. Hesitantly, I gripped the handle and twisted it. It moved, but the door didn't open. I pushed it, first gently and then harder. For a moment, it resisted, then suddenly it gave way and I tumbled forward into the darkness. Even before I hit the rough wooden floor, the smell inside struck me as hard as if I'd been punched in the face. Then I noticed something moving. The only light was coming through the open door, but as I scrambled to my feet I saw a human form moving slowly back and forth. Not knowing what it was, I bolted from the room and out into the daylight, expecting to hear the sound of footsteps chasing after me ... but there was nothing. I stopped and stared back at the hut as Rob's worried voice blared from the radio. 'What's wrong, CJ?'

'I don't know.' I paused as I considered the situation. 'There's someone, or something, in there, but I don't think it's an infected.'

The radio buzzed with static for a second before Rob replied. 'What is it then?'

I searched the darkened doorway as the door moved slowly in the breeze. I thought about the smell and then I realised what I'd seen. I pulled the sleeve of my jacket over my hand and pressed it firmly across my mouth before stepping back inside. In the darkness, the body moved, swinging gently from side to side, suspended from a coarse rope which had been wrapped around a wooden beam. A thick beard told me the body was male, but it was too dark to see much else. I stared at him, wondering how long he'd been there. His flesh was starting to decay and his belly was bloated, but it must have been too late in the year for flies because there were no maggots eating into his flesh. As I turned to leave, I noticed a notebook sitting open on a table, black writing scrawled across its white pages. I closed it and carried it with me as I emerged into the daylight once more.

'All clear?' There was a hint of anticipation in Rob's words as they emerged out of the radio.

'All clear,' I replied, hearing the excitement in my words as I spoke.

As I picked my way back to the dinghy, I thumbed through the pages of the notebook, stopping every now and then to read a sentence or two. It started out as a formal log, a record of the day's events, but gradually, as time passed, it became a diary and then a confessional, before descending into little more than scrawled ramblings. The final page was dated and I tried to work out how long ago the entry on it had been made. I'd lost track of time, but from what I could work out, it had been written only a few weeks before we'd finally reached the island. Perhaps if we hadn't been slowed by the storms, we'd have arrived in time to save him. I flicked back a few pages and scanned the writing. Maybe, by then, it had already been too late. I found the final entry again and read the single line scratched onto the otherwise blank page in a clear hand: *I can't go on*.

Rob ran his eyes over the slowly swinging figure. 'I suppose we should get him down.'

We crowded round the doorway, staring at the body hanging inside. Once I'd got back to the dinghy, I'd motored out to the catamaran and returned a few minutes later with the others. Jeff and Jimmy had run ahead excitedly, enjoying the feel of the land beneath their feet. Mike and Rob followed, both concentrating on the task ahead. As we'd climbed up the hill, I'd told them what I'd found and together we'd decided what we should do. Since the infected came into our lives, we rarely got to bury anyone we lost and it felt only right that we should do this for the lone man who had chosen to end his life rather than live in the world the way it now was.

The details of his final days were set out in black and white in the notebook. The hut, it turned out, was a small research station for scientists studying the local seabirds. The man was a postgraduate student, not much older than myself, sent ahead to open up the building for the annual field season, which would have started once the birds returned to breed. Yet, before anyone else could arrive, the disease had appeared on the mainland and swept across the country. He had an FM radio and knew exactly what was happening, but there was nothing he could do about it. Soon, he figured there was no one left who knew he was there, and having been dropped off by a local fishing vessel which had then departed, there was no way for him to get off the remote island.

He survived well at first, eating the supplies he'd brought with him and supplementing them with the wildlife he was meant to be studying, but after a while the birds left for the winter and the last of his supplies ran out. He tried catching the sheep that roamed the island, but they were too nimble for him to corner on his own. His descriptions of the way they'd sprint away as he lunged at them, only to stop a few feet beyond his reach before turning and staring at him, would have been amusing if it weren't for the desperateness of his situation. Soon, he was reduced to scouring the shoreline for anything edible he could find, living off a diet of shellfish and seaweed.

As time passed, the pressure of being alone started to wear him down. The radio stopped working soon after the outbreak on the mainland began, or rather it stopped picking up any broadcasts because there were no more broadcasts to receive. In the first weeks and months, he'd occasionally see a plane passing in the distance. While he thought there was no way of attracting its attention, its presence let him know he wasn't the only one who'd survived. Then one day he realised he hadn't seen it in a while. Days became weeks and weeks became months. Each morning he woke, hoping he'd see the plane again, and each night he'd return to the shelter of the hut, his spirits shattered once again.

He became obsessed by the plane, doing nothing but watching the skies, waiting for it to reappear. He built a signal fire on the tallest point of the island, cursing himself for not thinking of doing so before, but it remained unlit. As winter approached and the days shortened, he'd finally abandoned hope of ever seeing another human being again. He became fixated on the idea that he was the last man on Earth, and he couldn't cope with the weight of the loneliness that this piled on top of him.

I wondered if I'd have handled things any differently if I'd been in his position. While I'd lost a lot, at least I still had others around me. They'd become my family and they helped keep sane despite the madness of the world I'd suddenly found myself plunged into. If I'd been trapped alone on such a remote island, I'd probably have cracked too, and I may well have ended things in a similar way. If only he'd managed to hold on just a few weeks longer, he'd still have been alive when we arrived, but he had no idea of our plans; that we were meandering our way towards him even as he chose to end it all.

Rob stepped into the hut and I followed. While Rob held the dead man's legs, I dragged a chair across the room and stood on it, reaching up to cut the rope with a knife I'd brought ashore with me for just this purpose. Rob grunted as he took the full weight of the lifeless body and then carried it outside before laying it on the grass. In the daylight, I could see his hair was brown, almost black, but beyond that I couldn't make out any other features beneath the bloated and rotting flesh.

Rob wiped his hands on the grass. 'Where will we bury him?'

As I scanned our surroundings, my eyes settled on a place where a stone wall, topped with a cross, still reached into the sky. 'That looks like it used to be a church. D'you think there's a graveyard, too? Maybe we could bury him there. That way, he'd never be alone again.'

The others looked at me curiously. None of them had read the entries in the notebook which I had read, and none of them knew how utterly isolated and lonely he'd felt at the end. Only I knew how important it was for him not to be alone in death as he had been in his last few months of life.

'You see this soil?' Rob rubbed some of it between his hands. It was light and sandy, but with darker flecks mixed through it. 'This is why this island is perfect for us. It's so rich and fertile. It's not natural though. It's been made by people over hundreds of years, thousands even. They'd haul seaweed up from the beach and dig it into the sandy soil, filling it with nutrients from the sea. You can grow almost anything in it.' A chill gust of wind whipped across us, blowing the handful of dirt away. Rob watched it as it went. 'Well, anything which can withstand the weather.'

It had taken only a few minutes to find the old graveyard, the headstones visible above the undergrowth. Some were still readable, none of the dates more recent than over a century before, marking the point at which the island had been abandoned. Others had been worn smooth by the elements, eliminating all knowledge of who was buried there. We found a spot that overlooked the sandy bay where the catamaran was now anchored and dug a grave using spades which we'd found stored in a lean-to behind the hut. We took turns, Jeff and Jimmy tiring faster than the rest of us, and within an hour we had the grave finished.

Rob and I wrapped the body in an old tarpaulin we'd found with the spades, before carrying him over to the churchyard. In silence, we laid him to rest and marked his final resting place with a short plank of wood Jeff had found on the shore. We didn't know his name, so we had nothing to put on it, but nonetheless, we felt it was important to mark where he lay.

Back at the hut, we set about examining it in detail. Using the spades, Mike and Jeff levered open the shutters which had been nailed in place, while Rob and I opened the windows from the inside. Jimmy hovered by the door, not wanting to enter because of the smell of decay which still hung heavily on the air. With light now filling the wooden building, we could see it clearly: it was part bunkhouse, part research lab, the walls lined with maps and photographs. In one corner, there was a small wood-burning range that, when fired up, would provide heat and warmth, as well somewhere to cook. A roughly made wooden table ran along the wall under the windows, clearly designed to act as a workspace, while against the opposite wall four sets of bunk beds stood, each within touching distance of its neighbour. Two large solar panels lay near the door, next to a small wind turbine, similar to ones I'd seen before on the back of yachts. Alongside them, was a bank of large batteries of the type used to power golf carts. Rob examined these. 'Looks like a pretty good set-up; it shouldn't take us too long to get it up and running again. It's almost like he closed the whole place up, before he ...' Rob's voice trailed off.

I decided to change the subject. 'I wonder what he did for water?'

Rob walked over to the small kitchen area beside the range and turned one of the taps on a small sink, but nothing came out. He turned on the other one, expecting the same result, but instead a slow, but steady, stream of water, the colour of freshly brewed tea, emerged.

I eyed the water suspiciously. 'That looks pretty disgusting.'

Rob cupped a hand under the tap and once it had filled, he lifted it to his mouth and sipped it loudly before letting the rest fall into the sink. 'Not too bad, and perfectly drinkable,' he smacked his lips, 'if a bit of an acquired taste.'

I looked at him disbelievingly. 'But why's it so dirty?'

Rob dried his hand on his trousers. 'It must come from a stream somewhere further up the hill. The peat in the soil stains the water as it runs through it. It always happens when you get water running over peat. It doesn't look too appetising, but it's safe enough to drink.'

He turned the tap off again, but as he did so, I realised that, despite all that was here, something was clearly missing. 'There's no bathroom.' I looked again. 'Or even a toilet!'

'I guess there must be an outhouse somewhere.' Rob peered out of one of the windows. 'Maybe round the back.'

Before we could discuss this further, Jeff and Mike entered the hut, followed by Jimmy

'What *is* this place?' Jeff was examining one of the maps that were pinned to the walls.

'It's a research station. They used it to study the breeding habits of seabirds.' I walked over to him and peered at the map. It showed an outline of the island, with a cluster of coloured pins stuck in at one end, each labelled with its own unique number. 'I'm guessing these must be nest sites. I wonder what species they are.'

'How'd you know that?' Jimmy was now looking at the map, too.

I pulled the notebook out from where I'd tucked it away for safe keeping. 'I read about it in here.'

Rob took the notebook and flicked through it. 'Anything useful in it?'

'I don't know.' I took it back. For some reason I didn't want anyone else reading it. 'I've only skimmed it so far.'

Mike eyed the notebook, obviously curious about what it might contain. 'Does it say how he ended up here on his own?'

'Yes. He came here ahead of the main research team, to open up the field station and get it set up for the season, but there was an outbreak on the mainland, starting in Glasgow, and no one ever came back for him.' I tucked the notebook away again before anyone else had a chance to take it from me, and looked round. 'You know, we could turn this into a pretty civilised little place.'

Jeff wrinkled his nose. 'What about the smell?'

With the windows open, the scent of decay was already starting to dissipate, but it remained strong, assaulting our senses with every breath. Below where the body had been hanging, there was a damp spot where fluids dripping from it had accumulated. As I walked over to it, the smell intensified. I pointed to the fluids. 'Once we clean that up, I think it will go away.'

Jimmy stared at the damp patch. 'What *is* that?'

'Liquid human.' Mike laughed as he saw his little brother recoil in horror.

Rob chuckled, too. 'Not the best way to put it, but I guess it's accurate.'

For some reason, their flippancy annoyed me. After all, we were talking about another human life here, but I didn't say anything, figuring we each had our own ways to deal with things like this. Instead, I dug into a cupboard under the sink, finding some bleach, a scrubbing brush and some rubber gloves. Taking these out, I set to work, scrubbing the wooden floorboards as hard as I could. While I did this, Rob organised the boys, and together they took the solar panels outside. Soon, they had them set up and connected to the batteries, and by the time I'd finished, Rob was standing by the doorway, his hand on the light switch. 'Here goes nothing.'

He flicked it and the fluorescent light which ran along

the centre of the room pinged and flashed a couple of times before finally coming to life. The youngsters clapped and whooped in celebration, causing me to smile. It was a small thing, but it marked our first step towards taking back the land — or at least a tiny little part of it that we could hopefully, one day, call home.

'You two go that way, this time. I'll go this way, and we'll see if we can trap it against that wall there.' Mike glanced at Jimmy and Jeff. 'Okay?'

The two younger boys nodded.

'Let's go then!' With that Mike set off, the other two a few feet behind.

The three of them had been trying to catch a sheep for the last hour, but they were having little success. Just as had been described in the notebook, no matter what they tried, the sheep outfoxed them. It would let them get within a few feet, but no closer. The sheep didn't run far, though, and once it felt safe again, it would stop and turn, bleating belligerently at its pursuers. The effect was comical, but I could imagine that for a hungry man, alone on the island, it would have been soul-sapping.

While the boys chased sheep, I continued to tidy up the hut, moving things around, making space here and there for our stuff. Every now and then, I'd come across something of the dead man's and each time I made sure I put it somewhere safe. I didn't know quite why, but it felt like the right thing to do.

When I was finished, I walked to the door and examined my surroundings. Thirty feet from the back of the hut was another, much smaller wooden structure I hadn't noticed before. Above the door, stencilled in white paint, was the word 'Toilet'. Below this hung a handmade

made sign, which said 'Unoccupied'. I wandered over and opened the door, finding a simple wooden bench with a round opening that led to a deep, dark hole cut into the ground beneath. There was no plumbing, just the hole and an aroma to match its crude functionality. I closed the door again, unsure how I felt about using the outhouse. It wasn't what I was used to, and it would be unpleasant to have to venture outside to use it in bad weather, especially at night, but it would do the job it was designed for: keeping the inhabitants of the hut separated from their waste in such a way as to avoid the risk of contamination and disease.

Down below in the bay, I could see the boat riding gently at anchor. Rob was standing by the stern where he had two fishing rods dangling over the side. As I watched he grabbed one of them and started reeling something in. Moments later, I saw him pull a fish about the same length as his arm from the water and drop it onto the deck. I grinned, knowing we'd eat well tonight. I turned my attention to the island itself. The land nearest to the hut was green and fertile, and judging by the number of ruined cottages I could see, it had once supported a substantial population. Certainly, in the past, it had supported more than there were of us, even once the other people from Hope Town arrived. Further off, the island was more rugged, but in a world where infected roamed, this ruggedness was an asset that would prevent them from being able to make it ashore along most of its coastline. Coming here had been a risk, but Rob's gamble had paid off: this really did look like the perfect place to establish a community where we could live our lives, as far from the threat of the infected as was possible.

Chapter Three

'Mingulay calling Hope Town, come in Hope Town.' Rob released the transmit button for a second before pressing it again. 'Mingulay calling Hope Town. Come in, Hope Town.'

Again there was silence. I glanced at my watch; it wasn't our usual check-in time, but there might be someone listening on Jack's boat nonetheless. We were all back on the catamaran, having spent the afternoon exploring the island and double-checking that there really was no evidence of infected ever having reached it. Rob explained the local currents, and how they'd carry any drifters which came from the nearest inhabited islands away, rather than towards, us, making this very unlikely. Now we were anchored in still calm waters, it had only taken Rob a matter of minutes to climb up the mast and re-secure the radio's antennae near the top. Once he'd finished, we went inside to see if this was all we needed to do to re-establish contact with those who'd remained behind in Hope Town.

The radio hissed for a moment and then Jack's soft southern American accent emerged from it. 'Mingulay, this is Hope Town. You can't believe how good it is to hear your voice again, Rob. I was beginning to think we'd lost you. Are you all okay? Is everyone safe?'

'We're all fine, Jack. It wasn't the easiest of crossings,' Rob shook his head, remembering just how bad the voyage had been, 'but the important thing is that we got here in the end.'

'That's great to hear, Rob. You had us all worried for a while there when we lost touch.' Jack sounded relieved, and it was clear that our apparent disappearance had been weighing heavily on his shoulders. 'What happened?'

'Storms, Jack, one after the other.' Rob shook his head again. 'I've never seen anything like it. We were lucky to get through them in one piece, and we couldn't let you know what we were going through because our antenna got damaged. We couldn't get it sorted until we got here.'

'So you've made it then?' Jack asked the question eagerly. 'You've reached Mingulay?'

Rob smiled. 'Yes.'

'And?' There was a sense of anticipation in Jack's voice.

'Well,' Rob paused for dramatic effect, 'I'm happy to report that it's infected-free and just as good as I remembered.'

Jack's response was jubilant. 'That's the news we've all been praying for!'

I took the mic from Rob. 'It's perfect, Jack. I really wish you could see it: it's truly amazing. There's a nice sheltered bay to anchor in, but much of the rest of the island is lined with cliffs so there's no way any infected could ever climb up. That makes it almost impregnable to drifters. It's like a fortress or something ...'

I could hear myself starting to babble, but I was so excited that I didn't care. Jack, however, must have felt differently because he cut me off. 'Hi, CJ, good to hear your voice, too.'

There was genuine joy in the way he spoke, but there was an undercurrent of something else too. 'We might be seeing it sooner than you might think.'

The faces gathered round the radio froze, our earlier happiness evaporating in an instant. Rob took the mic

41

back. 'Jack, what's wrong?'

'It's the drifters; the ones from the hurricane. They're getting everywhere, and not just individually. There are whole flotillas of them clinging to the debris from Hope Town. We've had to move twice this week alone, just to keep clear of them.'

I remembered how the Hope Town anchorage had looked as we'd abandoned it after the hurricane had passed over us. Not only had the storm destroyed much of our community, but it had filled the bay with flotsam and jetsam. Infected clung to this, hundreds of them, possibly thousands. These same drifters were the reason we'd had to leave the place that had been our home for what seemed like forever, although in reality, it had only been a matter of months. Now it sounded like the debris in Hope Town was breaking up like pack ice in the spring, forming floating time bombs which, if they drifted into an anchored vessel, would discharge their infected cargo to attack and kill anyone on board. The existence of drifters, with their ability to turn up unexpectedly almost anywhere, anytime, was one of the biggest threats to our survival, and the reason we'd set off in search of an alternative place to live.

'Jack, I know it's tempting to set out now, but it's too late in the year.' There was a concerned look on Rob's face as he spoke. 'We only just made it through the storms, and they'll be even worse by now. You're just going to have to sit tight until the weather eases up in the spring.'

Jack sighed. 'I know. I was just letting off steam. When we lost touch with you, I began to think that this was it; that we'd have no other option, but to stay here and work out a way to cope with them. At least we now know that it won't be for forever. We just need to make it through the winter.'

Rob's brow furrowed. 'Are you sure you can last?'

There was a long pause before Jack replied. 'Yes. We'll make it; it's just going to take a lot of work. We have to be on our guard all the time; we can't relax even for a minute.' Jack sounded tired and run-down.

I took the mic from Rob again. 'Hey, Jack, you just need to keep your eyes on the prize. This place really is as perfect as Rob remembered it to be. We've spent most of the day on the island. It was so great to feel the ground beneath my feet again without having to worry too much about infected. Whenever things are getting you down, just think about how you'll be able to do that once you finally get here.'

Jack laughed tiredly at the excitement in my voice. 'That's certainly something to look forward to, CJ.'

'Rob, can I ask you something.' Rob and I were alone in the cockpit, watching the sun go down behind Mingulay. The sunset was spectacular, illuminating the thin wispy clouds that floated high in the sky, bathing us in a golden glow.

Rob turned to me. 'What?'

I didn't know when the idea had first entered my head, but as the day had worn on it had grown to become an obsession. 'I want to spend the night in the hut.'

Rob frowned. 'I'm not too sure it's okay for us to move ashore yet, CJ. We've still got to work out if it's really safe from drifters. If we were all inside the hut and a drifter somehow got on to the island, we'd be trapped there. It would be just like being back in the container, and I'm never going through anything like that again.'

I remembered the incident at Little Harbour. While they

were out looking for food Rob, Jon, Mike and Jimmy had been surprised by a pack of infected and trapped in an old shipping container, and Andrew and I had had to rescue them. Jon told me later that he thought they'd be trapped there forever, and that he'd even thought about killing himself if that had turned out to be the case.

'Actually, Rob,' I hesitated, not sure quite how he would take what I was going to say next, 'I wasn't talking about all of us. I was just talking about me, so there'd be no risk of that happening.'

Rob looked at me curiously, 'You finally got fed up of the rest of us, CJ?'

'No, it's just ...' I didn't really know how to explain it. Since Jon died, I hadn't spent a single moment alone; not truly alone. On the boat, there was always something happening and someone nearby. Now we were here, I felt I needed to spend some time on my own so that I could finally process all that had happened and work out how to deal with it properly. I knew that if I didn't, if I continued to keep it all locked away inside me, it would gradually consume me. I had to do something to stop that happening, and for some reason, I felt that spending some time on my own would be the first step towards doing this.

Rob nodded slowly. 'I know what you mean.' He glanced at his wrist — an old habit that had become pointless after his watch had stopped working the week before — and then looked back to the island. 'Okay, get your stuff. I'll run you ashore before it gets too dark for you to see anything. Take the hand-held radio with you, just in case.' He turned to me. 'Promise me you'll be careful, CJ. You know how important you are to me, don't you? I need another grown-up around here.'

I smiled. When we first met, Rob had treated me like

44

the child I was; now, here he was telling me, in his own way, that he saw me as his equal, and that he needed me. 'Thanks, Rob.'

I flicked the switch as I entered the hut and marvelled once more at the fact the lights came on. It seemed like an eternity since I'd been able to walk into a building and do that. We had lights on the boat, but they weren't real lights, just little twelve-volt ones that meant you needed to be right next to them before you could do anything like read ... not that I'd read a book in months. This wasn't because I didn't like reading, it was because I'd read everything we had on board — twice. In fact, I think I'd read pretty much every book on board every boat in the Hope Town community within the first couple of months of our arrival. I'd always been an avid reader, and reading something new was one of the things I missed most about the world having changed. It sounds weird to say that, given how much had gone, but it also felt odd to think there'd never be another book written, unless we wrote it ourselves. I didn't know about the others, but there was no way I was capable of writing a book.

I'd unearthed a couple of dog-eared paperbacks as I'd tidied up the hut earlier in the day, and I could see them stacked next to the bed I was intending to use, but for some reason, I didn't pick one of them up. Instead, I pulled out the notebook I'd found near the dead man's body and settled down on the nearest bed. The covers smelled musty and unwashed, and slightly of decay, but I was happy to have a place to bed down for the night that didn't move. Just as I opened the notebook, the hand-held radio burst into life. 'How're you doing, CJ?'

I picked it up, 'Hi, Rob. It feels a bit strange to be back on land after all this time, but I'm fine.'

There was a moment of static before Rob's voice came again. 'Have you locked the door?'

'Yes, and the windows, and I've pulled the shutters down again.' It was like I was back living with my parents, but, given the circumstances, it felt good to have someone out there, watching over me. I thought about the man we'd buried and how he'd died, lost and alone in this little hut on a remote island, far from anyone who'd ever cared for him. With Rob out on the water, I knew that no matter what happened, that would never happen to me.

The radio crackled again. 'Well, keep everything secured until the morning. I'll check out the situation from here, and let you know whether it's safe or not.'

'Goodnight, Rob.' I let go of the transmit button and then pressed it again. 'Thanks.'

I set the radio on the small shelf above the bed and snuggled down into the blanket with the notebook. Turning to the first page, I started to read.

***

I'd fallen asleep before I'd reached the end of the notebook, but I'd got far enough to reach the point where he was starting to fall apart. I was woken just before dawn by an unfamiliar sound, and I lay there for several minutes, tense and nervous, trying to work out what it was. Eventually, it came again and I realised it was the soft bleating of a sheep. Despite Rob's orders, I didn't wait for him to check on the situation before I ventured outside, figuring that there wouldn't be sheep nearby if there were infected. Taking the notebook with me, I walked along the narrow animal trail which led across to the graveyard, and to the freshly dug grave. Once there, I sat down and watched the sun coming up, the notebook open before me. I thought about Jon and what had happened to him. There was nothing I could do to bring him back and I knew I needed to let him go, but I wasn't quite ready to move on, not yet; everything was still too raw.

Suddenly, there was a noise and a shadow passed over me. I leapt to my feet, sending the notebook flying, and spun round, not knowing what I'd find. Behind me, Rob stood, a stern look on his face. 'I thought I told you to wait until I'd checked everything was safe before you came outside?'

'I can look after myself, Rob.' I was annoyed at him, both for scaring me and because he was treating me like a kid.

'I know you can,' He stepped forward until he was standing beside me, 'but you still need to be careful. We can't be complacent, not for a minute: complacency kills, CJ.'

My annoyance evaporated. 'You sound like one of those old-fashioned public information broadcasts.'

'I do, don't I.' Rob looked down at the grave. 'You okay?'

'Yeah,' I stared off into the distance, 'I guess.'

'You miss him, don't you, CJ?'

We both knew who he was talking about.

I cleared my throat. 'Yeah.'

There was a brief silence before Rob spoke again. 'It'll get easier eventually.' He reached out and put a comforting hand on my shoulder. 'It doesn't mean you'll forget him, but it does get easier. You get to concentrate on the good times rather than the bad.'

I thought about this for a moment, and then

remembered something. 'You've used that line before. You said it to Mike, the night after you almost got killed.'

'After all that's happened, you still remember that?' Rob shook his head. 'I never was very original with my advice.' He bent down and scooped up the notebook from where it had landed before flicking through the pages. 'Anything useful in here?'

'It's mostly just personal stuff, but there's one bit.' I turned the pages for him and then pointed. 'Here.'

I watched as Rob read the passage and then read it again. 'That's interesting.'

I nodded in agreement. 'I know.'

Rob's brow furrowed. 'What d'you think it means?'

I smiled at him. 'Same as you.'

It was the passage where the dead man had written about the plane he'd seen from time to time, off in the distance, and how it had finally stopped appearing. While he'd struggled on for several more months, this seemed to be the final straw which had sent him over the edge. Until that point he'd felt there were others like him, clinging on, surviving despite all that had happened to the world. Its disappearance stabbed at the very heart of his being, killing the hope it had kindled there. That was when he'd finally realised he couldn't face struggling on, alone in a world where it seemed he was now the only one left alive.

'Someone else survived the initial outbreak.' Rob sounded excited. 'Maybe more than one.'

I gazed towards the east, the direction in which the aircraft had always been seen, as if I somehow expected it to suddenly reappear over the horizon after all this time. 'What d'you think happened to it? To the plane, I mean.'

Rob rubbed the side of his face, where his beard grew wild and shaggy, as he thought about the possibilities.

'Maybe they just ran out of fuel. Maybe there are still other survivors around here somewhere.'

In a strange way, I found the idea thrilling. It was like when we'd first found out about the Hope Town community or heard on the shortwave radio that there were other communities out there, hanging on like we were. I could see from the look on Rob's face that he felt the same way.

'So what're we going to do?' Jeff looked from Rob to me and back again.

Once we'd returned to the catamaran, Rob and I explained to the others about what we'd found in the notebook and what it might mean.

Mike glanced round. 'Whatever we do, I think we need to be very careful.'

There was concern in his voice and it took me a moment to realise why. 'You think other survivors might not be friendly?'

'Well ... I mean ...' Mike struggled to put his thoughts into words.

Rob crossed his arms. 'You've got a point, but if there are other people around here, we need to know what we're dealing with.'

Jimmy picked absent-mindedly at a spot where his trousers were starting to wear thin. 'So how d'we find out?'

I leant backwards on the guard rail. 'We need to go looking for them, check out some of the other islands in this part of the world.'

Rob and I had already discussed this and together, we'd come up with a plan, but we wanted the boys to feel like they were being included in the decision-making process.

Jeff stared at Mingulay longingly. 'But we've only just got here.' He'd clearly been looking forward to spending more time with land beneath his feet.

I put my arm around him. 'We've all been dreaming of finally spending time ashore again, but I think that'll have to wait.'

Jeff looked crestfallen.

I pulled him close and squeezed him gently. 'Don't worry. The island's not going anywhere. It'll still be here when we get back.'

***

We didn't have charts for this part of the world, and why would we? We'd never expected to end up here on our delivery from Cape Town to Miami, but Rob had sailed these waters before and he knew his way around. He wanted us to start in the south, with the islands closest to the mainland and work our way north, before crossing over to another chain of islands which lay further from shore, then coming south again, back towards Mingulay. All in all, he thought it would take us a couple of weeks at the most. He'd spoken with Jack and Andrew over the shortwave radio and they seemed happy with the plan.

As we sailed south-east to the first island, I continued to read the notebook, searching back and forth through the pages, strangely attracted to the scribbled notes and observations. Its contents explained much of what had happened on this side of the Atlantic, and presumably what had happened to my family back in London. It was strange to read about it in the scrawled handwriting which was becoming so familiar to me that I could recognise it in my sleep, but it was also somehow comforting to be able to fill in some of the gaps. I'd never know for sure, but at least I now had some sort of an idea of what they'd been through.

In Britain, the first outbreak had started in Glasgow. No one knew quite how or why, but that's where it had begun. The army had been sent in to try to contain it, but no matter what they did, they couldn't bring the disease under control. There had been a few moments of hope, like when they'd hurriedly reconstructed Hadrian's Wall, but they were only temporary. By the time the radio stopped broadcasting, America had been overrun, and outbreaks were burning their way across every continent. In Britain, London was the last place to fall and my family might have survived until then. This was all before I'd even been aware that anything was going on, and it was disconcerting to think of them fighting for their lives while I was still blissfully ignorant of what was happening to the world.

While, officially, London had held out the longest, given the sightings of the plane — or was it *planes?* — by the lone inhabitant of Mingulay, it seemed that others had survived, unreported, amongst the islands of Scotland's wild west coast ... at least for a while, at any rate.

***

Rob passed me the binoculars and waited for me to look through them before speaking. 'What d'you think?'

Over the past five days, we'd checked out seven different islands, and in every case there was evidence that the disease had ripped through the communities that had once lived there. In most, it looked like there had been little time, or opportunity, to try to hold back the infected, but on the last island we'd visited, one called Iona, there was evidence of a fight-back of some kind. Here, around three of the houses, we saw the bodies of a large number of people scattered on the ground. While the remains had decayed, they weren't as far gone as I'd have expected if they'd lain there, exposed to the elements, since shortly after the outbreak in Glasgow had begun. We could see still-living infected nearby, haunting the shadows, so we couldn't venture ashore to investigate further, but something different had clearly happened there than elsewhere.

Now, we lay off what had once been a small town on one of the larger islands. The bay it was in was sheltered and the waters calm, reflecting the burned-out remains of houses, roofs gone, windows shattered and walls so blackened by flames that it was impossible to tell what colour any of them had once been. The only building that seemed unharmed was a large, gothic-looking one that stood on a hill above the rest, looking down silently on the destruction below. Despite its dereliction, there was something vaguely familiar about the place, but I couldn't quite put my finger on exactly what.

Skeletonised bodies lay scattered on the road that ran along the shore, most likely picked clean by the infected we could see lurking, waiting for something to attack. I focussed the binoculars on one of them; I could tell it had once been a young girl, maybe thirteen or fourteen years old. Her hair was matted and clung to the side of her head; her eyes were little more than dark holes sunk into her gaunt, weather-ravaged face, and the last remnants of her clothes hung like rags, clinging to her dirty and discoloured skin. Yet, while she looked close to death, there were others that, while they looked just as dirty, were less raggedly dressed and more well-fed. Well, perhaps not well-fed, but not nearly as close to starvation as the teenager.

I lowered the binoculars. 'There's something that doesn't quite seem right here. I mean, this is the only place where we've seen evidence of a fire.'

'That's not the only thing. Look there.' Rob pointed to one end of the row of burned-out buildings. 'And there.' He pointed to the other end. 'See the scorch marks on the road where the tarmac's been melted. It looks like there was some sort of barrier there that burned down, and then if you follow them down to the waterline, there's something sticking out. I think that's all that's left of a barricade of some kind.'

Now he pointed it out, I could see what he meant. There was something charred protruding out of the water, almost like the remains of a wall. Yet, whatever it was, it wasn't made of stone or any other building material I'd ever seen before. 'I think we need to take a closer look.'

Beside me, Rob nodded slowly.

'I know what it is,' Rob grinned, 'and it's genius!'

The two of us were in the dinghy floating just off the remains of the northern barrier. On the shore, infected stalked along the water's edge, driven into a frenzy by the sound of our outboard engine, but, as always, unwilling to venture into the water deeper than a foot or so. They roared and snarled, frustrated that we were so close and yet beyond their reach. The young girl I'd seen earlier was amongst them, the anger and rage clear on her face despite her advanced state of emaciation. I watched her for a moment, comparing her to the other infected nearby, before turning to Rob. 'Well, are you going to tell me? Or are you expecting me to guess?'

He leaned over the side of the dingy and pulled a fistful of something out of the water before holding it up. 'They're bales of straw!'

'Straw?' I looked at the matted strands in Rob's hand. 'What would they've been doing with bales of straw?'

Rob dropped the charred stems back into the water and together we watched as they drifted slowly away. Rob wiped his hand on the side of the boat. 'That's the genius bit. With a bit of know-how you could use them to build a barricade really quickly and easily, and I think that's what someone did here. Or more likely a whole bunch of someones. You'd need a lot of people to build barriers this long before the first infected reached here from the mainland.'

I ran my eyes over the infected that roamed the nearby land, thinking again about how some looked close to starvation while others seemed much further from it. Yet, there was nothing in between. The ones close to starvation outnumbered the healthier ones by about ten to one, but there were enough of them to make me wonder why the difference? Then it struck me. 'Rob, I think there were people here who survived the initial outbreak. I think they built the barriers, just like you said, and they managed to keep the infected out for quite a long time, I'm guessing until there was a fire and the barriers burned down, letting the infected in. Look at the infected,' I pointed landward. 'There are two separate types: some almost skeletal; and others in a better state. I think we're looking at those who were infected at the start of the outbreak, and then others who were only infected much later, when the barricades were finally breached.'

Rob stared at the infected, inspecting each one in turn. 'Well spotted! I think you're right.'

Rob sounded excited and I couldn't work out why,

Then he saw something and gunned the engine. On the shore the infected scrambled after us as we moved fast parallel to the beach, heading for a long stone quay which stretched out into the water. The dinghy bumped against the end of it and Rob leapt out before running the few short paces to where a number of barrels were stacked tightly together.

My eyes flicked to the pack of infected that had now reached the base of the pier and I saw they were starting to run. 'Rob, what are you doing?'

He said nothing and crouched down next to the barrels, examining them closely. Within seconds, the infected were halfway along the quay, their speed increasing with every passing step as they sprinted towards him. I called out again, this time more urgently. 'Rob, the infected!'

Rob looked up and scrambled to his feet, but he remained where he was, wrestling with a cap on one of the barrels as if he was trying to twist it open. As a group, the infected roared and I could hear their feet pounding on the concrete quay as they honed in on the prey they could sense ahead of them. I tried again. 'Rob! they're almost here!'

Rob finally managed to get the cap off the barrel and he threw it to the ground before peering inside. Only then did he finally turn and run. He was just a few yards from the end of the pier, but with the infected closing in on him with every passing second, it was uncertain as to whether he'd make it or not. I held my breath wondering if he'd left it too late and what I'd do if he had. He reached the end of the pier just before the infected and leapt into the dinghy, landing with a loud *whump*. The instant he was on board, I pushed us away from the dock and gunned the engine, clearing the quay before any of the infected could get aboard. Behind me, I heard a howl, and looked back to see an infected launching itself after us. For a moment, it flew through the air, and fear shot through me as it seemed like it might make it, but then it fell, landing just short, and I watched as it was swallowed up by the ever-increasing swathe of dark water that now separated us from the shore.

Once we were far enough out to be safe, I slammed the engine into neutral and the dinghy drifted to a halt. I glared at Rob, angry that he'd taken such a risk. 'What the hell did you do that for?'

Rob was still breathing heavily, but after a second or two, he managed to get a few words out. 'I had to make sure.'

'Make sure of what?' I snapped back, unable to believe he'd do anything so dangerous, not with infected so close.

Rob pointed back at the quay 'See those barrels? The ones I was looking at?'

I nodded, still mad at him, but now calm enough to at least hear him out, and he carried on. 'They're filled with aviation fuel; the kind of stuff you'd need to fly a plane. Here,' he thrust the binoculars towards me, 'look at the logo on them.'

I scanned the barrels. 'What am I looking f—? Wait. That's a seaplane in the middle!'

'Exactly!' Rob's face glowed with something I couldn't quite place, and then I realised it was hope. 'We already know there was a plane flying around here well after the outbreak started. I think it must have come from here. I think there must have been a pretty good-sized community holding out here for quite some time after the disease brought down the rest of the country.'

I ran my eyes around the bay, taking in the burned-out houses, the infected that still crowded the end of the quay, the boats riding gently at anchor. 'But where's the seaplane now?'

'Another good point, CJ.' Rob smiled again. 'Where indeed? That's the question we need to answer, because I'm guessing these people weren't the only ones to survive around here. And maybe the people in the seaplane managed to escape when this place was overrun, and that's why it's not here.'

Rob's excitement was catching and I could feel it starting to bubble up within me, too, but then a thought occurred to me. 'If they got away, then why did it stop flying past Mingulay?'

Rob's face fell for a moment and then it lit up as a possible answer popped into his head. 'Because they couldn't access their fuel supply anymore! I bet if we search long enough, we'll find them.'

It was one explanation, but for some reason I didn't find it as likely as Rob did. 'But how d'you know they're still alive? How d'you know that wherever they ended up, they've not been overrun there, too?'

I turned the dinghy away from the shore and started heading back to the catamaran. All the time Rob was talking rapidly and excitedly. 'Think about it. It was probably only because of the fire that this place was overrun. If that fire hadn't happened, then I bet they'd still be here now. This is a big island, though, and it looks like there were a lot of infected on it already, even before that happened. But on other islands around here, smaller ones, more remote ones, the infected wouldn't have been able to get there because of the currents and the distances between them. I mean, we haven't seen a single drifter around here, or even anything that one could cling to, have we?'

Rob was verging towards the euphoric, and I'd seen before what could happen when a person started to fixate on an idea like this. They stopped thinking rationally and started doing things that could easily get themselves, and others, killed. I did my best to calm him down. 'Rob, okay, I admit it's a possibility, but it won't be the end of the world if we don't find any other survivors.'

'But just think about it, CJ.' Rob grinned at me wildly. 'A lot of these islands are just like Mingulay: they're remote and far from anywhere that had a large population before all this happened. If Mingulay's safe, then they will be, too. If I can figure that out, other people must have as well, especially people who already knew these waters. My guess is that they'll have come together somewhere, just like we did at Hope Town. We just need to find out where!'

'That's a big ask, Rob.' The way he was acting was really beginning to worry me. He had been under so much pressure for so long and I wondered if he was finally starting to crack. 'I mean, how many islands are there around here?'

Rob looked taken aback for a moment, but he smiled again, this time less manically. 'I was getting carried away with myself, wasn't I?'

I was relieved that he could see this for himself. 'You most certainly were.'

'Just as well you're here to bring me back to Earth, CJ.' He paused for a moment. 'I still think it's worth looking, though, just in case.'

'Yes,' I answered slowly, 'but we can't spend too long doing it. We need to be go back to Mingulay at some point and start getting it ready for the others.'

***

'I'm worried about Rob.' Jeff had just emerged from the cabin before slumping down next to me in the cockpit. We were anchored in a narrow bay on the east side of a large island that I didn't know the name of. The shoreline at the head of the bay was dominated by a large sandstone mansion, built in the style of a baronial castle.

'Me, too.' I glanced back inside. 'D'you know where he is?'

'He's still in his cabin. He's been in there since we got here and found that.' Jeff nodded towards the shore. 'He hasn't even eaten today.'

Rob's mood had changed dramatically in the few days since we'd left the remains of the burned-out town, with its evidence of a community which had survived well beyond the initial outbreak. This was because of what we'd found on every island we'd visited since. On each was evidence of a community that had survived the initial outbreak, only to succumb at some unknown later date. We'd even gone ashore on a small island ringed by steep rocks that housed a still-functioning automated lighthouse, wondering if people might have been drawn to it, just as they'd been drawn to the lighthouse in Hope Town, but all we'd found were the remains of two people: one who'd clearly been ripped apart by an infected; the other with its head staved in by a large rock and which, even in the advanced state of decay it was in, bore all the hallmarks of having been the infected that had killed the other one. How an infected could have made it all the way up there was unclear, and all we knew about them suggested it should have been impossible. Yet still it had happened.

The island we were now anchored off had been the last straw. Even from a distance, we could see that the main sandstone building had been fortified, with the lower windows boarded up and barbed wire strung across the grass in front of it. Two large black boats had been hauled up on the beach, and equipment lay in piles between the beach and the barbed-wire defences, things such as solar panels and wind generators, which must have been scavenged from far and wide. There were makeshift corrals too, and I could see the remains of two cows tied to stakes which had been hammered into the ground. In amongst these, were human remains; detached limbs, skulls and rib cages, suggesting they'd been torn apart either when they died, or later, when their killers returned to feed on them.

There were infected there, too, hiding in the shadows of the building and amongst the piles of machinery. They stood, staring passively into space, waiting for something to happen. I knew from experience you should never get lulled into a false sense of security by the infected, no matter how placid they appeared, because all that would change the instant they realised you were near. I'd examined these infected with the binoculars: some were in normal clothes, but others wore the remains of what looked like military uniforms; a few still had machine guns hanging round their necks.

This had been a well-organised and functioning community, with the ability to protect itself with some pretty heavy fire power, and I think it was this that had upset Rob the most. The infected had reached even here, and in sufficient numbers that the heavily armed men couldn't hold them back. At the burned-out community, Rob had argued that if Mingulay was safe, then places like this would be safe too, for exactly the same reason.

Yet, it had turned out that all the communities we'd found had eventually been overrun, and that cast the viability of Mingulay, as a suitable location for us to try to rebuild a community on land, into serious doubt.

This had sent Rob spiralling downwards again, into the dark pit where he worried that he'd dragged us all this way for nothing; that he'd given false hope to those who'd remained in Hope Town; that he'd let Jack down; that he'd let us all down. In a few short days, our future had gone from looking very bright to once again being stalked by the dark spectre of the infected, and their apparent, and inexplicable, ability to reach even the remotest outpost. Worst of all, it looked like many of the communities where we'd found evidence that they'd survived the initial outbreak had all been overrun in a matter of weeks, as if a wave of infected had somehow swept across the islands where these people had clung to life.

I'd tried to talk to Rob about it, but he'd just shrugged me off before walking into the main cabin and going down to his bunk. That was the last I'd seen of him — that anyone had seen of him — in many hours. Now, I went below and tried knocking on his door, but I was greeted only by silence. I twisted the handle, but it seemed as if it had been jammed shut from the inside. I tried banging on it and shouting, but still I got no response.

Not knowing what to do, I turned to Jack, calling him up on the shortwave radio, but there was no reply. I looked up at the mountain which towered over us and figured it was probably blocking our signal. I went outside, and found the three boys talking rapidly to each other in hushed tones. When they sensed my presence, they fell silent, waiting for me to speak, but I didn't know what to say. Instead, I walked past them and up to the left-hand

61

bow. Once there, I lent on the guard rail, trying desperately to figure out what to do next. Like it or not, it seemed like I was now in command of the boat, and I was angry at Rob for having put me in this position. I felt abandoned and lost, knowing that everybody's survival now lay in my hands, but not knowing what I needed to do next. I yelled in frustration out across the water, and heard the infected on the nearby shore moan in reply, the sound drifting towards me on the gentle breeze. I hated that sound; the one that meant they were just letting us know they were still there; that they were still the ones in charge; that they now ruled the land; and that there was nothing we could do about it.

I worried about Rob, and his state of mind: he'd once been concerned that I might do something stupid, and now I found myself wondering the same about him, and whether, if he tried, there was anything I could do to prevent it.

'CJ, are you okay?' I turned to find the three boys standing behind me, clearly scared by the sudden turn of events. Rob must have always seemed so strong to them, and it worried them to see him fall apart like this. I guess how I was responding didn't help either.

I pulled Jeff and Jimmy towards me, my arms round their necks. 'Sorry, I didn't mean to frighten you. I'm just a little frustrated.' I let them go and we stood in a rough circle. I looked at each of them in turn, wondering how I could keep them alive, given how little I knew, and suddenly I understood how Rob was feeling and why he felt under so much pressure. I thought back to something Bill had told me when we'd first discovered exactly what had happened to the world. I'd lost it in the cockpit, unable to cope with the enormity of the situation. Bill had taken me inside and given me something to help me sleep. He'd also told me that we'd all have moments like that, even him, and that we'd need to help each other through them if we were to have any hope of surviving. I tried to work out how best I could help Rob, and there seemed to be only one solution: I had to somehow show him that he hadn't been wrong to bring us here in search of somewhere safe, where we could once again live on the land. I didn't know how I could do that, but I knew the answer wouldn't be found here, amongst the ruins of this once-thriving community. I cleared my throat, issuing my first order as captain, hoping against hope that the position wouldn't become permanent. 'Let's get out of here.'

Chapter Four

I'd decided to complete Rob's original plan of following a broadly circular route which would take us past as many islands as possible before returning to Mingulay. Once we were back there, we'd need to make a final decision as to whether to take our chances and remain, or whether we should abandon it, with all its potential, and seek somewhere else instead. I only hoped that before then, something would happen which would raise Rob's spirits. For now, he remained in his cabin, the door barricaded, refusing even to speak to me.

I looked ahead and saw that what I'd initially thought was one very large island was actually two, with a smaller one nestled just off the coast of the larger one. I picked up the binoculars and scanned the shore. I could see a few near-derelict buildings here and there, but nothing else. Then I spotted it, the lone infected standing on the crest of a low ridge. Its body was lanky, but the clothes it wore seemed to be in remarkably good condition as they flapped loosely on its frame. I was just about to turn away when it suddenly disappeared. We weren't making much noise so I was pretty sure it couldn't have known we were there, and yet, in my experience, infected only moved that fast when they sensed prey were near. The rest of the time they barely stirred, and if they did, it was little more than the occasional shuffle as they conserved as much of their energy as possible for any opportunities they'd have to attack in the future.

I swept the binoculars back and forth, trying to find it again, but I couldn't. I swore loudly enough to make Jeff and Jimmy jump, before stalking inside and banging hard on Rob's door. 'Rob, you've been wallowing in there long enough. I need you to get your arse out here right now. There's something odd going on and I need you up on deck.'

I paused for a moment, but there was no response. I thumped the door again. 'Rob, I know how you're feeling, but none of this is your fault. You took a gamble and I know it's not looking good right now, but at least you tried. We could still all be sitting in Hope Town, waiting for some random infected to drift by and climb on board, but we're not: we're out here trying to do something to make the situation better. It doesn't matter if we fail. What matters is that we keep on trying. We can't give in. We can't let the bastards win!'

I was just about to bang on the door again when I heard something move inside. A moment later, it swung open and a dishevelled figure appeared.

I stared at him. 'Jesus, Rob, you look like crap! What on earth have you been doing to yourself?'

He cleared his throat and pointed to an empty rum bottle. 'That.' He coughed, and then pressed a hand to the side of his head as he closed his eyes tightly. 'Jack gave it to me before we left. I was saving it for a special occasion, but ...'

I looked at him incredulously. 'You've been drunk this whole time?'

'No, just last night.' He blinked blearily at me. 'I only meant to have a couple, but it kind of got away from me.'

Anger flared up inside of me. 'D'you know how worried we've all been about you? About what you might be doing to yourself in there? And after all that, I find you've just been getting shit-faced. For fuck's sake, Rob, you're acting like a complete arsehole!'

'I ...' Rob closed his eyes for a second time and swallowed before opening them again. 'I guess I wasn't thinking straight.' He rubbed his bloodshot eyes and blinked slowly a couple of times. 'Sorry, CJ, you deserve better.'

I glared angrily at him. 'You can save your apologies for later. Right now there's something strange going on, and I need you on deck.'

Rob shook his head, as if trying to unfog it, but it didn't seem to make much difference and he stumbled as he emerged into the main cabin. Outside, the three boys avoided looking at either of us, clearly trying to make us think they hadn't heard everything that had just been said. Suddenly, I felt like we were parents who'd been caught fighting by their kids. I ignored their furtive glances as they tried to work out how things were between me and Rob, and picked up the binoculars. 'There was an infected on the island last time I looked and it suddenly vanished.'

Rob cleared his throat. 'But infected don't just disappear ...'

I scanned the shore slowly. 'Exactly, so where the hell is it? And just what's going on?'

'There!' Mike pointed as he yelled and I swung the binoculars round to focus on that spot. Quickly, I found them: two infected standing side by side; one of them was the one I'd seen before, whilst the other was smaller and, if I wasn't very much mistaken, female. For a moment, they just stood there, then they turned their heads towards each other, almost as if they were talking.

'That's weird. I've never seen infected act like *that* bef—' A thought struck me and I stopped mid-sentence. There'd been a time before when we'd mistaken a

66

normal person for an infected, and I wondered if we were doing the same again here. I passed the binoculars to Rob. 'Here, take a look and let me know what you think.'

Rob lifted the binoculars, but after a few seconds he lowered them again. 'I can't see them.'

'Oh, you're just too hung-over. Give them here.' I grabbed the binoculars back and trained them on the island again. After a minute, I lowered them and turned to Rob. 'Okay, so it looks like I owe you an apology.' The two figures really had gone.

'Not as big as the one I owe you,' Rob mumbled.

I shot him back a weak smile. 'That can wait until we work out exactly what we're dealing with here.'

'I can see them again!' This time it was Jimmy who'd spotted them. 'Down on the shore!'

There was only one figure again now, the tall, skinny one, and it was moving its arms back and forth over its head. We were now close enough that all of us could see it.

Rob was the first to speak. 'Survivors!'

Mike narrowed his eyes. 'You think they're safe?'

'I don't know.' My mind was racing as I tried to work through all the possibilities of what this might mean. 'Mike, go get the rifle.'

Jimmy piped up, 'But we don't have any bullets.'

I put my hand on his shoulder. 'They don't know that, do they?'

It was a further ten minutes before we were close enough to be within shouting distance of the beach and I gave the order for the anchor to be dropped. The rifle lay on one of the seats, easily accessible, but not visible to the person on the shore. Until I knew more about the situation,

I didn't want to go waving a gun around in case I made the situation more complicated, but I wanted it within easy reach, just in case I needed it. Now we were closer, I could see the person on the shore was a teenager, maybe the same age as Mike, maybe slightly older … or it could just be that he was taller. He looked skinny, but I couldn't tell if that was simply his natural physique or whether it was because he'd lost a lot of weight.

I took a deep breath and called out. 'Ahoy there. Is this island free of infected?'

The young man cupped his hands around his mouth and yelled back. 'Aye. We've no' got anythin' like that around here. Where'd you guys come from?'

There were whispers behind me from Jeff, Jimmy and Mike, but I ignored them. 'The other side of the Atlantic; the Bahamas to be precise.'

The man cupped his hands round his mouth again. 'That's a hell of a long way to come, especially with the way the world is.'

Rob stepped up to the guard rail. 'We're just looking for somewhere safe we can hole up.' He winced as his own words echoed round inside his head. It was clear that the sudden discovery of other survivors had done nothing to banish his hangover.

'Well, this is our island.' The young man sounded defensive. 'You can come ashore, but only if you agree to do what we say.'

I swept a stray hair away from the side of my face. 'Actually, we've got another island in mind that's much better than this one.'

'Oh!' The teenager looked deflated. He'd obviously been expecting that that would be the ace up his sleeve, but now he'd played it, it turned out to be a dud. 'D'you want to come ashore anyway?'

Now it was my time to be cautious. 'How many of you are there?'

The teenager looked uncomfortable, but didn't say anything.

I carried on. 'We know there are at least two of you. We saw a girl, too.'

'Aww, for fuck's sake! I told Sophie she needed to keep her head down.' He spoke more to himself than to us, but his words still carried out across the water. He turned and called over his shoulder. 'Sophie, you might as well come out. They know you're here anyway.'

As the girl emerged, the whispering behind me intensified. She was younger than the boy and was dressed in poorly fitting men's clothes which had clearly seen better days. She waved nervously.

Trying to reassure her, I waved back. 'Is it just the two of you?'

There was a rapid whispered discussion before the boy spoke again. 'Why d'you want to know?'

For a moment, I wondered what to say, and then I decided that the best option was to go with the truth. 'We've been looking for other survivors so we could see if we can make contact. We wanted to know if there was anyone else around here. We're trying to make sure we're not stepping on anyone's toes.'

There was another rapid discussion before the boy spoke again. 'An' you're really no' here to cause us trouble?'

'No. If you want, we can just leave you to it.' I made as if to go forward to pull up the anchor.

That clearly got them both worried and the girl called out 'Wait! Don't go.' There was a hint of panic in her voice. 'There're four of us. If you can pick us up, we can show you where the others are.'

The boy said something to her, but she shrugged it off and yelled out again. 'Well?'

The young man reached up. 'I'm Daz, an' this is Sophie.'

I shook hands with both of them as they climbed onto the catamaran. 'I'm CJ.'

It had only taken Rob a couple of minutes to nip ashore in the dinghy and pick them both up. Once they were properly on board, I carried on with the introductions. 'I presume Rob's introduced himself to you already.'

Rob gave a distracted wave. Even though the trip had been short and smooth, it seemed to have played havoc with his hangover and he was starting to turn a little green. I indicated towards the three teenagers. 'This is Mike and Jimmy, and this is Jeff.'

Sophie shook hands with each of them in turn, followed by Daz. Daz eyed us all carefully. 'So, are you all, like, related an' that?'

The boys stared at him for a moment, clearly confused. Jeff glanced across at me. 'What did he say?'

Daz looked at Jeff, bemused, and then spoke again, this time more slowly. 'I said, are you lot all related to each other an' that?'

Jeff remained nonplussed, and I realised he might be struggling with Daz's rather strong accent, so I stepped in. 'No, well, except for Jimmy and Mike; they're brothers. But apart from that we all just ended up together.'

Sophie nodded. 'Pretty much like us then.'

Daz's eyes drifted over to where the rifle was lying on the seats. 'You expectin' trouble?'

I shrugged noncommittally. 'We didn't quite know

70

what to expect. From what we've seen so far, there's been some odd stuff going on around here.'

Daz and Sophie exchanged a knowing glance.

'Where've you been?' There was an edge to Daz's voice that hadn't been there before. It wasn't distrust, but it was definitely guarded.

I didn't know the names of the places we'd visited, but I was able to describe them. Daz told me the one with the burned down barricades had been called Tobermory, while the island with the mansion was Rhum. Again, he and Sophie exchanged looks that told me that there was something more going on here, but that I shouldn't press things too far, not yet at any rate.

I decided to change the subject. 'Right, let's get going. Mike, you get the anchor; Jeff, you sort out the main sail; and Jimmy, can you get the jib?' I looked back to where Daz and Sophie were casting a critical eye over my crewmates as they bustled around the deck. 'Which way?'

'Oh yeah,' Daz glanced round to get his bearings. 'Just along the coast a couple of miles at the western end. There's a big stone pier an' an old buildin' with the roof fallin' in. We've been stayin' in there.'

Daz turned his attention to me, looking curiously. 'How come you're the one in charge?' He pointed towards Rob. 'I'd of thought it'd be the big man there.'

Sophie punched him in the arm. 'Why? Because he's a man?'

'No,' Daz scowled back at her, 'because he's older.'

'Oh!' She flashed a smile back at him that made me wonder what the relationship was between the two of them. 'Sorry.'

I did my best to pretend I hadn't noticed the apparent

undercurrent in their exchange. 'He usually is.' Rob was now laid out on one of the seats, one arm shielding his eyes even though the day was overcast. 'He's just temporarily a little bit under the weather.'

'Yeah,' Rob didn't bother to sit up. 'Just paying the price for, what was it you said again, CJ? Oh yeah, "acting like a complete arsehole".'

'Most definitely.' It was good to see Rob starting to relax a bit more, but despite the ferocious hangover, there was still concern etched deep into his face.

'Well, that explains a few things.' Rob sounded happier than he had in days. 'It all makes sense now.'

We'd reached the stone pier Daz had told us about in a little over half an hour and were now tied up alongside it. As we'd closed in on it, two people had emerged from a nearby stone building, a man and a woman, their clothes heavily worn and their skin deeply tanned from exposure to the elements.

Daz pointed to each of them in turn. 'That's Ben, an' that's Mitch.' He waved to them, enjoying the look of complete amazement on their faces. Soon, we'd all been properly introduced and then we started to exchange our stories. We told them about being at sea when it had all started, and getting back to shore to find civilisation gone; about Hope Town and all that had happened there. They told us about escaping from Glasgow as the outbreak ripped through the city, about Tobermory and the other communities, and how they'd come to be overrun. All of us avoided talking about the people we'd lost along the way.

Much like Hope Town, their community had been destroyed, not just by the infected, but by the actions of other survivors who'd thought they had the right to tell everyone else what they should be doing, and how they should be doing it. Even when the worst was happening all around them, it seemed that some people just couldn't resist the all-too-human urge to meddle in the lives of others. Yet, as we all knew to our cost, in the world of the infected, that could threaten the survival of everyone.

After mulling over all that I'd heard, I turned to Rob, 'You know what this means? It means the infected weren't spreading between the communities on their own. The water was keeping them safe after all. It means Mingulay's safe.'

Ben butted in, 'What's that about Mingulay?'

'It was Rob's idea.' I tilted my head in his direction as I spoke. 'He spent time there years ago. He reckoned it was the perfect place to try to establish a proper community on land.'

Ben scratched his chin, 'I hadn't considered Mingulay before. Isn't there a seabird research centre there?'

Rob nodded. 'Yes, and it's a pretty nice set-up.'

'There wasn't anyone there when the outbreak started?' Ben sounded cautious, but curious.

I shifted uneasily, not quite too sure what to say. I was just about to reply when Mitch beat me to it. 'No, I always flew them out at the start of the season.'

I cleared my throat. 'Actually, there was someone there, but we were too late.' I told them about the man we'd found hanging in the hut and about the notebook we'd found beside him. I was just telling them about the aircraft and how much hope it had given him, and how its disappearance finally sent him over the edge, when Mitch interrupted me. 'Oh shit! I never thought to check Mingulay when I was out looking for other survivors. I figured there'd be no one there.'

Rob's brow furrowed. 'What d'you mean?'

'That'll have been my aeroplane he saw.' Mitch explained. 'It was a seaplane. I'd fly out over the islands I knew were inhabited when the outbreak started every now and then, just to see if I could spot any survivors holed up anywhere who might need help. I never thought of going out as far as Mingulay.' There was regret in her voice. 'If I'd known, I could have got him out of there, or at least let him know he wasn't alone.'

There was silence all round, with none of us quite knowing what to say next. There was no way any of us could have known the dead man was there, or what he was going through, but we all felt like we had somehow failed him.

As we sat there, Jeff's voice floated in through the open cabin door. 'But what language is he speaking?'

While Rob, Ben, Mitch and me were exchanging our stories in the cabin, the others had remained in the cockpit.

I heard Sophie laugh. 'English, same as you guys.'

'But I can't understand a word he's saying!' Jimmy sounded frustrated and confused.

The next voice was Daz's, his Glaswegian accent clearly marking him out from the others. 'I'm no' that difficult to understand, am I?'

I glanced out to where they were sitting: Daz and Sophie sat close to each other on one side of the boat; Jimmy, Mike and Jeff on the other. Sophie looked the most relaxed, and despite her ill-fitting clothes, she held herself in a way that reminded me of my younger self. I tried to work out how old she was, and guessed she was somewhere around fourteen or fifteen, but with girls of that age it could be difficult to tell. Her hair was long and dark. Like mine, it was tied back in a ponytail, but unlike me she'd made more of an effort to keep it neat and tidy.

Daz, I guessed, was the oldest out of all of them, but I figured he couldn't be more than eighteen. His hair was wild, but not too long, suggesting he'd either found a way to cut it, or that it had started out pretty short in the first place. While he had a beard of sorts, it was patchy at best. He sat, arms crossed and shoulders hunched defensively, clearly uncomfortable with the situation. Sophie must have seen this too because she placed a reassuring hand on his forearm. She smiled across at the others. 'Don't worry, it's just his accent. Give it a few days and you'll get the hang of it.'

It was clear that Sophie and Daz came from very different worlds and, for a moment, I wondered how they had ended up together, but then it occurred to me that the disease would've thrown a lot of people together who previously would never have met. After all, it was the same for me and Rob.

I returned my attention to the cabin, and to Ben and Mitch. As far as I could tell, Ben was in his early thirties and underneath all the ingrained dirt, weather-beaten skin and overgrown beard, he was good-looking in a non-traditional, but by no means unattractive sort of way. He was clearly tired and run-down by the rigours of survival, but then again, I hadn't seen anyone who wasn't in a very long time. Mitch was a little older, maybe in her late thirties and she'd adopted the same functional hairstyle as Sophie and me, and probably for the same reason: it was the easiest thing to do.

Both Ben and Mitch were lean, but not from being underfed. Rather, they both had the type of body you got from working hard all day, every day. I didn't know what they'd been doing for food, but clearly they were getting enough, and I figured that the knowledge which had kept them that way could only stand us in good stead, if they chose to come with us to Mingulay.

Chapter Five

'I'm really not so sure about Mingulay.' Ben folded his arms. 'It's much more exposed and open to winter storms.'

'But that's just the point. We need somewhere which is that exposed to reduce the risk of drifters. This far in, the storms might drive drifters towards you as they come in from the south-west.' Rob pointed out to our left. 'Out there, there's no land for them to come from. Even if any did somehow manage to get there, they'd never get up the cliffs, and that would mean there'd be little chance of them being able to land.'

We were sitting in the cockpit of the catamaran, still tied to the old stone quay. At first, things seemed to be going well between the two groups, but by the following morning, when it came to deciding what to do next, the arguments started. Mostly, it was just between Rob and Ben, with neither one wanting to be seen to back down, but when Daz stepped in on Ben's side, Mike and the other teenagers in the crew of the catamaran felt they should join in too. It didn't help that they were still struggling to understand anything Daz said because of his strong and unfamiliar accent.

'Have we no' been safe here for somethin' like four months? If we've no' seen infected here so far, what makes you think they'll ever make it?'

'What?' Mike looked flustered, unsure exactly how to respond to something he'd not fully understood. 'Anyway, we've already been to Mingulay and it's much better than here. It's got a hut and everything on it. The building you've got here looks like it'd fall down in the next strong breeze.'

'Mike's got a good point.' Rob leant forward. 'And besides, we've got to think about the long term here. It'd be much easier to grow things on Mingulay. The soil's better and there's better grazing for things like sheep.'

'What would you know about soil and whether it's any good for growing things?' Ben sounded condescending.

'I'm an archaeologist,' Rob shot back. 'I've spent most of my adult life digging around in the stuff. I know it better than most farmers do. And I know the soils around here, I've studied them before, I know how they've been made and how to maintain their fertility with seaweed.'

Ben sat back. 'Yes, but I know the seas. I know where to get everything we need from them.'

Sophie caught my eye, and she rolled hers in an exaggerated manner. Clearly, she was as fed up with all the macho posturing as I was. I decided to step in. 'Guys, cool it.'

At first, they ignored me and kept talking loudly. I tried again, but still they didn't listen. I decided it was time to take a more direct approach. I went into the cabin and grabbed the hand-held foghorn. Before any of them realised what I was doing, I put it to my lips and blew, sending a deafening blast across the cockpit. 'Right, now I have your attention, I want you to listen.' I gave them a look that let them know I was serious. 'There are merits to both sides here, and they're not necessarily mutually exclusive. Rob, you want to go back to Mingulay, right?' Rob nodded.

'And Ben, you think we'd be better off staying here?' Ben nodded in agreement. 'Well, I've got a third option. Rather than sit here and argue about it, why don't we spend a few days here, so that we can get to know the place ...'

Rob opened his moth as if to say something, but I didn't let him get a word in. 'And then we can go back to Mingulay and you guys can come with us so you can see it for yourselves.'

This time it was Ben that looked like he was going to protest, but I held up my hand to stop him before he started. 'Rob, I know we usually make decisions as a group, but if you remember, you went AWOL for a couple of days, leaving me in charge.' Mitch and Ben looked curiously at Rob, causing his cheeks to flush with red. 'And I haven't officially handed the reins back to you, so right now, it's a matter of my boat, my rules, and what I say goes.'

Daz smirked and glanced at Ben. 'She's got a point there, Ben, doesn't she?'

Mitch and Sophie laughed openly. The tense atmosphere which had been building all morning evaporated in an instant and even Ben chuckled. 'Hoisted by my own petard!'

Daz explained. 'That's what *he* always says, too.'

***

For the next three days we remained on the island which, by then, I'd learned was called Soay, assessing its resources as well as its advantages and disadvantages. We foraged together and ate together, and slowly the two groups got to know each other. Ben and Rob circled warily around one another at first, but gradually they figured out how to work together without clashing too much, with each respecting the other's areas of expertise. I had to admit, I liked Soay, nestled as it was in the shelter of the larger island which lay only a few miles away. This made it amazingly picturesque, but I felt there was danger in it, too. There would almost certainly be many infected on the big island, and with the right conditions, it would be relatively easy for one of them to make it the short distance to Soay. Unlike Mingulay, it lacked high cliffs and there were many places where infected could drift ashore undetected, and that was a possibility I thought we needed to avoid at all costs. However, for the time being I kept these thoughts to myself.

According to Ben and Mitch, the house in which they'd been living was all that remained of a fishery that had once hunted basking sharks, one of the biggest fish in the oceans, which visited the local waters each summer to feed on the abundant plankton blooms. It was these same plankton blooms that attracted the seabirds back to Mingulay each spring, and which drove much of the local marine ecosystem. The fishery had failed after a few years, possibly a victim of its own success, or more likely, as Ben claimed with his marine biologist's hat on, because of a change in the local climate: the seas had cooled and the sharks disappeared. When they had warmed again, as man polluted the atmosphere with ever-increasing amounts of carbon dioxide, the basking sharks returned, and Ben and the others had watched them skimming through the surface waters around the island for much of the summer. What would happen now there were too few humans left to have an impact on the gases in the atmosphere high above our heads was anyone's guess, and all we could do was wait and see.

The building itself was falling apart, but it had provided them with some much-needed shelter. They'd used the life raft in which they'd come ashore to help provide a waterproof roof, and they'd managed to create a cosy and dry, if rather small, living space. Cooking was done on an open fire and there was no running water. Instead, it had to be collected each day from a nearby stream.

Mitch told me about their life on the island as we sat on some rocks near the water's edge, filleting mackerel we'd caught earlier in the day.

'After Ben's yacht sank, we ended up in the life raft, just drifting around. We were all a mess, both physically and mentally. We'd all lost so much in such a short space of time, but Sophie and Ben had lost the most. I wasn't sure they were going to make it, but I had no idea what I could do to help them. Ben, in particular, just disappeared into himself, barely doing anything other than lying against the side of the life raft. In all the years I'd known him, I'd never seen him like that before. Then Daz spotted that we'd drifted near an island and from the moment I recognised it, I knew we were safe.'

I frowned. 'Why?'

Mitch smiled. 'Because I knew it was uninhabited, and that meant ...'

I finished her sentence. 'No infected.'

Mitch pointed a fish at me. 'Bingo!'

She put the mackerel down and with a practised flick of the knife she was holding, she carved off a single fillet as she carried on. 'So we paddled ashore, but we didn't know for sure there were no infected here. It took us a couple of days before we were finally certain, and we felt it was safe enough to start looking around for somewhere to live.'

Mitch turned the fish over and sliced off another fillet from the other side before throwing the rest into the sea. 'I remember my grandfather telling me stories about this place and the basking shark fishery, but I'd never been here before. Yet, it seemed like the most appropriate place to set ourselves up. We knew there wasn't anyone else around here who was still alive, so we didn't keep a look out for people who might be able to rescue us. Instead, we just accepted that we were starting over again with nothing and this was what our lives would be from now on. It took time for each of us to come to terms with that, but gradually we did.'

Mitch picked another fish out of the bucket and set to work on it. 'I think that's why Ben's so keen on staying here. This island helped us to rebuild our lives, and get over what happened to us, and it almost feels like we'd be betraying it if we went elsewhere. I know that sounds a bit weird, but ...' Her voice drifted off as she remembered some past event.

I thought back to Hope Town and how it had felt to leave it after all the time we'd spent there, and immediately I knew what she was talking about. This brought back my own memories, and the rest of the time preparing the fish was spent working in silence.

***

On the fourth day, we left Soay, heading back towards Mingulay, but on the evening before we departed, I found myself alone on the foreshore with Sophie as we collected seafood for the voyage. I'd never done anything like this before and she showed me how to pull back the seaweed to find butterfish and crabs, and the technique for knocking the limpets from the rocks with the heel of your shoe. I was impressed by the productivity of what looked, to me, like nothing more than a pile of rocks covered with brown, slimy seaweed, and within twenty minutes we'd collected enough to feed us all. This was the mainstay of their diet on the island, and while it made a change from the fish we'd been living off since arriving in Scotland, I knew it would get pretty old very quickly. I'd already noticed the pile of empty shells from mussels. periwinkles and limpets which was accumulating beside the dilapidated house they'd been living in, indicating just how much they'd eaten since they'd arrived on Soay. Rob, always the archaeologist at heart, couldn't resist pointing out a similar pile eroding out of a bank at the top of one of the beaches, which had been created by Neolithic hunter-gatherers thousands of years before. It seemed we were rapidly reverting to the way our ancient ancestors lived — the way all humans lived — before we had been diverted by our own ingenuity, and the civilisation we'd created, and then destroyed, with it.

As we walked back to the house, I chatted to Sophie, trying to find out more about the relationships within her group. It was clear from how they interacted with each other that Ben and Mitch had known each other for a long time, but I wondered if it ran deeper. 'Are Ben and Mitch, you know, a couple?'

Sophie sniggered. 'No way. I don't know why, but they just don't see each other like that. They've known each other for years, apparently, so I think if anything like that was going to happen, it would have happened long before now.'

For a fourteen year old, that sounded like quite a mature assessment of the situation. She carried on. 'Anyway, Mitch was seeing Tom, Ben's best friend. They only met after the ... the ... after it happened, but they were pretty tight. It tore them both apart what happened to him ... to Tom I mean.' Sophie looked sombre, and I wondered how badly she'd been affected by his loss herself.

We walked along silently for a bit, and then I asked her another question. 'What about you and Daz?'

Sophie's face reddened. 'What about me and Daz?'

I smiled. 'I've seen the way you look at each other, and the way he acts around you.'

Sophie's face, still tinged with pink, shifted into a sheepish smile that told me all I needed to know. Before I could ask her any more questions, she turned the tables on me. 'What about you and Rob? Is there anything going on there?'

I playfully pushed her away from me. 'He's old enough to be my father!'

'Yeah, but you must get lonely.' She grinned impishly at me, and then stopped the instant she saw the look on my face change. 'Sorry, CJ, did I say something wrong?'

'No, it's okay. You're right, I did get lonely, but I found someone. It's just …' I swallowed. 'It's just he didn't make it.' I swallowed again. 'I'll tell you about it sometime, but not now. It's still too fresh.'

Sophie put her arm around me. 'I know. That's the way I feel about my mum.'

This was the first time Sophie had mentioned any of her family. I waited for her to say something else, but she remained silent, her eyes suggesting that, in her mind, she'd drifted off to memories that she found both disturbing and unpleasant.

'A bit tighter on the jib an' a bit more slack on the main sail. That's right.' Daz was at the helm and he was putting the catamaran through its paces, while Rob and I watched on nervously. We'd left Soay well before first light, which was about 8 a.m. at that time of year, and almost as soon as we'd got underway, Daz had asked if he could have a go at the helm. Ben and Mitch assured us he knew what he was doing, and that he could be trusted, but still we worried and Rob waited until the sun was well above the horizon before letting him take charge. Bill had told me a long time ago that catamarans were powerful vessels: if you didn't handle them right, they could easily capsize, and there was no coming back from that. In this respect, they're different from single-hulled boats which had a keel. You can lay one of them almost on its side and the weight in the keel will still haul it upright again; do that in a catamaran, and it'll flip. Bill had pointed out that, over the years, many experienced sailors had been caught out by this, and killed. This meant we had every reason to be concerned when Rob finally let Daz take his place at the helm.

Ben shielded his eyes against the light with his right hand as he watched Daz moving the wheel back and forth, trying to keep the boat heading in a straight line. After a moment, he spoke. 'Handles a bit differently from my boat, doesn't it, Daz?'

'Yeah.' Daz wore a look of intense concentration as he turned the wheel too far to the left to try to counter for the fact he'd just turned it too far to the right. Rob got up and stood beside him. 'You're doing good, but you just have to remember you can't go as close to the wind with a catamaran and you've got to make small movements not big ones.'

Daz took in what Rob said right away and within a few minutes the boat was moving more smoothly. Rob sat down again, clearly impressed by the speed at which Daz had picked things up.

Ben smiled, knowing what both Rob and I were thinking. 'Yeah, it surprised me, too, but he's a real natural out here, especially for someone who'd never even seen the sea before ...'

He didn't complete the sentence and I realised that the way we referred to all that had happened was gradually changing; it was no longer 'the disease', 'the infected', 'the outbreak' ... it was just becoming 'before'.

Daz's eyes narrowed as he stared off into the distance. 'Is that another boat?'

Ben, Daz and I were alone in the cockpit, while the others slept below. It was now early afternoon and we were about halfway between Soay and Mingulay.

'It is!' I scooped up the binoculars. 'It's an old sailing ship.' I paused for a second as I examined it further. 'It doesn't look in great shape, though.'

Ben stood up as I offered him the binoculars and he pointed them at the distant vessel. 'I think we're going to have to take a closer look.'

Daz frowned. 'Why? D'you think there might be survivors or somethin'?'

'No.' Ben handed him the binoculars. 'In case there are infected on board. If there are, we can't afford to leave something like that floating around anywhere near us.'

It took us an hour to reach the ship, and by then we could tell it was about ninety feet long, with three masts, the tallest reaching some eighty feet into the air. Tattered sails hung from the cross-beams while loose ropes swung back and forth as it rolled heavily on the gentle swell. It rode low in the water, suggesting it was close to sinking, yet it remained afloat. On its decks, infected stood, dressed in the remnants of some sort of naval uniform. We kept our distance as we inspected it, trying to assess the danger it might pose to our survival.

Mike handed the binoculars to Jeff and turned to Rob. 'Where'd you think it came from?'

Rob thought for a moment. 'I don't know. The flag on its stern looks Russian, and its name's written in Cyrillic, but it can't have come from there, not directly at any rate.'

Daz looked at him curiously. 'Why no'?'

Ben stepped forward. 'Because of the way the currents work around here. It must have come up from the south.'

Jeff lowered the binoculars. 'They all look pretty young.'

I felt myself frown. 'Who looks pretty young?'

Jeff lifted the binoculars again. 'The infected.' There was an element of sadness in his voice.' They all look like they're about my age.'

Ben took the binoculars from Jeff and scanned the vessel, stopping every few seconds as he concentrated on each of the infected he could see. 'He's right. It must've been a training vessel for sea cadets or something like that.'

'How long d'you think they've been out here? I mean d'you think they've been out here since the beginning?' Sophie shifted uneasily from one foot to the other. 'Or d'you think they managed to hold out for a while afterwards and somehow got infected later?'

I stared at the ship. There was nothing I could see that could tell us anything about how long it had been at sea, or, indeed, how long it had been since the infection had overwhelmed its crew.

Mitch rested her hands on her hips. 'Does it matter where they came from? Or how long they've been out here? Surely what's more important is that they're infected and we need to do something about it?'

Sophie looked confused. 'Why?'

Ben put a hand on her shoulder. 'Because if we don't, they might end up running aground on Soay, and then the island would be overrun.'

Rob huffed loudly. 'That's another reason not to stay there.'

Ben scowled at him. 'It could just as easily end up on Mingulay.'

Rob shook his head dismissively. 'Not with the way the currents run around here. You said so yourself; the currents will carry it northwards, not south towards Mingulay.'

I felt irritation well up inside me. Yet again, the ongoing argument between Rob and Ben about which island was best for our future survival was distracting us from what we should really be doing. 'Can we deal with one thing at a time? No matter where we end up, we can't leave something like that just drifting around out here, can we? So what're we going to do about it?'

Ben and Rob sat down on opposite sides of the boat, both avoiding eye contact. I looked from one to the other and then back again. 'Well? Any ideas?'

'Is everyone clear on what we're going to do? We're going to have to get pretty close for this to work, so we'll need to keep our wits about us.' Rob glanced round the group and everyone nodded. 'Okay, let's get started.'

Daz had been the one to come up with the solution to the problem which lay before us, and he'd explained it to the rest of us. 'I saw it on a TV programme once. It's how the Vikings buried their dead; they'd load the bodies into a ship an' push it out to sea, an' then they'd set fire to it; the whole thing'd burn down an' there'd be nothin' left.

Rob pursed his lips. 'I'm not too sure the Vikings ever

actually did that.'

Daz crossed his arms defensively. 'But I saw it on TV, in a documentary.'

'Yes, but ...'

'Rob, this isn't the time to get pedantic.' I was starting to get frustrated with him again. 'Whether the Vikings did it or not doesn't matter. It's a good idea, isn't it?'

Rob shrugged. 'I suppose so, but how would we do it?'

Daz's face suddenly lit up. 'You got any petrol on board?'

Daz and Ben now stood at the front of the catamaran, one on each bow, as we made our final approach to the sailing ship. Behind them stood Sophie and Mitch, a collection of mismatched glass bottles by their feet. Within the bottles, a liquid with a blue-green sheen sloshed back and forth, and some old sailcloth had been stuffed into their necks. We couldn't afford to waste much of what little petrol we had left, but Daz's suggestion seemed to be the only way we could hope to burn the ship down without getting close enough for the infected to be able to board us.

With Rob at the wheel, and Mike, Jimmy, Jeff and me standing in the cockpit, gripping makeshift weapons in case we needed them, we closed in on the vessel. As we did so, the infected started to sense our presence: those already on deck flocking towards the side we were approaching, while others streamed up from below. By the time we were within throwing distance, there were some fifty of them milling and growling as they prowled along the edge of the boat, all pushing and shoving to get themselves into the best position to attack. As Jeff had pointed out before, they were all just teenagers, the oldest about the same age as Mike, but this didn't reduce the ferocity with which they fought each other to get as close to us as possible. They lined the side of the vessel, reaching out, grasping the air, their emaciated faces contorted with rage and fury.

After staring at the infected crew for a few seconds, Daz turned to Sophie. 'Pass one over an' spark it up for me.'

Tentatively, Sophie picked up one of the glass bottles and handed it to Daz. She then took out a small box and pulled out a match. She went to strike it, but in her nervous state, she pressed too hard and it snapped in two. She took out another, and although she got this one lit, the wind blew it out before she could get it close enough to the petrol bomb to ignite it.

Sophie let out a frustrated cry. 'Oh, for fuck's sake!'

Ben chuckled at this outburst. 'I think you've been spending too much time around Daz.' He shook his head slowly. 'You used to be such a polite young lady, and now look at the language you're using!'

Sophie glared at him ferociously, clearly annoyed at her inability to do what would have been a simple task if it weren't for the distraction of the nearby infected, but she said nothing. Instead, she took out a third match so she could try again. I glanced at Rob, knowing that we were running low on matches. 'You think I should go forward and help?'

Rob leant forward on the wheel. 'Given the look she just gave Ben, I really don't think she'd appreciate it, but we can't let her keep wasting something as important as matches just to spare her feelings.' He considered the situation for a moment. 'How about you give her one more go, to see if she can get it this time, and if she can't, then you go do it.'

I nodded, and together we watched as Sophie made to strike the third match. She learned from her previous attempts, and this time she struck it gently and took care to shield it with her body, keeping it lit long enough to touch it to the petrol-soaked sailcloth that protruded from the top of the bottle Daz was holding patiently. As it burst into flames, a relieved look spread across Sophie's face. She picked up a second petrol bomb and lit it off the first. Ahead of her, Daz steadied himself and then hurled the one he was holding through the air. I watched it arc across the sky, leaving a black smoky trail in its wake, and then land on the ship's deck. Instantly, it exploded in a ball of liquid flame that washed across the deck, setting it, and some nearby infected, alight.

Mitch lit a bottle off the one Sophie was holding and passed it to Ben, who then followed Daz's lead. His throw, too, found its mark. This was quickly followed by a second one from Daz, then a third. The four of them were now working quickly and efficiently, Mitch and Sophie keeping Daz and Ben supplied with lit petrol bombs, while all the time ensuring that each new one could be ignited off a previous one before it was thrown, so avoiding the need to use any more matches.

By the time the last petrol bomb had been hurled across the sea that separated it from us, the vessel was well ablaze, but the infected took little notice: all they were interested in was us. We pulled back and watched the ship burn. Even as the fire consumed their clothes, the infected continued to pace angrily along the deck, howling with frustration rather than pain. We watched, horrified, as the flames licked across their skin, causing it to bubble and burn, and their eyes to boil and pop, but still they didn't stop. The smell of burning flesh drifted across the sea and forced itself into our nostrils, causing us to gag and wretch. Finally, they succumbed to the flames and their movements ceased, but, by then, they were little more than charred skeletons.

As soon as it was clear that the ship was starting to sink, we turned to continue our voyage, but for many miles a pillar of smoke stayed visible, rising up into an otherwise clear sky, marking the ship's final position. For the most part, we remained silent, the images of the burning infected etched vividly into our minds. So consumed were they by the virus that they'd done nothing to stop the flames as they were burned alive. But they'd once been human; each had once been someone's child. I knew what the infected were capable of, what they'd do to me if they ever got hold of me, but did anyone, infected or not, really deserve an end like that?

We pulled into the sand-fringed bay on the east side of Mingulay just as the sun was going down, and once again it was setting the western horizon on fire. In keeping with the time of year, the temperatures were dropping fast and it was threatening to be a cold one. Rather than go ashore straight away, we decided we'd wait until the morning. This meant that, for the first time since we'd left South Africa a little over seven months before, we were short of bunks, but it would only be for one night.

After supper, I went out into the cockpit, finding the main cabin too crowded after it being just the five of us on board for so long. I sat in the dark, remembering the times when Jon and I had stayed up talking into the night, often falling asleep in each other's arms, despite the risk from drifters which might've come alongside and clambered aboard. Now, with hindsight, I shuddered at our stupidity, but back then, we'd felt it was the only way we could spend time alone with each other.

We'd called Jack almost as soon as we'd arrived back at Mingulay. As always, he was glad to hear from us, and he was heartened by the fact that we'd found more survivors. Less good was the news that the problem with the drifters in the Hope Town community was continuing to worsen, with one boat having been boarded the night before. They'd managed to deal with the problem without anyone getting hurt, but still, it was a worrying development.

I don't know how long I'd been in the cockpit, lost in my own thoughts, when Sophie and Daz came out, obviously hoping for some time alone themselves. They saw me and stopped, both looking slightly uncomfortable. They were about to go back inside when I rose, wishing them a good night as I passed. I thought I'd afford them the same luxury I knew Rob had done for me and Jon. After all, with the way the world now was, I knew you had to make the most of your time with those you loved.

***

'Hey.'

Startled by the unexpected voice, I looked up to find Ben standing behind me. I'd got Rob to run me ashore at first light and I'd been sitting in the churchyard where we'd buried the dead man the week before. I didn't know why I'd been drawn there once again, but I had, and as usual, his notebook lay open in my lap.

I returned the greeting. 'Hey.'

'Rob dropped me off so I could take a look around and see how this place stacks up against Soay.' He glanced off towards the horizon for a second. 'Mind if I join you?'

I shook my head and closed the notebook. I still didn't quite understand why I was being so protective of it, but for some reason I wanted to keep the unknown man's writings to myself. I felt a connection to him through it and I didn't think I wanted to share it with anyone else.

Ben sat down on the grass beside me and pointed to the notebook. 'What's that?'

I shrugged defensively. 'Nothing really; just a journal he,' I nodded towards the fresh grave in front of me, 'kept while he was on the island.'

I expected Ben to ask if he could see it, but he seemed to sense how I felt about it and he didn't pry. I don't think he realised how grateful I was to him for that.

I glanced over at Ben. 'You know, he almost made it. If we'd got here just a couple of weeks sooner, he'd still be alive.'

Ben sighed. 'I can't imagine what it would've been like for him being stuck out here all by himself. I mean, I've been at sea on my own for weeks at a time, but always by choice, and I always knew there'd be other people when I got back to shore. He must have thought he'd be on his own forever.'

I nodded, but didn't say anything.

Ben looked at the crude grave marker we'd made. 'Do you know his name?'

'No.' I fiddled with the notebook, riffling the edges of the pages absent-mindedly with my thumb. 'He never wrote it down. I've looked everywhere in the hut, but there's no record of it anywhere.'

Ben pulled his knees up and wrapped his arms around his legs. 'So it's kind of like the grave of the unknown soldier?'

I frowned. 'What d'you mean?'

'After the First World War, there were so many people who'd just disappeared on the battlefields, their bodies never found, or maybe found but never identified, so they were dumped into mass graves. Their families had nothing to bury, nowhere to mourn them, so someone came up with the idea of having a monument to all those who'd been lost, and inside they buried the remains of a soldier they couldn't identify. That way, those who'd lost people could imagine that it might be their son, or brother or father, and it gave them somewhere physical to hang their grief.'

As Ben spoke, I realised that, unknowingly, this was what I'd been doing here. I'd been projecting my feelings about losing Jon on to this other man, so similar in age to him. After Rob had shot Jon, we'd not been able to recover his body and we'd had to leave him, lying there amongst the infected, his body slowly decaying as the elements gradually eroded it to dust. Losing him had been bad enough, but not being able to bury him, to say good bye one last time, had made it so much worse.

While I hadn't been able to bury Jon, I'd been able to bury this unknown man, and in my mind, by doing this for him, it was as if I was doing it for Jon.

'Thanks, Ben.' I smiled at him.

He looked puzzled. 'For what?'

'For helping me understand a few things.' I gazed out over the bay where the catamaran rode at anchor. Despite the lateness of the year, I could see Jimmy, Mike, Daz and Jeff taking turns to dive over the side as Sophie watched, laughing.

Ben turned his attention to the sea as well. 'The grave of the unknown survivor: a monument to all those who made it through the initial outbreak, only to be lost later on. Somehow their deaths are more painful because they happened individually rather than all at once. A million nameless people killed on a single day is just a statistic; the loss of one friend is a tragedy.'

I looked across to see Ben wiping his eyes. 'You want to talk about it?'

It was as if a barrier had broken and it all came spilling out. About how Ben had known Tom for what seemed like forever; how it had been pure luck they'd been together when the outbreak started in Glasgow; about getting out of the city, the near misses, and Tom's eventual death at the hands of a psychopathic madman; about how Ben had watched him die, horribly and painfully, unable to do anything to prevent it. Just like Jon's, Tom's death wasn't caused by the infected, but instead, it had been caused by the need that some humans have to manipulate and control the actions of everyone around them. I know how this sounds, but I couldn't help thinking that if the disease allowed us to get rid of such people once and for all, and somehow start again, to rebuild a world without them, then maybe, just maybe, some good could come of it. It wouldn't be much, given how many had died, but at least it would be something positive that I could cling to.

Chapter Six

'Hope Town calling Mingulay. Come in, Mingulay.' Jack's voice burst out unexpectedly from the radio. I watched as Rob raced across the cabin to answer it. We usually checked in with each other at a set time every evening, and a call at noon potentially meant trouble.

'This is Mingulay. What's up, Jack?' I could hear the concern in Rob's voice and I listened intently.

'Hi, Rob. Don't worry, there's nothing wrong here.' There was a brief pause before Jack continued, 'When was the last time you heard from Tristan?'

Tristan was Tristan da Cunha, the radio name for a small group of survivors stranded on an isolated rock called Gough Island, situated close to where the South Atlantic met the might of the Southern Ocean. Like the lone man on Mingulay, they'd been on a research expedition to the remote outpost when the disease struck and with no one left to come and pick them up, they'd been there ever since. Unlike Mingulay, there hadn't been just one of them; there'd been fifteen. Yet, the harshness of life was taking its toll and gradually their numbers had been whittled down by accidents and ill-health. By the time we'd first made contact with them, they were down to nine, and they'd lost two more over the next month.

'Last week sometime, I think.' Rob looked across at me for confirmation and I nodded, 'CJ thinks the same, but we haven't been scheduled to speak to them recently.'

'We were meant to check in with them three days ago, but we've had no answer.' I could tell by his tone that Jack was worried. 'I'm hoping they just can't hear us for some reason. Rob, would you be able to see whether you can raise them?'

We hadn't known about the other groups of survivors for a long time, and we'd sometimes wondered whether the Hope Town community was all that was left of humanity. Then, in preparation for our trip across the Atlantic, we had finally got round to repairing our damaged shortwave radio and had been amazed to suddenly find there were others, just like us, clinging on in the remotest corners of the planet. These were the places the infected had yet to reach: remote mountain refuges; distant islands; a few large ships anchored far from shore; a couple of oil rigs standing on the shelf edge in the Gulf of Mexico. At the time we first made contact, with twenty-seven members, ours had been the largest surviving community any one had heard from, but it had given us a much-needed boost to our morale when we'd found there were others out there too; that we weren't all that remained of humankind.

The surviving communities made a plan to check in with each other on a regular basis, and we more or less kept to it, although the need to survive under harsh conditions often meant previously arranged check-ins were missed. However, missing several in a row was unusual, especially for Tristan. There were just the two of them left now, the remaining five having succumbed to an unknown illness that had flared up out of nowhere while we were crossing the Atlantic. I watched as Rob picked up the microphone again and pressed the transmit key. 'Mingulay calling Tristan. Come in, Tristan.' He released the button and waited a few seconds before pressing it again. 'Mingulay calling Tristan. Come in, Tristan.' Again there was no reply. He tried a third and a fourth time with the same result. Rob glanced at me, a troubled look on his face. 'This isn't good.'

I shifted uneasily on my seat, not knowing what to say.

Rob turned back to the radio and pressed the transmit button once more. 'Mingulay calling Hope Town. Jack, are you still there?'

Jack's voice instantly crackled out of the radio's speaker. 'Yeah, Rob, I'm listening. No luck then?'

Rob leant forward, eyes closed, and pinched the bridge of his nose. 'No.'

'Damn!' Jack sounded weary and run-down. 'Thanks, Rob. I guess they're gone.'

We waited for Jack to say something else, but the radio just hissed quietly to itself. Eventually, Rob turned it off to conserve battery power and came back over to the table where we'd been discussing whether we'd stay on Mingulay or go back to Soay. As before, the discussion had become polarised; while Mitch and Sophie were leaning towards Mingulay, Ben was still dead set against it. I could see Daz was in two minds, but he clearly felt a certain loyalty to Ben and was supporting him, despite the dirty looks Sophie was giving him.

Now, everyone remained silent, not quite knowing what to say. This was the first of the other communities which had been lost since we'd discovered they still existed, and this was the one we'd made our initial contact with, which meant we felt their loss as badly as if we'd lost people from our own group.

'Is there no' a chance they've just run out of power or somethin'?' Daz was trying to find a bright side.

Rob cleared his throat. 'It's possible, but unlikely. They've got a solar set-up just like the one in the hut here so I can't see them running out of power.' He lowered his head. 'Besides, they were both pretty sick when we last spoke to them. They've had no choice but to live off seabirds and fish, and you can't survive on that forever. By the sounds of it, they'd got scurvy.'

Daz's eyes narrowed. 'What's scurvy?'

Before Rob could say anything, Sophie beat him to it. 'It's when you don't get enough vitamin C. The human body needs vitamin C to function properly, and without it, it starts to break down. It's a horrible disease: you know you're dying, but you can't do anything about it unless you can get some vitamin C. Your joints ache, your gums start bleeding and your teeth fall out. Eventually, your skin turns black and peels off.'

Daz was horrified. 'That sounds like an awful way to go.'

'It is.' Sophie gave him a stern look. 'That's why we keep making you eat the sea lettuce we gather off the beach, even though you don't like it.'

Daz hunched his shoulders defensively. 'If you'd told me that was what was goin' to happen to me if I didn't, I'd no've complained so much!'

Surprised, I eyed Sophie with curiosity, wondering how a fourteen-year-old girl knew so much about a disease which had become increasingly rare in the Western world in the last couple of centuries. I'd certainly never heard of it until Jack and Rob had started discussing it as a possibility in the Hope Town community if we didn't get enough fresh vegetables. This had led to us creating floating gardens in old and abandoned boats, but those efforts were short-lived and they'd been destroyed in the hurricane that had devastated so much else in our community. It was the need to be able to grow the food we needed to stave off ill-health that had eventually driven us to try to find somewhere new where we could set up on land, and so led to us setting off for Mingulay. I turned to Sophie. 'How d'you know all that?'

Sophie shrugged. 'My mum was a doctor. She used to work in refugee camps.'

For reasons she'd yet to explain, Sophie didn't like talking about her family and this was the first time she'd revealed anything about her mother to me. There was a level of sadness in her voice when she spoke that made me wonder exactly what had happened to her mum, but I knew I shouldn't press her on it. Instead, I'd let her tell me when she was ready, and I moved the conversation back to the matter at hand. 'That's actually one of the reasons we came to Mingulay in the first place. If we're going to survive in the long term, we need to be able to grow food to prevent diseases like that. As Rob said, the soil's better here than on Soay.'

Ben opened his mouth to say something, then stopped and thought for a moment. 'I guess you're right. I think I was just clinging on to Soay because we'd worked so hard to try to build a life there and it's been good to us for so long.' He glanced across at Rob, 'Mingulay's the better option.' He paused again for a few seconds. 'And besides that hut up there's a damn sight more civilised than living in an old ruin.'

***

When Ben and the rest of his group moved ashore, I moved with them. While part of me felt like I was deserting Rob and the boys, the rest of me felt I needed to move on with my life and I couldn't do that while I was still living in the cabin I'd shared with Jon. Besides, it gave the boys more of a chance to be boys without having me always chasing them round to clean up. I knew Rob would keep them in line, but I also knew they needed their own space, too.

On the shore, I gradually found myself spending less and less time sitting at the unknown man's grave, or, indeed, reading through his notebook. Ben had made me realise that it wasn't his death I was mourning whenever I visited it, but rather it was Jon's, and I could do that anywhere. I still went there from time to time, especially when I was feeling low, but I was no longer obsessed with spending so much time there.

While I usually visited alone, it was not uncommon to arrive there and find one of the others sitting, staring out to sea. As Ben had suggested, the grave had become our equivalent of a war memorial, and we each found ourselves drawn there from time to time, especially when we felt the need to commune with those we'd lost. We didn't talk about it, and it wasn't something we, as a group, decided to do; it was just that we'd all lost people and each of us was naturally drawn there by some innate human instinct, as though it acted as a portal between the living and those we'd lost.

I found Ben up there one day and sat down beside him. At first I didn't speak, but there was a question I very much wanted to ask him and I felt this was as good a time as any. 'Ben, why did you change your mind about staying here rather than returning to Soay?'

Ben had been so set against staying on Mingulay until we'd heard about the loss of Tristan, but afterwards he'd conceded almost immediately. I was curious as to what had led him to change his mind so dramatically, in such a short space of time.

For a few seconds, I thought he hadn't heard me, then finally he spoke. 'It was listening to Rob talking about Tristan; it just reminded me about what we'd lost. And why.' Ben stared out to sea, picking absent-mindedly at the scrubby grass on which we sat.

'We lost our whole network of communities because a few people refused to change their minds about how we should be doing things.' He sniffed and wiped his eyes with his sleeve. 'And I realised I didn't want to be like that; I didn't want to be the one getting in the way of doing what was right.'

He turned to face me, his eyes glistening. 'Besides, I don't think it's necessarily important where we are: what's more important is that we work together as a group.'

'He made a difference, too.' Ben glanced at the wooden grave marker. 'There isn't a day goes by when I don't miss Tom, and having a place like this to come when it's bringing me down really helps.'

I looked at the grave marker, too. The unnamed man had been alone when he died, but now he was helping the rest of us to move on. While it was still tragic, it at least gave some meaning to his otherwise pointless death.

***

Once Ben and his crew had settled in on Mingulay, we set about the task of assessing our situation and working out how to improve it. We could get as much fresh water as we needed from the stream which fed the sink in the hut, and while it was hard work, we could get fish from the sea and other seafood from the rocky shore to the south of the main bay. It was repetitive, eating the same few things again and again, and we were always on the lookout for anything that we could find to vary our diet, but getting enough food to keep the nine of us from going hungry wasn't proving to be a major problem. We could gather seaweed from the rocks, too, which, while it didn't taste great, provided us with much-needed vitamins and minerals. Yet, a regular supply of food wasn't the only thing we'd need if we were to build a life on Mingulay.

Sitting in the hut, Ben was addressing the group. 'At the moment, the biggest risk we have is that we only have one boat. If anything happens to that, we're going to be in real trouble. So, I say the first thing we need to do is find a second boat.'

Daz smirked at him. 'You just want your own boat, so you can be captain an' order everyone else around again!'

Ben shook his head vigorously. 'No, I'm being serious!'

Daz continued to needle him good-naturedly. 'I dunno, you were no' too pleased when CJ started orderin' you around back on Soay.'

I crossed my arms and settled back into my seat. 'He's got a point there, Ben. Are you sure that's not why you want to get another boat?'

Mitch echoed my movements. 'Yeah, Ben, you sure that's not the reason?'

Ben held up his hands, 'Okay, okay, I'll admit that there's a certain level of truth in that, but in all seriousness, we can't rely on a single boat.'

Rob leant forward. 'I think Ben's right; it's a big risk being here if we only have one boat, so maybe that should be our first priority. But what else do we need?'

'How about a generator for the hut?' There was a slight nervousness to Mike's voice, as if he was worried his suggestion might not be taken seriously. 'You know, in case there's a problem with the solar panels or the wind turbine?'

Rob nodded. 'Good idea.'

Mike beamed, pleased at Rob's response. Meanwhile,

Rob turned to Sophie, who was sitting next to him, making notes. 'Let's add that to the list, and if we're going to have a generator, we'll need to get diesel from somewhere. We'll also need that for the boats, because there'll be times when we'll want to use engines rather than sails.'

'How about seeing if we can get some of the old buildings around here rebuilt?' I looked round the group. 'Once the others get here, we'll need more accommodation, won't we?'

'In that case,' Rob leaned across and ran his eyes down Sophie's list, double-checking what was already on it, 'we'll need to see where we can get something to make roofs from, and also see if we can get some more solar panels and wind turbines.'

Sophie was scribbling furiously, trying to get everything down, but suddenly she stopped and looked up. 'What about farm animals? Couldn't we do with things like chickens for eggs and maybe a cow for milk, and stuff like that?'

Ben and Rob nodded, and Sophie added them to the list.

Jimmy frowned. 'How're we going to get cows and chickens when we can't even catch a sheep here on the island?'

'Yeah.' Jeff was sitting beside Jimmy, 'We've been trying for days, and we haven't even got close.'

This was true. The boys, along with Mike and Daz, were becoming obsessed with the idea of eating red meat again, but they were out of luck and the sheep had managed to evade their every attempt at capturing one.

Mitch lifted her hands in an attempt to quieten the two teenagers down. 'We don't need to work out how we're going to get things quite yet. We just need to work out what we need.'

With that, we returned to our discussions and before we knew it, we had a long list of things. These we then divided into three categories: the essentials which we needed to sort out immediately; the staples which we'd need in the longer term; and the luxury items, like new clothes, which we'd deal with if and when the opportunity arose. Of the essentials, the first items on the list were getting a second boat, finding a generator and sorting out a reliable supply of diesel. With this in mind, and even though the days were growing ever shorter as the year grew to a close, and the weather gradually worsened, we set out to see what we could find.

***

'What about that one?' Rob pointed to a twenty-five-foot sailboat anchored close to the shore. 'It looks in pretty good shape.'

Ben shook his head. 'It's a bit on the small side. What about the one over there?'

'Okay.' With a clunk, Rob put the dinghy's engine into gear. 'Let's see if there's anyone home.'

We were in a large bay with small boats dotted all around, either riding at anchor or attached to moorings. Daz, Ben, Rob and I were in the dinghy, while the rest remained on the catamaran, which we'd anchored near the entrance. The edge of the bay was fringed with houses and other buildings, while what looked liked a ruin of a small Roman amphitheatre stood on the hill above the small town. Silhouetted in one of its stone arches, I could see a lone figure: an infected staring out over the bay, waiting for someone, anyone, to come near.

We didn't venture ashore, but everywhere we went that had once been inhabited, we saw infected haunting the land, lurking in the shadows and hovering in doorways. Most were almost skeletal, but some looked better fed than others. How, I wondered, were these individuals surviving so well? Were they preying on their fellow infected? If this was the case, this was a behaviour we'd never seen before. Were they feeding on something else? If so, what? On the odd occasion or two, we'd seen infected chase stray animals in Hope Town, but we'd never been sure why they were doing it. Maybe when they got hungry enough, the infected were capable of hunting other prey, but only if uninfected humans weren't available.

Ben saw me staring at the building on the hill and nodded towards it. 'McCaig's Tower; started at the end of the 1800s, but never finished.'

Daz frowned. 'Why'd anyone want to build somethin' like that in Scotland?'

Ben shrugged. 'Why do rich people do anything?'

'That's us almost here.' Rob slowed the engine. 'CJ, you know the drill.'

We all knew the dangers posed by going onto a strange boat, and Ben had first-hand experience, but we'd developed a well-honed strategy in the Hope Town community for making sure that small boats were empty before we climbed on board. All you needed to do was come up alongside and bang hard on the hull, all the way along. If there were any infected inside, you'd hear them screeching and crashing around as they tried to work out where you were and how to get to you. As we pulled up beside the yacht Ben had picked out, I reached out and hammered hard on the side. Almost immediately, it was answered by the unmistakable sound of infected. As always, the moans and growls sank deep into my soul, and I shuddered involuntarily as I turned to Ben. 'Looks like you'll need to pick another one.'

After an hour of searching through the available vessels, we finally found one which was both free of infected and acceptable to Ben. We left him on board, and Daz, Rob and I went back to one of the vessels which, while there were no infected on it, had nonetheless been rejected by Ben. We tied the dinghy to the stern and climbed on board. Rob looked round, 'I don't know why Ben didn't want this one; it's perfectly acceptable.'

I scowled at Rob. 'When have you ever settled for *perfectly acceptable*? When we were looking for the hulls for the garden boats, I seem to remember you were very … '

'Selective?' Rob ventured.

I shrugged noncommittally. 'I was going to go with *picky* myself.'

Daz looked confused. 'What's a garden boat?'

'Oh,' Rob sounded slightly flustered, and I knew why. 'It's an idea CJ's boyfriend and Jeff's father, Dan, came up with about how we could grow things without having to go ashore. We turned some unused boats into gardens by filling them with soil.'

'That's a brilliant idea,' then Daz's eyes narrowed. 'Did it no' work or somethin'?'

'In principle.' Rob bent down, pretending to examine a winch. 'It was just in practice that things went a little bit wrong.'

'What happened?' Daz eagerly shot back.

Rob and I glanced at each other, unsure exactly what to say. Eventually, I was the one that answered. 'The short answer is that they sank in a hurricane.'

'An' the long answer?' Daz was clearly curious, but neither Rob nor I wanted to go into the details. They were still too painful to talk about. Instead, we went down below and started examining the boat's engine. After a few minutes, Rob straightened up. 'I think this'll do.' He wiped his hands on his trousers. 'Now all we've got to do is work out how to get it out of here.'

By nightfall, we were ready to leave. Not only had we gained a second boat, and an engine we could use as a generator to help charge the hut's batteries, but we'd ransacked pretty much all the other unoccupied boats, removing dinghies to act as spares in case our own was ever damaged and searching for anything that might prove useful. Through our scavenging, we'd topped up our supply of matches, as well as obtaining several still-functional cigarette lighters, a number of half-full petrol cans and a selection of clothes to add to our rather limited wardrobes. These were particularly welcome as our existing clothes were starting to stink, no matter how frequently we tried to wash them. Part of this was simply because we lacked things like detergents and easy access to hot water, but also because once clothes had been worn for as long as ours had, it was pretty much impossible to get the smells out completely. It didn't help that washing our clothes by hand was laborious and time-consuming, and most of the time we had better things to do.

While Sophie and the boys sat inside with Ben, Mitch, Rob and I remained in the cockpit. We could have left straight away, but we were in no rush, and it made sense to wait until first light before heading off. There was already a chill in the air and it didn't seem like it would be long before winter was upon us.

I glanced at the others. 'So that's the first two essentials ticked off. Anyone got any ideas where we can get the third?'

Back in the Abacos, finding a reliable source of diesel had been relatively easy. There were plenty of fuel docks filled with vast quantities of diesel which we could access with little danger of being ambushed by infected. Here in Scotland, such fuel docks were much rarer, and of those that existed, most were mounted on the tops of tall stone piers that would require us to go ashore in order to get to them, and that would be too risky.

Rob ran a hand through his ever-increasingly out-of-control hair. 'I was thinking about that earlier. Did you see those fishing boats tied up to the quay? That type of boat has a pretty big fuel tank. Even if it's only half-full, one of those could give us all the fuel we'd need for the foreseeable future.'

Mitch thought about this suggestion. 'That could be pretty dangerous, Rob. They're still tied to the shore.'

Rob nodded. 'I know, but if we're careful, we might be able to get one of them untied and away from the dock without attracting the attention of any infected, then we could use it like a floating fuel tanker.'

I narrowed my eyes, watching Rob closely. 'Isn't there a risk that there will be infected on board?'

'Possibly.' Rob stared out into the darkness as if trying to see whether there were infected on the boats or not. 'But we could at least take a look in the morning before we leave.'

***

As the sun started to rise above the horizon, Rob and I took the dinghy and puttered, as slowly and as quietly as possible, towards where the fishing boats were tied alongside each other to one of the stone quays. Above them on the shore, the outlines of several buildings were visible, but I couldn't work out what they were, beyond the fact that they were industrial rather than residential. The bay was mirror-calm and the ripples from our wake were the only things that disturbed its glassy surface. We stopped twenty feet from the nearest fishing boat and examined the situation closely. The boats were stacked four deep, with only the final vessel secured to the dock itself. The sides rose almost six feet above the water, but by standing up, we could see their decks were cluttered with winches and fishing gear, and there were many places where infected could be hiding.

'I don't like the look of this, Rob.' I shivered, partly because of the early morning chill, but mostly because I was scared by the prospect of what might be hiding, unseen, on the fishing boats. 'It's too risky.'

Rob ignored me and motored forward before reaching out and banging on the hull. Unlike the fibreglass yachts, which echoed loudly when you did this, the thick metal of the fishing boat's hull made little noise. Rob thumped the hull again, and again there was no response. Rob looked at me questioningly. 'You think it's empty?'

I listened intently, but heard nothing moving inside. 'I can't hear anything, Rob, but that mightn't mean that there are no infected on board. They might just not have heard you.'

Rob thumped the side of the boat for a third time, still nothing stirred inside. He took a deep breath. 'I'm going to take a look.'

'Rob, no.' I tried to stop him, but he'd already

grabbed hold of a rope hanging down from the side of the fishing boat and was pulling himself upwards. A moment later, he'd disappeared over the gunwales and a quiet *thunk* told me he'd landed on the deck. It had been several months since we'd encountered the infected in any sort of truly dangerous situation, and I was worried this had led Rob to become complacent. Holding onto the end of the dinghy's rope, I climbed up until I could see Rob over the side of the boat, and from there I watched nervously as he crept around the deck, his eyes darting back and forth, ever alert for danger. Eventually, he reached the far side and set to work undoing the first of the ropes that attached it to the next boat along. His fingers must have been cold because several times he stopped to blow on his hands and rub them together before starting on the rope once more.

After several minutes of struggling in silence, he got it free and moved towards the next one. He'd just started pulling at it, when a circling seagull noticed him and floated down, landing on the edge of the boat a few feet from where he was working on the second rope. Unperturbed, Rob carried on, the seagull watching him intently, clearly used to having been fed by the local fishermen, wondering if this might mean it could get a free meal. It took a step forward and lowered its head, threatening to get in the way. Rob tried to bat it away with his arm, but the seagull simply floated up on out-stretched wings and landed again just beyond his reach. It stood for a second, staring at Rob with a dark beady eye, then threw back its head and let out an ear-shattering squawk that echoed across the bay.

Almost immediately, half a dozen heads, skin sallow, hair lank and lifeless, appeared amongst the equipment on the deck of the fishing boat closest to the quay. I hissed to Rob, 'Infected!'

Rob glanced up and saw them, their rage-filled eyes moving left and right as they tried to work out where the sound had come from. Rob froze, doing his best to blend in with his surroundings, but while the infected were fooled, the seagull wasn't. It waddled forward and pecked at Rob's sleeve. Rob tried to ignore it, but the bird persisted, grabbing his jacket with its beak and tugging, then he tried to push it away; the gull responded by throwing its head back again and crying out for a second time. This, combined with Rob's movement, was all the infected needed to hone in on him and with a collective scream, they were on their feet and running across the deck. The infected weaved in and out of the equipment, the remains of tattered yellow waterproofs flapping around them, before scrambling over the side and onto the second boat. The seagull screeched again, this time in alarm, and shot into the safety of the sky.

Unable to escape so easily, Rob turned and ran. He'd made it halfway across the deck when, in his haste to get away, he clipped the edge of a large, flat metal object which had been leaning against a winch that was as big as a small child. For a moment it wobbled, then it crashed to the deck with a metallic clang that was loud enough to rebound off the nearby buildings and reverberate around the town.

I saw a movement out of the corner of my eye and looked up to see the heads of more infected appearing over the top of the quay. At first, there were only one or two, but within seconds there were too many to count. They pushed forward, leaping the short drop down to the deck of the boat closest to the dock, and then, roaring and howling, they raced across its deck. Some were dressed in oilskins, while others wore thick jumpers, or the last shreds of flimsy t-shirts decorated with tourist-friendly slogans. One or two were naked: maybe their clothes had disintegrated in the time since they'd been attacked, or maybe that was just the way they'd been when they were infected. They were all thin and weather-worn, but their movements remained as fast as ever. As I watched, more streamed over the edge of the stone pier, following those which had gone before. I turned back to Rob, ready to urge him on and saw, to my horror, that his left leg was now pinned to the deck by the heavy metal plate. He was struggling to free himself, but as hard as he tried, he couldn't get the plate to move.

Without thinking, I made the only decision I could, and I threw myself over the gunwales and onto the deck, not even pausing to tie the dinghy off. I cursed my stupidity almost immediately as I glanced back and saw the dinghy bump against the hull of the boat before drifting away. I pushed this problem from my mind for the time being and raced over to where Rob was trapped. By then, the first of the infected had made it onto the boat next to the one we were on, and the decks of the ones nearer the dock were covered in a seething mass of infected that was surging towards us; still more poured over the edge of the quay with every passing second, drawn by the ever-increasing screams and snarls from the infected that already had us in their sights.

Rob turned his attention from the infected to me. 'CJ, get back in the dinghy. Now!'

I shook my head as I ran towards him. 'I'm not leaving you behind.'

'CJ, this'll take too long to move, you've got to go.' Rob sounded desperate. 'You've got to save yourself.'

When I reached him, I bent down and grasped the side of the metal plate. 'Just shut up and help me get this shifted.'

Rob tried to push me away. 'CJ, go. It's my own stupid fault I'm trapped here. There's no point in both of us getting killed.'

I ignored him and struggled to get the metal object lifted. I felt it move slightly and Rob must have felt it too because suddenly he stopped trying to force me away and started pushing it from below. Just then, there was a roar and we turned to see an infected crouching on the side of the neighbouring boat, readying itself to leap the short distance that separated the two vessels. As I turned back to the metal plate, I heard the infected land on the deck with a sickening thud, then the sound of more following. With all my strength, I pulled upwards while Rob pushed. For a second nothing happened, then suddenly it shifted. It was only a few inches, but it was enough for Rob to slip his leg free. I grabbed him and yanked him to his feet, but his leg gave way the moment he tried to put any weight on it.

A terrified look shot across Rob's face. 'CJ, I think it's broken. I'm never going to make it.'

I didn't need to look back to know how close the infected were. I could hear their feet clattering against the metal deck as they pounded relentlessly towards us. I threw an arm around Rob and yelled. 'Hold on.'

Half-carrying, half-dragging, I manhandled Rob to the nearest side of the boat and pushed him over the edge. Behind us, the mass of approaching infected let out a roar that engulfed us as it shattered the still morning air. Knowing what was coming, I didn't dare look behind me. I could already imagine their fetid breath on the back of my neck and the pain of their hands clawing and ripping at my flesh. I climbed onto the gunwales and launched myself forward, flying through the air before crashing into the water and disappearing far below the surface. The sea was freezing and I had to fight against my suddenly waterlogged clothes to stop myself sinking any deeper. To my left, I could hear more splashes and saw infected that had flung themselves after me in a vain hope of reaching me before I escaped, plummeting into the water. Yet, they couldn't swim and I watched their emaciated forms sink into the depths, still struggling frantically, uncomprehending of why they could no longer make any headway. I glanced around for Rob, but I could find no sign of him. I looked down, hoping against hope not to see him sinking downwards into the darkness along with the infected, but he wasn't there.

After what seemed like forever, and with the last of the breath in my lungs, I gave up my search and kicked upwards. Finally, I broke the surface again, spluttering and gasping for air, and almost instantly felt a hand grab the collar of my jacket. Fearing it was an infected I struck out, only to hear Rob yell. 'I'm trying to help!'

Realising I was okay, he let go, and together we swam the twenty feet to where the dinghy was now floating. We dragged ourselves on to it and lay there, shivering and breathing heavily. As Rob inspected his injured leg, I glared at him. 'Not one of your brightest ideas, was it?'

'It would have been fine if it hadn't been for that bloody seagull.' He pressed his leg, and winced with pain. 'I don't think it's broken, just badly bruised.'

I looked towards the fishing boats, their decks now covered with a swarm of infected that jockeyed for position, those at the back still pushing forward, crushing those in front or sending them over the side and into the water, the seagull circling lazily above them. It was clear we were going to have to find another way of getting diesel.

Chapter Seven

The return trip to Mingulay was, thankfully, uneventful and, despite Rob's injured leg, we soon had the old boat engine installed as a generator for the hut. This meant we'd be able to keep the batteries topped up on the still days of weak sunlight, which Mitch told me were often found in late autumn and early winter in this part of the world, at least as long as we could find the diesel to run it.

As the days grew ever shorter, the greater the proportion of what daylight was available to us was spent foraging for food, meaning we had little time to do anything else. We still went out scavenging from time to time, but these trips were few and far between, both because we had to work hard to feed ourselves, and because, as we moved into winter, there were fewer and fewer days where the weather was calm enough for us to be able to set out to sea.

Our days on Mingulay followed a regular routine. Rob, Jeff, Mike and Jimmy slept on the catamaran, while Ben, Mitch, Daz, Sophie and I slept in the hut, at least at first. Once we'd obtained the second boat, Ben and Daz moved onto that, giving Sophie, Mitch and me more space, and more privacy. Each morning, we'd wake with the sunrise and our first duty was always to check the island was still safe and infected-free. When we first arrived, we'd patrol every inch of the shoreline, looking for any evidence that infected might have drifted ashore in the night, but as time went on, with no sign of this happening, we reduced this to scanning the island from the top of the hut, accessed by a ladder Ben had made from slats he'd taken from the lean-to that had previously been used for storage. We were growing to trust that the cliffs would keep drifters from landing anywhere other than the sandy beach of the main bay, or the smaller rockier beach where we frequently foraged, and which lay a mile or so to the south. Both these locations could be seen from our vantage point on the hut's roof and, with the aid of the binoculars, could be examined closely for any signs that infected might have come ashore.

Despite the security that the cliffs gave us, there was always a period of worry after we woke, but before we'd ensured that Mingulay remained free of infected, and it was always an anxious wait until we got the call from one of the boats that there were no infected near the hut itself. This meant we could open the door, knowing the immediate vicinity was safe enough for us to venture outside.

After we'd ensured that nothing had happened during the night that would affect our safety, those on the boats would come ashore, and we finally be able to start thinking about breakfast. This was usually leftovers from whatever we'd eaten for supper the night before, and it was rarely something we looked forward to, but we had few other options.

Breakfast finished, and regardless of the weather, we'd head out to forage. We fished when we could, and we scavenged food from the rocky beach which lay to the south of the main bay when we couldn't. Here, there was plenty to eat, with crabs, mussels, limpets and butterfish all readily available, even on the coldest and windiest of days. These we supplemented by catching the occasional seagull. The gulls were wary, but they could be lured, with fish scraps, into an ingenious trap that Jimmy and Mike had cobbled together, and while they tasted rather gamey, they made a welcome addition to our diet whenever the boys caught one.

After food, fuel was our most pressing need, not just diesel for the generator and the boats, but things we could burn in the hut's range. At first, we relied on driftwood, but that was an unpredictable resource, and after a while we shifted over to peat. As someone who'd grown up locally, Mitch told us that peat was a traditional fuel in Western Scotland. Somewhere between plants and coal, it formed in the bogs on the western half of the island and we could follow the age-old method of digging it out and piling it on to stone platforms that had been created millennia ago for just this reason and which still peppered the north-west side of the island.

While soaking wet at first, once exposed to the elements, the peat dried to form crumbling dark bricks that could be burned in the range to provide the heat we craved to keep us warm, to cook our food, boil our water and to dry ourselves out in the naturally wet climate. The peat smoke infused the hut, curling out of the stove in blue-grey tongues that had a distinctive tinge I could never quite describe, imprinting itself on our minds, our clothes, our hair and, eventually, even our skin. It wasn't necessarily unpleasant, but it was certainly distinctive, and it was something that made me long for the clean and scentless central heating system, with its water-filled radiators, that had warmed the house where I grew up.

Some days, our food and fuel needs were met by lunchtime, and we had the rest of the day to ourselves, but more often, particularly when the weather was bad, we'd be lucky to be finished by the time it got dark. When we had the free time, we'd wash our clothes and ourselves in the nearest stream, downstream of the upper end of the pipe which provided water for the hut. Being shy, Sophie liked this the least, but Jimmy and Jeff were almost as uncomfortable with these arrangements. Mike put up with it, while Daz, Mitch, Ben and Rob did their best to take it in their stride. Myself, I preferred the feeling of being clean over being embarrassed, and I regularly exposed myself to the elements, almost regardless of the temperature, in order to feel clean, even if it was just for a few moments before I had to slip back into my increasingly grimy clothes.

If, after all that, there was still daylight to spare, Daz, Sophie, Jeff, Mike, and Jimmy turned to their obsession of tasting red meat again and would spend their free time trying to catch a sheep, but no matter how hard they tried, they were always outsmarted by the famously small-brained mammals. It was probably just as well: I wasn't really too sure they'd know what to do with a sheep, if they'd ever managed to catch one.

Rather than waste our energy chasing sheep we could never catch, Ben, Rob, Mitch and I concentrated our efforts on maintenance. With a hut and two boats to keep in good working order, there was always something that needed done, and we were never short of work. All the time, we kept a careful eye out for any evidence that infected might be approaching the island. It became automatic: every few minutes, one of us would straighten up from whatever we were doing and scan the surrounding seas, checking for drifting vessels, or flotsam and jetsam to which infected might be clinging. We rarely saw anything that caused us more than a fleeting worry, but the implications of even a single infected reaching the island were so terrible, it meant we could never completely relax.

Each day, as the sun started to set, we'd make a final check that the island remained infected-free, and then we'd all return to the hut for supper. As we ate, we'd make plans for the following day. Usually, this was more of the same, but if the weather looked like it was going to be good, and we had enough food left over from the previous day, we'd plan a scavenging trip to one or other of the surrounding islands to see what useful items we might be able to find. With our bellies full, and the next day sorted, we could finally settle down for the night. Sometimes we stayed up talking, sometimes we played games or sang, just to pass the time, but mostly we were so tired that all we wanted to do was sleep.

The scavenging trips away from the island were a welcome break from the monotony of our regular routine and, more often than not, they brought back a surprise or two, some of which improved our lives dramatically. One was a small flock of chickens which Jeff had spotted pecking along the shoreline on Eriskay, one of the islands which lay to our north. We managed to tempt them, in ones and twos, into a trap made of an upturned box wedged open with a stick attached to a length of string. It took us a few hours to capture them all, but the opportunity to vary our diet with fresh eggs made it well worth the effort.

On returning to Mingulay, we set up a makeshift henhouse in what was left of the lean-to behind the hut. From then on, the hens spent their nights roosting inside and their days pecking and scratching amongst the tussocks of grass that surrounded it, feeding on whatever titbits they could find, supplemented by the leftover scraps of food we'd throw to them after every meal. Even though they were only chickens, it quickly became clear that each had its own unique personality, and although we contemplated it from time to time, none of us could bring ourselves kill any of them, especially when we had plenty of other food available to us from the surrounding seas. Anyway, the eggs that they supplied each day meant the chickens were more valuable to us alive than dead, and we had to focus on what was best for the long term, even if we'd all appreciate the one-off feast each would provide if we chose to dispatch it there and then.

Another unexpected surprise was the dog, which Jimmy took under his wing and christened Dougie, although he couldn't understand why Daz found this quite so amusing. To this day, I don't know where Dougie came from or how he'd survived, all on his own, for as long as he had, but when he appeared in our lives one day, he improved it in ways we never thought possible. He provided both companionship and an early warning system against infected, as well as a way to finally corral the semi-wild sheep with which we shared Mingulay.

Rob, Jimmy and I had been sailing parallel to one of the beaches on the west side of Tiree, when we saw a small group of infected racing along it. At first, we couldn't work out what they were doing, but then Jimmy spotted the lone dog: he was running flat-out and was little more than a black and white blur, but the hunt had clearly been going on for some time. His tongue was hanging from his mouth and we could see he was starting to tire. Jimmy pleaded with Rob to do something about it. 'Come on, you can't just let them catch him. They'll tear him apart.'

After his very near miss on the fishing boat, Rob had been reminded just how dangerous the infected could be, and how quickly things could go wrong because of factors beyond our control. This meant he was standing firm. 'We can't risk our safety, or the boat's, for a dog. The others are depending on us.'

I'd always grown up around dogs, and I knew where Jimmy was coming from. 'How about this, Rob; Jimmy and I will take the dinghy and see if we can get to him before the infected do. The first hint of danger and we'll come straight back.'

Rob frowned. 'But what're you going to do?'

I glanced towards the shore, where the dog was still running as fast as he could, the infected close behind. 'I don't know, but if we're going to be able to do anything, it'll need to be fast.'

Being outnumbered two to one, Rob relented. 'Okay, go; but be quick about it. And stay safe!'

By the time Rob finished speaking, both Jimmy and I were in the dinghy and had the engine started. A moment later, we were skimming across the water as fast as it would go. By that time, the dog had doubled back on himself in a desperate attempt to escape the infected, but they were still hot on his tail, and were gaining with every passing second. I set a course that meant we'd meet the beach just ahead of the dog, and then sent Jimmy up front. 'Call him. Get his attention, so he knows we're here.'

Jimmy cried out, but the dog showed no sign of having noticed.

We were nearing the beach by then, and both the dog and the infected were racing towards us.

'CJ, he's not going to make it.' There was desperation in Jimmy's voice. 'Do something!'

I cranked the throttle up a notch, taking the engine into the danger zone, and us dangerously close to the water's edge: one wrong move and we'd be stranded; if that happened, we'd be dead in seconds. At the last possible moment, the dog finally saw us. He swerved and leapt, whipping his tail out of the grasping hands of the leading infected.

As he landed on the rubber pontoon, his back legs

dangling into the water, I shouted to Jimmy. 'Grab him and hold on!'

Jimmy pounced, gripping him tightly so that he wouldn't slip backwards into the water, just as I slammed the engine into reverse and turned the throttle. The engine strained and, for a second, it seemed as if the dinghy was still going forward, taking us towards the infected, but finally we started moving backwards and with ever-increasing speed, we shot away from the beach.

Once we were far enough away from the shore to be safe, I helped Jimmy pull the dog fully on board and he lay on the bottom of the dinghy, panting, his limbs weak from the overexertion of his escape. Jimmy stroked his head and whispered to him that he was safe now. The dog seemed to understand because he made a half-hearted attempt to lick Jimmy's hand, but he was so spent, he could barely lift his head off the deck. Back on the land, the infected, with no prey to chase, lost interest and started to drift away from the water's edge, and from each other.

Dougie rapidly recovered from his ordeal and soon became an integral part of our group. The only long-lasting effect of the whole episode was that while he spent most of his time with Jimmy, Dougie developed a bit of an abandonment complex. This meant he'd bark and howl whenever we left and then greet any of us over-eagerly on our return, even if we'd been away for as little as a few minutes. Being a border collie, Dougie also had a natural instinct to herd things and was adept at rounding the island's sheep into tight groups, whether we wanted him to or not.

***

Our main issue, beyond the daily grind to find enough food, dig out peat for the stove and ensure that the island remained infected-free, continued to be getting enough diesel to meet our needs. So far, we'd managed to keep our stores topped up by siphoning fuel from the tanks of uninhabited boats which were anchored or moored far enough from shore to allow us to avoid the infected. The problem was such vessels tended to be small, as well as few and far between, and many had been emptied before we'd even reached Scotland. This meant we were rapidly depleting what little diesel was safely available to us. The other obvious option was to try the fishing boats again, but after the experience Rob and I had had, no one was keen on that option. This meant we still needed to find a permanent solution to this issue, or accept that we'd soon have to give up on using the boat engines and the generator, which would make life much more difficult.

Ben had one possible solution, but to begin with, the rest of us were sceptical. We were sitting around in the hut one night discussing, once again, our options for getting more fuel when Ben first mentioned it to the rest of us. 'I was thinking about Soay again, and that old basking shark hunting station. You know, one of the reasons they hunted them was for their livers.'

Daz frowned. 'I thought we were talkin' about where to get diesel. What do baskin' shark livers have to do with that?'

Ben laughed. 'Where d'you think oil comes from?'

This puzzled Daz further. 'But oil comes out of the ground. Everyone knows that, don't they?' He glanced round at the rest of the room. The other teenagers looked just as nonplussed as he did, but Mitch and Rob were both smiling.

I didn't know where they were going, but I knew enough to know that you could burn almost any type of oil in diesel engines. Jon was the one who'd told me: he'd run out of fuel once on a boat delivery and they'd used cooking oil from the galley to get them the last few miles to shore.

Ben leant forward. 'You can get oil from loads of things: plants, peanuts, whale blubber and, most importantly, fish livers. A basking shark's liver makes up a quarter of its mass and most of that's oil. Given that a big basking shark can weigh more than five tons, that's an awful lot of oil.'

Sophie's eyes narrowed. 'But can you actually run an engine on it?'

Ben pointed at her. 'That's the million-dollar question.'

'How're we going to find out?' It was Mike's turn to join the conversation.

Rob sat back. 'That's another very good question.'

'Aye, how big d'you say they can get? Five tons?' Daz sounded incredulous. 'You'd need one hell of a big fishin' rod to catch somethin' that size!'

Ben chuckled, 'I'm not saying we use a fishing rod, I say we do it the old-fashioned way.'

Mitch turned to him. 'You mean harpoon them, like Maxwell did?'

Jeff's forehead furrowed. 'Who's Maxwell?'

Sophie's eyes lit up. 'He was the one who set up the hunting station we were staying in on Soay, wasn't he, Ben?'

Daz nodded. 'Aye, I remember Ben tellin' us about it.'

Rob glanced across at Ben, 'You know how to harpoon a basking shark?'

'No,' there was a slight pause before Ben continued, 'but the basking sharks won't be back until the spring. The way I see it, we've got all winter to work out how to do it.'

Rob rubbed his beard thoughtfully. 'I suppose it would give us something to do, and it wouldn't hurt to try.'

Daz nodded again. 'Yeah.' He stood up and mimed throwing a harpoon into something on the floor near the door of the hut. 'I'd be up for givin' it a go.'

***

As we approached mid-winter, I began to notice that Rob kept disappearing, sometimes for hours at a time. I started to worry that the situation was beginning to get him down again, but I couldn't work out why: while life was hard, and our diet somewhat monotonous, we were, on balance, doing well. Not only was Mingulay more than living up to Rob's anticipations, according to Jack, the problem they'd been having with the drifters since the hurricane was finally beginning to ease off. What on earth, I wondered, could be getting Rob down? Unable to work out what was going on, and deeply concerned, I decided to follow him one day. Halfway to the empty bird colonies at the southern end of the island I stopped and, smiling to myself, I turned back.

The next morning I went down to the beach with Mitch to forage for food. I started to speak several times, but each time the words failed to come. Eventually, Mitch stopped and turned to me. 'You know, don't you?'

I played dumb. 'Know what?'

Mitch looked at me. 'About me and Rob.'

I grinned. 'Yeah.'

Mitch seemed slightly surprised by my reaction. 'And you're okay with it?'

'Of course I am. I'm happy with anything that makes

Rob happy.' I narrowed my eyes, no longer smiling. 'Just don't hurt him, or you'll regret it.'

Mitch put her hands on her hips. 'Don't worry. I'm not going to hurt him. We're both adults. We've talked about it; we talked about it before anything happened between us. We both know where we stand with each other.'

I was confused. 'So why hide it?'

'Partly because we wanted to see how it went before we let anyone else know,' Mitch turned and walked along the beach again. 'And partly because we were worried how other people might react.'

I followed her. 'You mean Ben, because Tom was Ben's best friend and you were seeing him before he was killed?'

Mitch smoothed away a hair that the wind was blowing across her face. 'Actually, Ben knows. We've been friends for years. I wanted to know how he'd feel about it before I even thought about starting anything.'

I frowned. 'So who were you worried about?'

'You.' Mitch stopped again. 'Rob was worried about you, CJ.' She quickly, and automatically, scanned the sea, searching for anything that might mean approaching infected, before carrying on. 'I told him you'd be okay with it, but he was worried it might remind you too much of you and Jon.'

'Men!' I shook my head. 'Why do they always think they know best? I'm going to have to have a word with Rob ... making you sneak around like that!'

Mitch put a hand on my arm. 'CJ, when you do, just remember his heart was in the right place.'

'Hmmm.' Then a thought occurred to me. 'You want to have some fun with this?'

I stood near the empty seabird colony at the southern end of the island looking out to sea, waiting for Rob to arrive, the hood up on the waterproof jacket I was wearing. I heard him approach, but resisted the urge to turn around. When he reached me, I felt his arms close around me and he bent in to kiss me on the neck. That was when I spun round. At first, Rob was confused, and then he froze, a look of complete and utter shock written across his face. I stared at him, eyes narrowed and lips pursed. 'Rob, what the hell d'you think you're doing?'

'I thought you were ... I ... I mean.' Rob was stuttering so heavily he could barely get the words out.

I could feel his arms still around my waist. 'Do you mind taking your hands off me?'

Rob leapt backwards, his face redder than I'd ever seen it before. 'Oh shit! Yes, of course. Look, you're wearing ... I was meant to be meeting ... I thought you were ...'

The look on his face was priceless and I could no longer hold back the laughter.

'Why are you laughing?' Rob was more confused than ever. 'Aren't you mad at me?'

'Rob, I know.' I could hardly get the words out because I was laughing so hard. 'Mitch and I set you up. She told me you'd arranged to meet her here, and I borrowed her coat.'

'And you're really not mad?' Rob sounded relieved.

'A little, but mostly because you thought you had to hide it from me.' I finally managed to rein in my laughter. 'I know you were trying to protect me, but bloody hell, Rob, I've got this far. I mightn't have been able to stand on my own two feet when all this started, but I can now. If I couldn't, I wouldn't still be here, would I?'

'Yeah.' Rob sank down onto the grass. 'Yeah, I know. Sorry, CJ, it's just ... I know how much you miss him; I know how much it hurt you when he died.'

I sat myself down beside him. 'Jon's gone. It's taken me a long time to get over that. I'll never forget him, but I've got to find a way to move on. I can't have the rest of you putting your lives on hold, or feeling you need to keep your relationships hidden, just in case it hurts me.'

Rob turned to me. 'When did you get so grown-up, CJ?'

I stared out to sea, trying to quell the pain I could feel welling up inside me. 'When I had to.'

***

While Mitch and Rob might not have confided in me about their relationship, Sophie was another matter. Although she'd known Mitch longer, she seemed to feel that since I was closer to her age, I was better positioned to provide her with the advice she felt she needed from time to time. In the old world, she'd have had friends to discuss these questions with, and whose opinions she could seek out when she needed them, plus, magazines she could read, websites she could search out. Now, with the way the world was, it fell to me to fulfil all those roles.

She always seemed to wait until we were on the rocky beach at the south-eastern corner of the island, foraging for food amongst the seaweed, before we had one of these conversations. In fact, it had got to the point that I could tell she wanted to talk about something just because she'd ask me to go on one of these foraging trips with her. The rest of the time she'd go with Daz, glad of the opportunity to get some alone time with him well beyond the prying eyes of the rest of us.

In mid-December — or at least what I thought was mid-December, although I had to admit I'd long ago lost track of the date by then — she approached me once more and we set off down the island. We'd barely gone more than a few yards when the question she was dying to ask burst out of her. 'CJ, how old were you when you, you know, when you first …?' Her voice trailed off.

'If you're asking what I think you're asking,' I glanced across at her, 'you're probably not old enough to be thinking about doing it if you're not mature enough to talk about it.'

We walked in silence for a few minutes as my words sank in.

'CJ, how old were you when you first …' she paused and then spat the last two words out as quickly as possible as if she was scared they'd get stuck in her throat if she spoke them any slower. '… had sex?'

I'd been wondering how long it would take for this subject to come up, and I'd been dreading it. I think she was, too, because I got the impression she'd been wanting to talk about it for a while, but that she'd kept chickening out at the last minute. Suddenly, I knew how my mother had felt when she'd had to have 'the talk' with me. I thought about her for a moment and about all the conversations we'd never have: about getting married; about whether or not I'd decide to have children; about which order to do these two things in, if I decided to do either, and a sense of sadness settled over me. I wondered if she'd have liked Jon, if she'd have approved of him. My dad wouldn't have done, but then my dad was old-fashioned and he'd seemed to think it was his job to never be happy with any of my boyfriends.

'CJ, are you okay?' Sophie was concerned by my silence, and slightly red-faced. 'Sorry, I shouldn't have asked. It's none of my business.'

'No, it's alright. I was just thinking about ...' I heard my voice peter out. I cleared my throat. 'Anyway, it doesn't matter what I was thinking about.'

With that I took a deep breath and started a conversation I'd only ever had from the other point of view.

Chapter Eight

Near the end of the month, Rob gathered us all together and led us towards a gentle slope on the western side of the island. The weather was blustery and the cold wind whipped across our faces, bringing tears to our eyes. Rob had woken us early, and despite the protestations of the teenagers, he'd forced us out of our beds and into the slowly dawning day.

'Rob, why are you making us do this?' Jeff whined.

'Yeah, Rob,' Jimmy stifled a yawn. 'It's not even properly light yet.'

'An' I've no' even had any breakfast; I'm starvin'.' As if on cue, Daz's stomach rumbled loudly.

Sophie punched him playfully on the arm. 'You're always thinking with your stomach. Sometimes there are more important things than food.'

Unfortunately, the intended effect of Sophie's words was ruined by her own stomach choosing that exact moment to make a noise louder than Daz's. Sophie scowled, but everyone else laughed. While I wouldn't admit it out loud, I was none too pleased at having been woken up so early either. I'd been having a dream in which, while I couldn't quite remember the details, I'd felt safe and warm, and I begrudged Rob for yanking me back to reality with quite such a harsh bump. In fact, the only one who seemed happy to see us out and about so early was Dougie, and he bounded around, trying to persuade each of us in turn to throw an old tennis ball he'd found on the beach for him to retrieve.

On reaching Rob's intended destination, we found a carefully constructed pile of stones which I was sure hadn't been there last time I'd passed through that part of the island. It seemed I was not alone in thinking this.

Ben nodded towards it. 'That's new.'

Rob smiled. 'I built it yesterday.'

Jimmy and Jeff ran forward and inspected it closely. After completing their circumnavigation, Jeff looked up. 'What's it for?'

Rob smiled again. 'D'you know what day it is today?'

Jeff wrinkled his nose in concentration. 'Christmas?'

Rob put a hand on his shoulder. 'Close. It's the winter solstice.'

Daz frowned. 'The winter *what*?'

'Solstice.' Rob repeated. 'It's the shortest day of the year. After today, the days start getting longer and it means that we'll have passed mid-winter.'

'Oh, yeah.' Daz's eyes opened wide in recognition. 'It's like the hippies' New Year, is it no'?'

Rob gave Daz a disapproving look. 'I wouldn't quite put it that way, but yes, it marked the New Year in many traditional societies. It was an important day for them because it signified that from that point onwards, things would get better again: new shoots would start appearing; birds would soon be returning; and it would almost be time to start thinking about planting the next year's crops. But d'you know how they knew it was coming?'

I could see the concentration on Daz's face as he tried to work it out, but before he could come up with an answer, Sophie cried out. 'Stone circles!'

Her eyes darted to the newly piled rocks. 'We're going to build a stone circle, aren't we?' There was a level of excitement and anticipation in her voice I hadn't heard before. 'Like Stonehenge!'

Rob nodded. 'Well, nothing quite as big as

134

Stonehenge, but something along the same lines; something so we can easily know what time of year it is, so that we can know what's coming and can plan ahead.'

I looked at him incredulously. 'But Stonehenge was huge. We can't possibly move stones like that; not just the nine of us.'

'I'm not thinking of anything that grand, just some carefully placed piles of stones, like this one.' Rob gestured to the cairn he'd made the previous day. 'We'll build them so they'll line up with the setting sun on particular days of the year.'

Mitch crossed her arms. 'But how'll we know where to put them?' She sounded sceptical.

'That's why we need to build it today. The sun sets pretty much due east on the spring and winter equinoxes no matter where in the world you are.' Rob pulled out a compass he'd brought ashore from the catamaran. 'That places it about there.' He pointed off into the distance. 'That's because the sun's directly over the Equator. If we know where it sets on the winter solstice, we can then build a line of stone cairns which will mark out where the sun will set between these two points to tell us how far away we are from each one. We can then make a mirror image of this on the northern side to allow us to mark out the rest of the year.'

Ben turned to Rob. 'That's brilliant! How on earth did you know how to do that?'

Rob shrugged. 'It's the same principle behind any ancient calendar, and I've studied a few in my time.'

Ben lowered his head sheepishly, 'I keep forgetting you used to be an archaeologist.'

Rob held out his arms, palms open and facing upwards. 'Once an archaeologist, always an archaeologist.'

Jimmy patted Dougie's head before finally taking the tennis ball the dog had been carrying since we'd left the hut, and throwing it as far as he could. Dougie streaked after it as Jimmy turned to the rest of us. 'But how d'you know today's the shortest day?'

'That's a good point.' I knew I'd lost count of what day was what, and I was keen to hear how Rob could be so certain he was right.

'Partly because I've been keeping a log,' Dougie returned with the ball, and this time it was Rob's turn to throw it, 'but also because I've been using the sextant to measure the height of the sun above the horizon at noon, and then comparing this to what the tables say it should be for this latitude on a specific date. With the weather around here, I haven't been able to do it often, but just enough to keep myself on track, at least so far, although I'll lose track eventually.'

I was confused. 'But when we were crossing the Atlantic, none of us could use the sextant properly. How come you're able to use it now?'

Rob smiled. 'It's much easier to use when you're stationary on land and not rolling around on a boat. It also helps if you already know where you are.'

Sophie looked perplexed. 'You don't have a watch, though. How d'you know when it's midday?'

It was Ben, rather than Rob, that answered her question. 'It's when the shadows are shortest.'

Rob nodded. 'Exactly.'

'But why can't you just keep using the sextant if you want to know what day it is?' Mike had sat himself down on the ground a few feet away and was leaning back, his arms supporting his weight. 'Why d'we need to waste our time making something like this?'

'Because eventually the sextant will break, or we'll lose it, or the tables we need to do the calculations will become unreadable, or ...' Rob's voice stalled for a second, '... or something might happen to me.'

'Enough talking.' Mitch cut Rob off before the full implication of what he'd just said could sink in. She was rubbing her hands together and stamping her feet, trying to warm herself up. 'I'm happy to accept that Rob knows what he's talking about on this one. Shall we just get started?'

It took most of the day, and some careful measuring, but by the time the sun was going down, we had the stone calendar finished. It was a line of seven equally spaced stacks of rocks. The two at each end were the largest and most complicated, forming rough arches rather than just rocky pinnacles like the rest of them. If everything had been calculated correctly, the setting sun would shine directly through these arches on the winter solstice for the southern-most one, and on the summer solstice for the one at the northern end. There was a slightly smaller and simpler arch in the middle, consisting of two piles of rocks connected by a large, flat stone on the top, which marked the position of the sunset at both the spring and autumn equinoxes, while the smaller piles between these represented each passing month.

Once we were finished, we gathered at the cairn Rob had built the day before, and from which all the measurements had been taken when deciding on where to place the others. While it had been overcast all day, just as the sun was starting to set, the clouds began to part, promising to let us have our first glimpse of whether or not we'd got the stones in the right places.

We waited with bated breath as the sun dipped closer and closer towards the western horizon. There was a palpable air of anticipation, but none of us dared speak. Even Dougie seemed to sense something important was going on, and for once he sat still, watching us carefully rather than racing around as he usually did. First, the sun disappeared behind the cairn which was meant to mark this day and then, a second later, it reappeared, shining directly through the arch we'd constructed, lighting our faces with a pale golden glow, before finally disappearing from sight.

As we returned to the hut through the gloaming, Dougie running around excitedly between us, Mitch took Rob's hand. 'That was amazing!'

He smiled at her. 'I really wasn't too sure it would work, but it looks like we did a pretty good job.'

While Mike, Jimmy, Jeff and Daz trailed some way behind, Sophie was walking alongside them. 'Can we mark things on it?'

Rob glanced across at her. 'Like what?'

Sophie thought for a moment. 'Special events, like birthdays and that sort of thing.'

Rob reached out and ruffled her hair. 'Of course you can. All you need to do is put something in the right place relative to the cairns we built. It can be anything: rocks, seashells, pieces of wood, whatever you can find.'

Daz had run up to join them and was listening in. 'But how'll we know where to put them?'

'You can either put it in place at the end of the day itself, or you can calculate where it should go, based on the distance between the existing cairns.' Rob bent down and took the ball Dougie was now offering him. He threw it ahead of us and watched as the dog disappeared after it into the growing darkness. 'If we put markers for things which happen between mid-winter and mid-summer on the far side of the stones, and the ones for things which happen between mid-summer and mid-winter in front of them, we'll have a calendar which moves in a clockwise direction.'

Daz nodded.

'Can we mark other things, too?' Sophie now sounded solemn. 'Things we want to remember, even if they're not necessarily good things?'

Rob stopped and looked at Sophie. 'You can mark anything you want on it; we all can. There are things we'll all want to remember. If you need a hand working out where to put anything, just let me know and I'll make sure you put it the right place. You don't even need to tell me what it is, if you don't want to.'

Sophie smiled at him. It was a sad sort of smile, as if she was thinking of someone she'd lost, someone she missed immensely. 'Thanks, Rob.'

***

Creating the calendar had an odd effect on us, and it was one I hadn't expected, although I think Rob might've. Now we had a way to measure what day it was, we started to live less in the past and anticipate the future more. I caught Jimmy and Jeff out there one afternoon, pacing off distances, each holding a large and distinctive stone in their hands.

I was curious. 'What're you doing?'

Jeff kept his head down as he counted out his steps. 'Working out how long it is to our birthdays!' He took another couple of steps and placed his stone carefully on the ground. 'That's mine there.'

As Jimmy continued to pace out his position, I looked at the line of stone cairns and arches: spread around them were all kinds of objects, each carefully placed to mark a special date. Some were happy days, like birthdays, while others were functional, like the date we estimated the seabirds were likely to return, offering us a new and easy-to-access food supply. Ben had done his best to work this out from the information in some field notes he'd uncovered in the hut before marking it on the calendar.

There was a third kind, too, and that was the reason I was there. I waited for the boys to depart, racing each other back to the hut across the uneven ground, and for the sun to start to set. Once it did, I took a small metal tube from my pocket and placed it vertically in the ground in just the right position. Around this, I built up a pile of small stones until it was completely covered. I couldn't be certain, but I'd found the empty rifle cartridge wedged into a corner of the cockpit when we'd tidied the boat up after the hurricane. It seemed like it had fallen there after Rob had fired the shot that had finally put Jon out of his misery, and by some miracle it hadn't been washed into the sea in the storm that followed.

I don't quite know why I'd kept it, maybe in an attempt to hold on to Jon for as long as I possibly could. Now I knew this was the perfect place to bury it, so I'd always remember him. I could've chosen to mark the day he died, but that was too painful. Instead, I chose to mark today, which would have been his twenty-fifth birthday. I hadn't got to bury Jon, but at least now I had a way to mark his presence in the world, and a way to make sure I'd never forget him.

The stone calendar was our first modification of the island; our first attempt to alter it to fit our needs, rather than just trying to blend into its existing landscape. In many ways, it marked a turning point in our life on Mingulay; a shift from just struggling to survive to trying to live better lives there. We started to view the island differently, looking for ways in which we could adapt and improve it.

One day, Ben and Daz returned from a scavenging trip with a very old and battered enamel bath they'd found close to the shore on an otherwise uninhabited island. For years, it had served as a drinking trough for livestock, but now Ben and Daz had other plans for it. They floated it ashore and dragged it up to an area of grass close to where the stream we used for washing met the beach. Here, they built a stand for it from rocks and stones and then dug a channel that would allow us to divert part of the stream and fill it whenever we wished. There was space for a fire to be lit beneath it, meaning we could warm the water, affording us a luxury I'd often thought I'd never experience again: a long, relaxing soak in hot water. Yes, it had to be done in full view of everyone else, but I wasn't going to let that stop me enjoying the experience. This set-up also provided a much more effective way of washing our clothes, as well as ourselves, leaving us feeling properly clean for the first time in ages.

We also set to work on the old stone buildings, deciding which we might able to reconstruct using stones taken from ones that were too far gone for us to be able to do anything with. Once Jack arrived in the spring, we'd have many more people to house, and while they could live on their boats at first, there was no doubt they'd all want to move on to the island as soon as they could.

The work rebuilding the stone cottages was back-breaking and time-consuming, and we had to fit it around our foraging and scavenging. We also had to learn the required skills by trial and error, which slowed us considerably, but gradually, over several months, the skeleton of the first new building grew out of the ruin it had been on our arrival. By the time the winter storms started to wane, the walls and the chimney stack were complete, and all that was left was to add a roof, and to work out what we were going to use for windows and doors. While Rob assured us that Mingulay would have once had trees which could have provided sufficient timber for both roof beams and shutters, he also told us that these had all been cut down within a few centuries of the first people arriving on the island thousands of years before. Now we'd have to look elsewhere or work out another way to make the buildings weather-tight.

When we rebuilt the walls, we followed the traditional design and used centuries old building techniques that required no bricks, tools or mortar. Stones were stacked on top of each other, carefully positioned based on their shape so they locked together and held each other in place, to build walls that were several feet thick and rose no more than one storey above the ground. The knack of fitting the stones together so that they remained where they should was difficult, but some of us were better at it than others.

Oddly, it was Mike and Daz who were the best, and they were responsible for much of the rebuilding, while the rest of us concentrated on foraging for food and supplies. One of the reasons they worked so hard was they acted like typical teenage boys, competing against each other to see who could complete individual sections of the wall the fastest. While Mike did well to keep up with Daz, he was a year younger and his body that little bit less physically mature, meaning Daz usually won. You would've thought the competitive element they brought into it would've led to poor quality construction, but it didn't, and both seemed to have a natural instinct for selecting just the right stone to fit into any given space. Daz explained why he thought he was so good at it. 'It's just like that computer game ... y'know, the one where you have to stack the blocks up, but in 3D?'

I thought about it for a moment and saw he was right: he was a child of the computer game age, and while others might have criticised him for the amount of time he'd spent playing them, by doing so, he'd picked up skills that were useful even in a world where such games no longer existed.

While Mike and Daz took to dry-stone walling, I, along with the others, tried to turn our hands to similarly ancient skills in the few snatches of free time that we had. As the spring equinox approached, the sheep started shedding their thick winter coats, and we could see it dotted around the island, caught on rocks and jagged weeds. Mitch was the one who pointed out its potential. She gathered handfuls of the shed fleece and brought it back to the hut, setting it in front of the rest of us. 'I think we're going to have to work out how to use this stuff; our clothes aren't going to last forever, and I, for one, don't fancy wandering around out there stark bollock naked when that happens.' She shook her head. 'It would be too bloody cold!'

There were some stifled giggles from the youngsters, while I could see that Rob and Ben were doing a better job at not laughing at what Mitch had just said.

Ignoring them, Mitch carried on. 'People around here

have always been very good at turning wool into things like tweed that'll keep you warm and dry. I just wish I knew more about how it was done. All I know is that you weave yarn into sheets of material, and then soak it in urine …'

'You soak it in piss?' Daz was flabbergasted by this revelation.

Mitch chuckled at his reaction. 'Yes. It's how tweed was traditionally made around here; it's what makes it waterproof.'

Daz was disgusted. 'I'm no' wearin' anythin' that's been soaked in someone else's piss.'

Rob leant forward and slapped Daz on the shoulder. 'You'll just have to use your own then, won't you!' He grinned at Daz before picking up some of the discarded fleece. 'But before you can do that though, you'd need to turn this stuff into yarn. I know the basic tools you need to do that, I used to come across them on digs all the time, but I've got no idea how you use them.'

'Hmmm,' Ben picked up some of the fleece, too, pulling it into smaller pieces. He glanced across at Rob. 'Could you make them? The tools we'd need to do it?'

Rob mulled this over for a few seconds and then nodded slowly, 'I think so. They're not too complicated.'

Ben looked back at the small pieces of fleece in his hands. 'Then it shouldn't be too difficult to work out how to use them.'

It turned out Ben greatly underestimated the ease with which we could work out how to process the scraps of fleece into yarn, even once Rob had cobbled together the right tools from various things he found lying around the hut and on the two boats. The fleece needed to be soaked, washed, dried, brushed to align all the fibres and only then could the work of spinning it into yarn begin. This was done with something Rob called a drop spindle, which was a thin wooden rod with a flat, round weight attached to it near one end. A group of us sat down with some processed fleece and a number of these spindles, trying to work out what to do next. Mitch picked one up and examined it. 'You know, I think I remember my great-grandmother using something like this. I was only seven or eight at the time, but I remember her sitting by the fire and spinning with it.' Mitch scooped up a handful of fleece. 'Something like this.'

Mitch spun the spindle and sent it clattering across the floor. She swore loudly as she chased after it. A moment later she sat down and tried again, with the same result.

Eventually, between us all, we worked out how to use the spindles, and we were managing to produce a thread that, while too thin in some places, and too thick, or even lumpy, in others, at least vaguely resembled the yarn we'd need to weave into cloth.

With time, though, we improved, some more than others. Jeff and Sophie seemed to pick it up best, perhaps because they were the youngest, although Jimmy couldn't quite get the hang of it, no matter how hard he tried. While he was adept at other things, his hand-eye coordination just didn't seem to be able to cope with the combinations of movements needed to turn the fleece into yarn. Mitch, like me, was happy to leave the spinning to Jeff and Sophie. Both of us could do it, but found the repetitive nature of it very dull, and neither of us could produce yarn with as consistent a quality as they could.

With yarn to work with, Rob, with Ben and Daz's help, and with Mitch providing advice based on ones she'd seen on the islands in her youth, managed to create a very simple loom on which a tweed-like cloth could be woven. It was little more than a wooden frame a couple of feet long on each side to which lengths of yarn could be tied vertically, while others were passed horizontally between them, but it seemed to work. The first scrap they completed could've made little more than a loin-cloth, and didn't look like it would survive even a moderate gust of wind, but it was a big step towards being able to make our own clothes, at least at some point in the far-distant future. This meant it marked another advance towards creating our own fully self-sufficient community. This was one of our long-term aims, as the less time we had to spend foraging and scavenging at locations away from Mingulay, the lower the chance we'd have of encountering any infected.

***

While we'd managed to regain some ancient skills, getting through the winter had been long and hard. The position of the island far from the mainland meant we were spared the coldest temperatures, but it also meant we were open to the full brunt of mid-winter storms that made those we'd passed through on our way across the Atlantic seem like a summer's breeze. They could last for days on end, with winds reaching well over a hundred miles an hour that tore at the rigging of the boats and the very fabric of the hut. At these times, we didn't dare venture outside for fear of being blown off our feet, let alone manage to get down to the water's edge to seek out food. On the worst days, we could hear the spray from the massive waves that pounded the island land on the roof above our heads, despite the fact we were well above the shoreline.

Our biggest fear in these storms was that one, or both,

of the boats would either become badly damaged and sink, or break free and be lost forever. We soon realised it was unsafe to leave any one on board in case that happened, because we'd have no hope of rescuing them if something went wrong. Instead, to minimise the possibility of the boats breaking away in a storm, we had them secured with several anchors, each laid out in a different direction, and enough rope to allow them to move around in the wind without hitting each other or ripping their anchors from the seabed, but they were still at risk in such strong winds.

We also worried for the safety of the hut, and as soon as we realised a storm was brewing, we'd take down the wind generator and pack away the solar panels, before pulling down the shutters, going inside and locking the door behind us. We'd then huddle in the darkness, listening to the wind and the rain rattle off the walls, wondering how long we'd be trapped in the hut for this time round. With nine people and a dog, the atmosphere within the boarded-up building quickly turned thick and ripe. It didn't help that, because of the power of the winds, it was often unsafe to risk a trip to the outhouse in such weather, and we had to resort to using a makeshift chamber pot that we'd empty later. It wasn't pleasant, but there were times when we had no other choice.

Once a storm had passed, we'd split into two teams: one of which was dedicated to getting as much food as quickly as possible, while the other's job was to check for damage and start working on any repairs that were urgently required. All the time, we needed to keep a careful eye out, just in case the storm had somehow swept still-living infected into either of the two bays where they could make landfall. When we were lucky, we'd have plenty of time to rebuild our food stocks and fix whatever needed fixed, but when we weren't, we'd only have a few hours respite before the next storm hit.

***

Eventually, the spring equinox arrived and, with it, the end of the winter storms, and we chose to mark the occasion with a celebration at the stone calendar. Jimmy had been working hard with Dougie, learning how to signal to him and get him to respond to his commands. This meant that when we decided we should finally work out how to capture one of the sheep so that we could have a feast, it fell to Jimmy and Dougie to do it. Dougie had a natural instinct for herding, but it required careful planning and instructions from Jimmy to get him to guide and chivvy a sheep to the exact location we wanted it to be in. On this occasion, it was one of the half-completed cottages, which Rob and Ben figured we could use as a temporary corral.

As the rest of us watched, Jimmy stood on a low hillock to the north of the hut, Dougie beside him. Jimmy picked his target and nodded his head forward; in response, Dougie shot off into the distance, following a circular route that would take him behind the sheep without getting so close as to spook it. Once Jimmy felt the dog was in the right position, he lifted his hand and called out. Dougie stopped and sank down onto his belly. Jimmy whistled and waved, and Dougie crept forward keeping his body as close to the ground as possible. The sheep sensed the dog approaching and bleated loudly. Jimmy yelled and Dougie started forward more quickly, causing the sheep to turn and run towards the cottage, but before it could reach it, the sheep veered off to the left. Jimmy waved, but he needn't have: Dougie had already spotted this and reacted accordingly. Working together, Dougie and Jimmy made it look easy, and within ten minutes the sheep was safely within the cottage walls as the rest of us barred the entrance.

Jimmy joined us, rubbing Dougie's head as he did so. 'Now what?'

'One of us is going to have to go in there and kill it.' Rob held out a large knife he'd taken from the catamaran's galley. 'Any volunteers?'

In the confines of the cottage, the sheep suddenly looked much bigger than it had outside, and there was a gleam in its eyes which suggested it wasn't going to go down without a fight. Daz and Mike exchanged looks as if each were daring the other to step forward, but neither did. Jimmy and Jeff stood off to the side, Jimmy restraining Dougie, who clearly wanted to keep herding the sheep despite the fact that it was already where we wanted it to be. Sophie was beside me, holding onto my arm, while Ben was shifting uneasily back and forth. We'd waited so long to capture one of the sheep, but now we had, it seemed none of us were keen to end its life. Finally, Mitch broke the deadlock, reaching out and taking the knife before entering the still-unfinished building. 'If you can pin it down, I'll do it.'

Rob took off his jacket and handed it to Jeff. 'Deal,' He followed her inside, 'but be careful, won't you, Mitch?'

Given that all they were going to do was kill a sheep, hardly the wildest of animals, Rob's concern seemed a little over the top.

Sophie frowned at Mitch. 'Have you ever done anything like this before?'

Mitch nodded. 'Yes, when I was a kid. My parents had a croft, and I used to help them out when it came time to slaughter the year-old lambs each spring. I haven't done it in a while, but I think I still remember how.'

With that, Mitch and Rob started to make their way across to where the sheep was standing, but just as they were about to corner it, it leapt to one side, knocking Rob to the ground. He picked himself up and brushed himself down before looking back at where the rest of us were still blocking the doorway. 'I think we might need more help.'

It took another twenty minutes, but working together, Rob, Ben and I finally manage to trap the sheep and hold it down while Mitch slit its throat. It struggled at first as blood gushed out onto the ground, but soon this slowed to a trickle and the sheep fell still. Next, Mitch set to work, first gutting the carcass, and then skinning and butchering it so we could cook the cuts of meat over an open fire. By then, Jimmy, Jeff and Mike had lost interest and wandered away, but Daz, Sophie and I remained, half-intrigued, half-horrified. Like most people who'd grown up in cities, we'd never seen the process of turning a living animal into food before, certainly not up close. I think if I'd known back then the sights and smells that it entailed, I'd probably have become a vegan on the spot, but now, as I watched, I found my mouth watering at the very thought of the meat we'd soon be eating. Daz, in comparison, could barely conceal his disgust. 'Aww, that's mingin'. There's no way I could ever do somethin' like that.'

Killing infected, it seemed was one thing, but for him, butchering an animal was quite another. I guess the difference with the infected was that it was done on the spur of the moment: it was you or them, and you had no time to think about what you were doing. Now, with the dead animal lying opened up in front of him, Daz had all the time in the world to dwell on his actions and it wasn't sitting well with him. Sophie stood beside him. 'Maybe you should become a vegetarian then.'

Daz was shocked by the suggestion. 'What? And no' eat meat? Don't be daft!'

Mitch glanced up. 'If you're not willing to get your hands bloody, then maybe you should stick to eating seafood.'

Daz was dismayed. 'But we've no' had proper meat in absolutely ages. I'm no' missin' out.'

Mitch held out a blood-covered knife. 'Your choice.'

Daz tentatively took the knife and knelt down beside Mitch, looking pale and squeamish. All credit to him, though, he managed to get through the rest of the preparations without throwing up.

Once the meat was ready, we set out across the island and gathered at the calendar. Mike, Jimmy and Jeff were already there, having spent the time it had taken us to process the sheep collecting driftwood and forming it into a large fire. On our arrival, they lit it using an ember they'd carried carefully, cradled in an old metal bucket, across the island from the stove in the hut, and soon the smell of roasting meat was tantalising our taste buds. As we waited for it to cook, Rob took the opportunity to make a bit of a speech. 'Well, the sun will soon be setting on the day that officially marks the first day of spring. This means we've made it through our first winter.' Rob paused until the various whoops and clapping died down. 'Now, you may be wondering why we've gone to all this effort with the fire and the meat and all.'

Daz butted in. 'Cos it's about bloody time we had a party?'

Jeff, Jimmy and Mike cheered.

Rob waved his hand to signal them to calm down.

'There is that, Daz, but there's also a couple of other things which, in my book at least, are worth celebrating. First, I spoke with Jack earlier today and we both agreed that given how well things are going over here, it's about time the Hope Town community started planning their trip across the Atlantic. In fact, they'll be setting off as soon as the weather allows, which, with a bit of luck, will be in the next couple of weeks.'

Inside, my heart leapt. I'd missed Jack, Andrew and the others terribly since we'd left and it felt great to think that soon we'd all be together again. I could see Rob, Jeff, Mike and Jimmy felt the same. Sophie, Mitch, Ben and Daz were more cautious: the arrival of the rest of the Hope Town community would be a great upheaval to a way of life they were already settling into, but they could see the benefit of having a larger community around them, and generally their response was positive.

'Secondly.' Rob beckoned Mitch to stand up beside him. 'Some of you may've noticed that Mitch seems to have been eating more than her fair share of the food lately. This isn't just because she's being greedy ...'

Mitch turned and punched him gently on the arm, and in the early evening light I noticed, for the first time, the bulge in her belly. A thought suddenly popped into my head, and I blurted it out without even stopping to think: 'You're pregnant!'

Mitch gave me a withering look. 'Way to spoil the surprise, CJ!' Then she nodded, smiling as she did so. 'Yes, I'm pregnant.'

There was a brief moment of silence and then yet another round of whooping and clapping, although I noticed Sophie remained silent and still. Mitch bowed.

Daz cupped a hand round his mouth and called out.

'Any idea who the father is?'

Mitch scowled at him, but then laughed along with everyone else.

**

Early the next day, Sophie accosted me and dragged me off up the hill, away from the others. Something was clearly upsetting her, but I couldn't tell what. Eventually, we reached an ancient marker cairn, where she stopped and dropped down onto the ground before staring off into the distance, a dark and disturbed look on her face.

I sat down beside her, and as I waited for her to be ready to tell me what was troubling her so much, I surveyed the landscape that surrounded us. Below us, I could see the ruins of the village laid out, hugging the edge of the sheltered bay and creeping up the hill towards our vantage point, the outlines of what were once houses visible in amongst the scrubby grass. To our right, long thin lines formed undulations along the hillside. These were, Rob had told us, the remains of an ancient farming system developed by the islanders to help increase the amount of fertile land for growing crops. We scoured them endlessly whenever we had the chance, looking for the offspring of plants, like potatoes or barley, that might've been missed in the final harvest before the island was abandoned and gone feral, but we'd found nothing. Yet, much of the eastern side of the island was covered in these strange, linear structures, and we lived in hope that if we searched for long enough, we'd find some and be able to set about domesticating them once again.

Down on the shoreline, I could just make out Rob, Daz

and Mike wrestling to disentangle a string of lobster creels which they'd found the week before. These traps offered us the potential to collect food much more efficiently than foraging along the shoreline or fishing with rod and line, and now we had them, we were keen to start making use of them as soon as we could. Once they were deployed in the waters around the island, it would mean we could spend a lot less time foraging, giving us more time to do other things, such as rebuilding enough cottages for us all to use.

'CJ,' the sound of Sophie's voice drew my attention back to where we were sitting high on the hill above the hut, 'd'you think it's right, what Mitch and Rob are doing?'

I was puzzled. 'You mean having a relationship?'

'No. I mean ...' She struggled to get the words out, just like when she'd asked me how old I was when I'd first had sex. She hadn't seemed prudish in the discussion we'd had afterwards, but I wondered if it was different when she thought about other, older people doing it.

I decided I'd try to finish her sentence for her. 'Having sex?'

'No, not that either.' I could tell she was irritated with me for interrupting her. 'As far as I'm concerned they can do *that* as much as they want ... so long as they keep it to themselves.' She shuddered at the thought before carrying on. 'I mean having a baby. How can they possibly think about bringing a child into this world? What's a baby ever done to deserve that?'

I was surprised at the anger she seemed to be feeling about it. The thought of Mitch having to give birth out here, and without medical help, worried me, but I hadn't considered whether the very act of having a baby was a good thing to do or not. Instead, I'd just accepted that it was something that was going to happen. 'I don't think they planned it, Sophie. I think it's just one of those things.' I shot her a look. 'And maybe that's something you and Daz should bear in mind.'

'We're not *actually* doing anything, CJ,' Sophie retorted, her face flushed with teenage derision and embarrassment. 'Well, nothing that could get me pregnant.' She glanced down, muttering, 'not yet, anyway.' She was getting more flustered with every passing word. She looked up again. 'But that's beside the point. We're talking about Mitch and Rob here. Is it right what they're doing?'

'I don't think it's a matter of whether it's right or wrong. Mitch's pregnant, and there's nothing any of us can really do about that. All we can do is give her, and Rob, all the support they need.'

'But what about the infected? Surely it's not right to bring a baby into a world with infected in it?'

'Sophie, I think Mingulay is about as safe as anywhere in the world. I think it's well-protected from the infected. I can't say for certain, but given how things have gone so far, I think that if there's anywhere left on earth where it's safe to bring up a child, then it's Mingulay. It might not be a childhood like you or I had, but it'll still be a good place to grow up.'

Sophie said nothing and, instead, pulled her knees up to her chest, hugging her legs tightly as she rested her chin on them. I put my arm round her. 'What're you really worrying about?'

She turned to me. 'What if, after they have the baby, something happens to them? To Rob and Mitch? Who'll look after it? The baby, I mean. This is no world for a child to grow up in without parents, without a family. A child needs a family ...' Sophie's voice faded out and I wondered whether she was only talking about Mitch and Rob's future child, or whether she was also, at least in part, talking about herself. She had the rest of us, but we weren't related to her; we weren't the people she'd grown up with; we couldn't replace those who'd once been closer to her than anyone else in the world and who she'd now lost forever.

It wasn't until that moment, that I realised quite how Sophie felt. She hid it so well, the pain she was going through, the loneliness, the sense that her entire world was over and that she was only just hanging on to some semblance of reality. I squeezed her. 'Not that I'm saying anything's going to happen to Mitch and Rob, but if it did, if the worst happened, the baby would still have us: you and me; Daz and Ben; Mike, Jimmy and Jeff. We're like a family already. We'll be there for it, all of us will. We'll be there for it, even if nothing happens to Mitch and Rob. We'll be its family and it'll be ours. It doesn't matter that we're not related. What counts is that we know we'll be there for each other, no matter what.'

I glanced across at Sophie as she stared out across the ruined village that lay below us. I didn't know whether I was helping or not, but I didn't know what else to say. Eventually she spoke. 'D'you really see us all as family?'

I nodded.

'Not just Rob, Jeff, Jimmy and Mike?'

'No, not just them. All of you.'

'Even me?' She asked the question quietly and tentatively, as if she wasn't sure what the answer would be. In that moment, I knew what she needed to hear, and in some strange way, I needed to hear myself say it too, and for the same reason. I was living just as much of a lie as Sophie was, pretending that things were okay when they weren't; not admitting, even to myself, how much I missed people from what was now my past. I knew how much I missed Jon, but my love for Jon had come after the world had ended. Before that, I'd lost others, people so close to me I could never forget them, but who I'd never know what had happened to, and this ate away at my very soul. In Sophie, I'd found someone who, while she couldn't replace them, at least allowed me to pay some sort of penance for the fact that I'd survived while they had, almost certainly, died.

'Especially you, Sophie.' I smiled at her sadly and stroked her hair. 'You remind me so much of my little sister. I'll never get to see her grow up, to help her become the person she wanted to become, but I can do that for you, Sophie. If you want me to, that is?'

'I'd like that, CJ.' Sophie smiled back at me. 'I'd like that a lot.'

***

While it seemed all was going well on Mingulay, and we were, indeed, coming together to form some sort of makeshift family to help and support each other when we needed it, the same couldn't be said for the other communities which we were in contact with on the shortwave radio. Indeed, the only other group that we knew about to have survived until the spring was the one in Hope Town. Gradually, as the winter months passed, the others had disappeared one by one. Some had finally been overrun by the infected they'd been fighting to hold back for so long, the garbled and terrified messages we received telling us what was happening before their broadcasts finally ceased, but that wasn't the fate of all of them. Others were lost to disease, accidents or hunger. One simply stopped broadcasting mid-sentence, and we never heard from it again.

The loss of the other communities was worrying. Even though we'd never met them, just knowing they existed was somehow comforting. There was something reassuring about knowing there were other people out there, going through similar things to those that we were experiencing. It was also good to know for sure that we weren't all that was left of humanity. Now, with the other communities gone, we felt more lonely and isolated, like the last bastion of civilisation, but at least we still had the comfort of knowing the rest of the Hope Town community was not only still out there, but would soon be setting out to join us, and this helped to keep our spirits up.

Chapter Nine

The sound of gunfire echoed round the cabin. It seemed close, and we could hear shouting in the background. We looked at each other, panic written across both our faces. Rob and I were alone on the catamaran for our daily check-in with Jack on the shortwave radio, and we'd been halfway through a discussion on how soon it would be before the rest of the Hope Town community were ready to leave when the first shots rang out, then the radio fell silent.

Rob grabbed the mic from me. 'Jack, are you alright?' He let go of the transmission key for a second and then pressed it again. 'Jack?'

Still there was no reply.

'Shit!' Rob thumped the chart table hard with his fist and then stared at me, shocked and confused. 'What d'you think that was all about?'

I bit my lip nervously and looked away, avoiding his eyes. 'I don't know, but whatever it was, it didn't sound good,' I glanced back at Rob, 'did it?'

Rob picked up the microphone again. 'Jack, are you there? Jack?'

The radio remained unsettlingly quiet.

Rob tried again. 'Mingulay calling Hope Town. Come in, Hope Town ... Jack? ... Andrew? ... Anyone?'

We waited, but there was only silence and static. The shots had sounded like they were in the same room as us, but, in reality, they were almost 3,000 miles away, and whatever was happening in Hope Town, there was nothing we could do, but worry.

'Are they going to be okay?' Jimmy's face was as white as a sheet.

We'd spent almost an hour trying to reach Jack again, but no matter what we tried, there was no response. Afterwards, while Rob remained on the catamaran, I'd gone ashore to tell the others what was going on.

I slumped down onto a seat in the hut. I wanted to say something reassuring, but I couldn't think of anything, not without lying, and I didn't want to do that in case it gave any of them false hope. 'I don't know, Jimmy.'

Sophie frowned. 'Is there anything we can do?'

'No.' Ben stood up and stared out the window, almost as if he was trying to see what might be happening on the other side of the ocean. 'They're too far away.'

Daz glanced at me. 'What d'you think happened?'

I shook my head. 'I've no idea. It was all so sudden. One minute we were speaking to Jack and the next there was gunfire and shouting, and then Jack was gone.'

In the silence that followed, I ran over those last few seconds of the radio conversation in my head again and again: I'd asked Jack how long he thought it would take them to make the crossing, and he'd just started to reply when there was shouting, and then the gunfire began. It sounded so close, almost as if it was in the cabin of Jack's boat, but as I replayed it in my mind, I wondered whether that was just my imagination and whether it was really further off.

Mitch watched me, concerned. 'Are you okay?'

'Yeah.' I stood up. 'I just wish we knew what was going on.' I moved towards the door. 'I should get back to the boat. Maybe by now, Rob's heard from them again.'

Jeff stood up. 'I'll come with you.'

Jimmy and Mike joined him, both speaking at the same time. 'Me too.'

I slid open the door to the catamaran's cabin and called out. 'Anything?'

Rob was still by the radio, waiting. He shook his head. Behind me, the boys trooped inside and sat down, each of their faces creased with concern.

Jeff shifted uneasily. 'What'll we do if we don't hear from them again?'

This thought had crossed my mind too, but I didn't want to think about it. When we'd lost contact with the other communities, it had been sad and depressing, but we only knew them as disembodied voices on the radio. With Jack and the others, we'd lived with them, fished with them, and when we needed to, we'd fought the infected alongside them. My mind focussed on the word 'infected'. Maybe they'd been attacked by some drifters and the gunfire was them trying to defend themselves. After all, I knew Jack had a shotgun, but as I replayed the shots again in my head, I realised that they weren't from a shotgun. They were from an assault rifle. I'd never really shared it with the others, but my father had been, unusually for a Brit, a bit of a gun nut. On a holiday to the States when I was thirteen, he'd dragged us all along to a gun show and we'd watched, bored, as he played with all the guns on the firing range. His favourite had been a Russian-made Kalashnikov assault rifle, and it had a very distinctive sound. While that was a long time ago, I was pretty sure I'd heard the same distinct sound coming out of the radio just before it went dead.

I sat down and put my arm around Jeff, as much to comfort myself as to comfort him. 'I don't know, Jeff,' I hugged him to me. 'I just don't know.'

161

Rob and I remained within a few feet of the shortwave radio for the next two days, barely sleeping or eating for fear we might miss something that would tell us what was going on. Ben ran Mitch out to the boat several times, but Rob barely spoke to her, so she stopped coming. On the evening of the third day, I finally went ashore again, leaving Rob to continue his vigil. I was worried what effect all this would have on him and whether it might send him spiralling downwards once more. Yet, I was just as worried about what had happened to Jack and the others.

Up ahead, I could see light pouring from the windows of the hut into the rapidly approaching night, and I knew the questions I'd be asked if I went inside. Rather than face them, I took the trail which branched off to the right and walked up to the graveyard. When I got there, just as I'd done so often before when I was feeling like the world was getting on top of me, I sat beside the grave of the unnamed man and stared out across the bay as the sun set behind me.

I don't know how long I'd been there when I heard a quiet cough. I turned to find Ben standing a few feet away. 'Mind if I sit down?'

I shook my head and he lowered himself onto the ground next to me, but rather than speak, he joined me in staring out into the growing darkness. Eventually, I broke the silence. 'Why's life so shit? Every time things seem to finally be getting better, something happens and makes it worse again.'

Ben pulled some grass from the ground and started tearing it apart with his hands. 'I don't think there's an answer to that question, and you'll just drive yourself nuts if

162

you keep looking for one. You just have to accept that that's the way the world is.'

I snorted. 'That's easy for you to say.'

'No, it's not: I learned it the hard way and it took me a long time to reach that point. When we first landed on Soay, I spent so long trying to work out why everything that had happened had happened, but one day I realised that even if I ever found the answer, it wasn't going to make things any better. The world wasn't going to change: it wouldn't suddenly all be okay again; everyone wouldn't mysteriously come back to life. It would be the same crappy world and the only thing that would've changed would be that I'd know why. That's when I decided that if I was going to have any chance of staying sane, I'd need to just accept that the world is what it is, and do my best to keep myself, and the others, alive in it.'

'So you've somehow just managed to forget everything that's happened, forget everyone you've lost and move on?' I shook my head. 'That's cold; I could never do that.'

Ben eyes remained locked on a distant horizon that was no longer visible in the inky blackness of the night. 'I didn't say I'd forgotten anything, I just stopped trying to work out why it had happened. I still think about the people I've lost. In fact, that's why I came up here tonight: it's Tom's birthday today; or at least it would've been if he was still alive. There isn't a day goes by when I don't miss him, but tearing myself apart won't bring him back, and I know he wouldn't have wanted me living like that.'

There was a quiver in Ben's voice and I glanced across to see him wiping his eyes. 'Ben, I'm sorry; I should never have called you cold, It's just the worry, it's eating me up inside.'

'That's just my point: there's nothing you can do about it. The past is the past; whether it's good or bad, you can't do anything to change it. You're feeling guilty because you're still alive, and they might be dead. You're blaming yourself because you're here, safe, while they remained over there and might not be, but you can't live like that; not without driving yourself insane, and we need you here, CJ, for Rob, and for Jeff and Mike and Jimmy, and for Sophie.'

I was surprised by the last name on the list. 'Sophie?'

Ben glanced across at me. 'I don't know whether you've noticed it or not, but Sophie really looks up to you. She listens to you; she cares about what you think. She speaks to you about things she doesn't speak to me and Mitch about, and I know you've been giving her advice about her and Daz. She really needs you, CJ.' Ben paused. 'Hell, Mitch and me need you, too!' He smiled at me weakly and then looked away.

I sat in silence. I knew that if, as seemed likely, something bad had happened to Jack and the others, none of them would want me to rip myself to pieces when there was nothing I could've done about it, but it wasn't as simple as that.

'Life goes on, CJ, no matter what.' Ben gently put his hand on my arm, and I felt an unexpected sensation course through my body. The thrill that ran through me both enlivened and troubled me: how could Ben's touch make me feel this way when I still missed Jon so intensely? I knew I liked Ben, but this was something that went well beyond just liking him, and it caught me by surprise. Almost instantly, I felt guilty for the way my body was reacting, and confused as to why it even was happening in the first place.

Ben seemed unaware of the turmoil he'd accidently

sparked inside me, and he carried on. 'And while it can be pretty messed up at times, there's beauty in it, too. And if you need a sign to remind you of that, I don't think you could get a better one than that.' He pointed off to the north.

I looked round, not quite knowing, at first, what I was meant to be looking at. There was a red glow along the horizon, but it was just the sunset, wasn't it? Then the rays of light spread out across the sky, changing from red to green as it did so. My eyes widened as I took the spectacle in. 'What is *that*?'

Ben stared upwards, his face illuminated by the strange, and ever-changing, glow from the sky. 'The northern lights; you don't often get them this far south, but when you do it can be spectacular.'

The lights changed again and it seemed like the whole sky was moving to a rhythm I couldn't hear. I leaned back so I could see it better. 'Wow!'

Ben leant back, too. 'Some people call them the heavenly dancers, and on nights like this, you can see why.'

'Should we get the others?' I felt we should, but I didn't want to move in case I somehow broke the spell.'

Ben lay down, supporting himself on his elbows. 'We could, but I think it'd be okay if we just kept this between us.'

I felt relieved. That was what I wanted to do, too. As I watched the lights shimmer and change, I realised Ben was right: there was nothing I could do about Jack, but there were things I could do for the people who were already here. As the lights finally started to fade, I pulled myself up onto my feet and brushed myself down. I walked a few feet and then stopped. 'Thanks, Ben.'

He frowned. 'For what?'

I smiled at him. 'For knowing what to say.'

'It was nothing.' There was something in the way Ben responded that for some reason made me think that if I could've seen him properly, I'd have seen he was blushing. Again, a sensation ran through me that made me feel uncomfortable. Why was being with Ben making me feel like this when I still cared for Jon so much? Not wanting to address the issue, I did my best to push these feelings from my mind.

'Thanks anyway,' With that, I turned and headed down towards where the dinghy was pulled up onto the beach.

'Any news?' Back on the catamaran, I found Rob staring so hard at the shortwave radio I thought it might explode.

He looked round, surprised to see me standing there. 'Huh?'

I asked again. 'Any news?'

Rob turned back to the radio. 'No, nothing.'

I walked over to the radio and turned it off.

'What're you doing?' Rob turned it back on.

I turned it off again. 'Rob, you've got to stop.'

'Stop what?' He reached out to turn the radio on again, but I stepped in front of it. 'This: sitting here, not sleeping, not eating; there's nothing we can do about Jack and the others, but there are people here who need you, and you can't keep treating them like shit just because things are happening and there's nothing you can to do stop them.'

'I hadn't realised I was treating you *that* badly, CJ.' There was anger in Rob's voice.

'Not me, Rob,' I was angry, too, 'Mitch.'

'Mitch?' Rob seemed taken aback. 'What's Mitch got

to do with it?'

'In case you hadn't noticed, she's having *your* baby, and she's been out here half a dozen times because she's really worried about you, and all you've done is ignore her and stare at that ruddy radio.' I slumped down onto one of the seats by the table. 'I'm worried about Jack and the others, too, but there's nothing we can do about it. Sitting here watching the radio, willing it to burst into life won't help. We need to turn it off and only put it on at the pre-arranged check-in time. We can let ourselves worry then, but we can't let it take over the rest of our lives.'

Rob's shoulders drooped. 'You're right, CJ.' He ran his hands over his face several times before getting up and walking across to the cabin door. Once there, he stopped and turned. 'Are you coming?'

I was confused by Rob's action. 'Where?'

'Ashore.' He glanced across to the island. 'The lights are still on in the hut, and as you so rightly pointed out, given the way I've been acting, I've got quite a bit of apologising to do. I might as well get it over and done with.'

***

I woke early the next morning and resisted the urge to switch on the shortwave radio. Rather than go ashore with Rob the night before, I'd stayed on the catamaran with the boys. I lay there for a while, wondering what to do next until I heard Jeff and Jimmy start moving noisily around the main cabin getting their breakfast together. Knowing if I left them alone much longer, the galley would soon look like a bombsite that I'd inevitably end up having to clean, I got up, too.

When I entered the cabin, I was greeted by grunted 'heys' and saw that I was already too late. While there were only two of them, it looked like they'd used pretty much every dish in the galley.

Jimmy lifted a pan off the cooker and waved it in my general direction. 'You want some breakfast?'

I took the lid off and peered inside. 'What *is* it?'

He smiled proudly. 'Scrambled eggs. Fresh from the hens. I got them last night.'

Given what I could see, that wouldn't have been my first guess; or indeed any of my guesses. While the boys where picking up new skills all the time, it seemed that cooking wasn't one of them. I dropped the lid back onto the pan. 'I think I'll pass.'

Jimmy shrugged. 'Your loss.' He divided the contents onto two plates. 'And all the more for us.'

The two boys descended on the food, swallowing it, barely chewed, in large mouthfuls, burnt bits and all. I guess even the collapse of civilisation couldn't stop teenage boys being teenage boys, but that still didn't make it a nice sight to see, especially first thing in the morning. Before they could put me off the idea of breakfast altogether, I went into the cockpit and looked towards the shore. The sun was only just rising, but I could make out two figures walking arm in arm along the sand of the bay. It seemed like Rob's apology had been accepted, and I hoped he hadn't done their relationship any permanent harm.

***

The door to the hut burst open, and Jeff flew in, quickly followed by Jimmy. 'There's something in the bay!'

Before any of us could ask what, they dashed off

again. Rob, Ben, Mitch and I had been updating the list of things which we needed to do, checking off those that had been done and reprioritising those which hadn't. Getting diesel to run the boat engines and the generator was still our most pressing need, but working out how we were going to roof the rebuilt cottages was also high on the list. This was a touchy subject because with the future of Jack and the others uncertain, we didn't know how many buildings we'd eventually need. Mitch and Rob would definitely want some space of their own on shore, especially once the baby came, and both Ben and I were increasingly feeling that we'd each like our own space, too, so we needed some additional functional buildings, but beyond that, the exact number was unclear. The lack of news from Jack weighed heavily on all of us, yet it remained unspoken.

Jeff stuck his head through the door again. 'C'mon!'

I sighed tiredly. 'I suppose we should go and see what's up.'

The others nodded, and together we got up and headed for the door. Outside, Daz had a pair of binoculars trained on the bay below. He heard us approach and lowered them. 'It must be about twenty feet long: what the hell *is* it?'

I glanced down into the bay: there, just beyond the anchored catamaran, a large, dark triangular object broke the water; several yards behind it, another smaller one followed. Below the surface, connecting these strange objects, was a massive shadow, visible through the calm waters and contrasting sharply with the sandy seabed far beneath it.

A smile spread across Ben's face. 'A basking shark; first of the season.' He looked at Daz and clapped his hands together. 'Let's go!'

Ben and Daz had been assembling equipment for just this moment ever since Ben had first raised the possibility of using oil from the giant fish's liver instead of diesel to run our engines. Three large harpoons had been created from stout metal poles fixed to old oars we'd found on one of our scavenging trips. Lengths of rope had been gathered and attached to the harpoons at one end and to fifty-five-gallon plastic containers at the other. We'd found these on an abandoned fish farm and they'd since been sealed to ensure they were airtight. Ben had explained the basic plan to us. 'The thing that will allow a basking shark to get away is diving below the surface where we can't get at it. The containers will act like giant fishing floats and they'll stop it being able to do that. Then we can get a rope round its tail and drag it on to the shore.'

Ben made it sound easy, but I wasn't so certain it would be as simple in practice. Now, as I watched Ben and Daz hurrying around, getting all of the equipment they'd cobbled together down to the beach and into one of the dinghies, I wondered whether it was a wise thing to even attempt. A few minutes later, and Daz and Ben were racing towards the shark. The shark itself was still swimming lazily through the still waters beyond the catamaran, unaware of what was about to descend upon it.

Sophie came up beside me. 'Is this not a bit dangerous? I mean, it is a shark after all.'

I patted her arm, trying to reassure her. Ben had told me about basking sharks and the fact that, despite their size, they were filter-feeders, meaning they had sieve-like gill rakers rather than teeth. 'Don't worry. Basking sharks don't have any teeth so they're not that dangerous.'

This didn't seem to ease Sophie's concerns. 'I know, but it's still pretty big.'

I returned my attention to the bay. As they

approached the unsuspecting shark, Ben slowed the dinghy to a snail's pace, trying not to spook it as they inched close enough for Daz to throw the first harpoon. He stood at the bow, harpoon at the ready, trying to keep his balance. When they were within a few feet of their intended target, Daz steadied himself and then hurled the first harpoon, but he was obviously worried about how the shark would respond and his throw lacked conviction. This meant that while his aim was good, the harpoon didn't pierce the shark's thick skin. Instead, it bounced off as the giant fish disappeared in a swirl of water that caused the nearby dinghy to rock violently.

Mike was watching through the binoculars. 'I can't believe he missed something that size.'

Sophie leapt to Daz's defence. 'That's easy enough to say when you're all the way up here. And anyway, he didn't miss, he just ...' Sophie tailed off, unable to come up with a justification for what had just happened.

Before Mike could respond, Jeff pointed off to the right. 'Look, it's back up!'

Sure enough, the giant fish had surfaced again, about sixty yards from the dinghy. Together we yelled and pointed; Ben must've heard us because he gave us a thumbs-up and, as Daz pulled in the harpoon using the rope attached to it, he put the engine into gear and motored towards the shark once more.

This time, when they were near enough, Daz threw the harpoon with all his strength, and when it struck, it held. A moment later, one of the yellow plastic containers was racing through the water as it was dragged by the fleeing shark. Daz and Ben chased after it in the dinghy until it eventually slowed, then stopped, the fins of the shark becoming visible above the surface once more. Daz readied himself again and soon the shark had two barrels attached to it; then three. By that point, it was clearly tiring and it barely reacted to the third harpoon, but it was still another hour before it was finally exhausted and it came to a halt.

Sophie glanced up a me. 'What're they going to do now?'

I bit the inside of my cheek nervously. 'Try to get a rope round the tail so they can pull it into shore.'

Sophie's brow furrowed. 'Is that easy?'

'I don't know, but ...' Before I could finish, there was a commotion down below. Daz had been leaning over the side, trying to slip a loop of rope around the animal's tail as Ben manoeuvred the dinghy into place, but he must've let the rope touch the shark too soon. Feeling their presence, the shark thrashed its massive tail wildly, sending a wave of water over the small boat. The tip of the tail caught Daz across the side of the face and sent him spinning into the water. Beside me, Sophie yelped and gripped my arm tightly.

'He's okay. Look.' I pointed to where Daz had just resurfaced, coughing and spluttering. As we watched, Ben helped him back into the dinghy. The shark, despite everything that had just happened, was so drained of energy it had only moved a few yards and soon they were alongside it again. This time, Daz succeeded, and with the shark secured to the back of the dinghy, they motored slowly towards the shore while the rest of us raced down to the beach, eager to see the shark up close.

'On the count of three, pull. One. Two. Three. Pull!' Under Ben's instruction, we worked together to try to drag the dying fish from the water. At about fifteen feet long, it was

172

smaller than we'd first thought and dark brown in colour. Unlike any other fish I'd ever seen, its skin glistened and glinted in the sun, but not from scales. Instead, it was covered with a sheen I couldn't quite identify. I reached out and touched it, finding it slimy at first, but beneath this covering of mucus, it felt rough, like sandpaper. The side of Daz's face bore testament to this roughness as his skin had been rasped raw where the shark's tail had made contact. Luckily, it had only been a glancing blow so the damage was superficial, but nonetheless, Sophie had fussed over Daz's injury as soon as he'd got back to shore before allowing us to set to work pulling the giant fish ashore.

After forty minutes, we were all sweating heavily, but the shark was still only halfway onto the beach. The further we dragged it from the sea, the less the water supported its weight, and the more we struggled to move it. The shark was exhausted, but still alive, and every now and then, it would summon up the energy to try to escape, flapping its massive tail frantically from side to side. Whenever this happened, we had to let go of the ropes and leap backwards to make sure we remained out of its reach, only to return to them when the shark had drained its energy stores and calmed again. Eventually, Rob released the rope he'd been hauling on and straightened up. 'I hate to say this, Ben, but this isn't going to work; it's just too heavy.'

The others followed Rob's lead as Ben wiped his brow and then dried his hands on his trousers. 'You're right. We're just going to have to do it here.'

Daz looked on expectantly. 'Do what?'

Ben walked over and picked up a spade he'd brought down from the hut. 'Kill it, and then cut it up.' With that he raised the spade over his head and brought it down, edge first, onto the shark just behind its head. It didn't even leave a mark; instead, it sent the shark into another frenzy as it tried to flip itself back into deeper water. We waited for the shark to calm down, then Ben tried again, with the same result. Ben threw the spade aside and glanced round. 'Any ideas?'

Mitch pointed to the harpoons sticking from the shark's back. 'How about using one of them? Would that work?'

'Worth a try.' With that, Ben stepped forward and grabbed the handle of the nearest harpoon. He twisted and pulled, again causing the shark to writhe with pain, until the harpoon was finally free. He walked up to the head of the shark and lined up his shot, aiming for just above and behind the eye, before thrusting it home. This time he was successful, and finally the shark was still. Well, not completely still: its muscles rippled from time to time, but its tail no longer flapped around and it no longer squirmed whenever it sensed our presence nearby.

Jeff fidgeted excitedly. 'Now what?'

Ben pulled out the harpoon and stuck it vertically into the sand next to his feet. 'We'll need to cut it open and get the liver out.'

Due to the toughness of its skin, slicing open the shark proved more difficult than Ben originally thought. It didn't help that, despite the fish being dead, its muscles still twitched and spasmed, causing the knife to skip across its body. Yet, after a ten-minute struggle, the shark had finally been opened up so that Ben and Daz, with the help of Rob and Mike, were able to set to work to remove its oil-rich liver. This was then cut up and placed into an empty metal barrel which had had its top removed. Once it was full, a fire was built underneath it and the slow process of boiling out the oil began. The smell was horrendous, and those of us not working directly on the shark moved away to a safe distance upwind where we could avoid the worst of the stench. When the hunt had started, I'd wondered whether we might be able to eat the shark's meat, but now I could smell it, I realised that even if it were edible, we'd have to be in pretty dire straits to be willing to consume it.

With the liver removed, Ben and Daz climbed back into the dinghy and towed the rest of the carcass out beyond the entrance to the bay before setting it loose, counting on the tide and the currents to carry it away from Mingulay before it started to rot. Given how badly the freshly killed shark smelled, I couldn't imagine how much worse it would be when that happened.

Once they had returned, Daz walked towards Sophie, wiping his hands on his t-shirt as he did so, but she was having none of it. She stepped backwards, pulling the sleeve of the old jumper she was wearing over her hand before clamping it across her mouth, muffling her words. 'Daz, you're not coming anywhere near me smelling like that. Go wash yourself.'

At first Daz looked hurt, but then he sniffed at his shirt and recoiled at the odour emanating from it as Sophie carried on. 'And wash your clothes. In fact, maybe just burn them, I don't think you'll ever be able to get that stench out!'

Daz was dismayed. 'But these are my favourite trousers. They're the only ones that fit me properly! Where am I goin' to get another pair that fit this well?'

Sophie wasn't backing down. 'You should've thought about that before cutting up a shark in them.'

Daz opened his mouth to say something in reply, but by this time Rob, Ben and Mike had joined him. Ben lifted his hands and sniffed them. 'I think she's right, Daz. We absolutely reek.'

Daz looked dejected, but he seemed to accept the situation. As the rest of us walked back up to the hut, he joined the other hunters as they began to strip off. Once they were naked, they cast their ruined clothes into the fire beneath the metal drum before diving into the sea, where they scrubbed themselves with handfuls of sand in an attempt to rid themselves of the odours that clung to them like limpets.

As I watched, I realised that we'd need to start taking better care of the few clothes that we had left, at least until we worked out exactly how to make replacements, and we were still a long way from being able to do that. Each item that became too badly torn, or worn out, or too dirty or smelly to wear meant one less item we had in our wardrobes, and there were few places left where we could hope to get any replacements. For tasks like killing sharks, we'd be better off doing it naked, skin being easier to clean than clothing, or wearing dedicated outfits which we could keep aside for such tasks, and which we wouldn't care how disgusting or malodorous they became. They wouldn't be fun to wear, but it would save us from ruining otherwise functional clothes that we needed to keep ourselves clad and warm.

By nightfall, the fire had died down and Ben explained what would happen next. 'If we let it cool overnight, all the oil which has been released from the liver should float to the top and we can then separate it out from any water and the remaining bits of flesh.'

Daz frowned. 'Will it be ready to try in an engine then? Or will we need to do somethin' else to it first?'

Ben mulled this over for a moment before replying.

'That should be it … at least in theory, but I've never done anything like this before.'

Rob scratched the back of his head, clearly nervous about what we'd need to do to find out. 'Which engine d'you want to test it on?'

'I figured the generator.' Ben looked round at the others. 'It'll be the easiest one to replace if something goes wrong.'

Mitch leant forward. 'Is that likely?'

Ben shrugged noncommittally. 'Diesel engines are pretty tough, so it shouldn't, but you never know.'

***

'Is everything ready?' Ben glanced round and there were muttered yesses from those of us gathered nearby. 'Here goes.'

Overnight, the boiled mixture of basking shark liver had, indeed, separated out, and the top half of the container was filled with a clear liquid tinged with a slightly yellowish hue. Ben had stuck a finger in and then pulled it out before rubbing it with his thumb. 'It's oil alright. Now, let's see if it works.'

With the help of Rob and Mike, he'd decanted some of the oil into a battered and rusting five-gallon jerrycan and carried it up to the generator. There, he siphoned off the diesel which was already in its fuel tank and replaced it with a small amount of the shark oil. He checked everything over and then once he was ready, he pushed the starter button. The engine coughed and spluttered, but didn't catch.

Daz looked crestfallen. 'Does that mean it's no' goin' to work?'

Ben held up a hand. 'You need to give the oil a chance to work its way through the system.'

He pressed the starter button again; it turned over, but still it didn't start. On the third attempt, it ran for a few seconds and then died.

'That sounded promising.' Rob pulled out a screwdriver and knelt down beside it. 'I'll adjust the idle.'

He slotted the screwdriver into a small screw and gave it a quarter of a turn. 'Try it now.'

Ben pressed the button once again and this time the engine not only roared into life, but, after an initial rough patch, it settled down and ran smoothly. Daz punched the air enthusiastically. 'Go on, ya dancer!'

After a few minutes, Ben shut the engine down, a broad grin on his face. The shark oil, it seemed, could, indeed, be used as a replacement for diesel. It was a shame that such a majestic creature should have to die just so we could run our engines, but it was much safer than trying to get diesel from elsewhere, and as long as we used the shark oil sparingly, and were careful not to kill too many of them, the few sharks we'd take would be unlikely to affect their numbers.

The fact that we could now make our own fuel marked another step towards creating a community which could survive, not just by picking through the remains of what had once been our civilisation, but by making its own way in the world in which we now found ourselves.

'Ready' Rob's hand was hovering over the power switch of the shortwave radio.

I nodded and Rob turned it on. This was the fourth evening we'd gathered, along with Jimmy, Jeff and Mike, in the cockpit of the catamaran, hoping that today would be the day we'd finally hear from Jack again. Tentatively, I picked up the microphone and spoke. 'Mingulay calling Hope Town. Come in, Hope Town.'

I set the mic down and waited, but there was nothing. I glanced round the room: faces, which moments before had been wide-eyed with anticipation, were now, yet again, looking dejected. Once more, it seemed there would be no news. In the silence that followed, I wondered how long we'd keep on doing this. At what point would we finally give up and accept the ever-more likely possibility that Jack and the others were gone? We'd lost people from our community before, but we'd always known, more or less, what had gone wrong. Now it was the uncertainty about what had happened that was tearing us apart. Might they still be out there? Was there something, anything we could be doing to help them? Should we set out to try to find an answer? Or should we remain here and grieve for those we might've lost forever?

As the hour we'd allotted to trying to contact Jack crept by, the others gradually drifted off until it was only me and Rob left, staring at the still-silent radio. Eventually, Rob looked up at the clock: the time for today was over. 'I guess we should ...'

He didn't finish his sentence. Instead, he reached out, but just as his hand touched the switch, the radio burst into life. 'Hope Town calling Mingulay. Come in, Mingulay.'

The signal was weak, but there was no doubt it was Jack. Rob's delighted shout as he scooped up the microphone brought the others running, and by the time he was ready to speak, we were all once again crowded round the radio. 'Hope Town, this is Mingulay. It's so good to hear your voice again, Jack. We thought we'd lost you. What happened?'

Rob released the transmit button and we waited for an answer, but there was only static. As the seconds ticked by, Rob glanced at me, wondering, like I was, whether we'd somehow imagined the voice we'd heard coming over the radio. Then it came again. 'Rob, are you there?'

Rob twiddled the knobs on the radio, trying to boost the signal before he spoke again. 'Jack, I can hear you, can you hear me?'

'Rob, I can hear you!' The joy in Jack's voice was obvious.

I took the mic. 'Jack what happened? Where've you been? We heard gunfire.'

'We were attacked; they came out of nowhere: two speedboats.' The radio crackled for a second before we heard Jack's voice again. 'They had guns; they tried to board us.'

I pressed the transmit button again. 'Is everyone safe?'

'Yes, somehow. It's a miracle really. I got my boat started, and I was able to drive them away, at least for a while, but then we saw them coming back with another pair of boats. I knew we wouldn't be able to hold them all off, and that we needed to get out of there, but mine was the only boat which was ready to leave, and which was fast enough to outrun them.'

Unlike the other boats remaining in the Hope Town community, Jack's boat was a large and powerful sport-fishing boat, capable of running at high speed if, and when, it had to.

'Andrew and me got everyone on board, and we high-tailed it out of there, except they chased us. We tried to lose them amongst the islands, but we couldn't shake them, so we decided we'd have to head out to sea and start the crossing.'

Rob took the microphone from me. 'Why didn't you let us know sooner?'

There was a loud burst of static before we heard Jack's voice again. 'Because they kept chasing us, right out to sea; it must have been a couple of days after they first attacked before they finally disappeared. After that, I was worried they might be able to find us again using the radio signals, so I thought it was better to keep quiet until we were far enough out that there was no way they could find us again.'

Rob's brow furrowed. 'Where are you now?'

There was a brief pause before Jack replied. 'We're about 700 miles north-east of Hope Town; we should be passing Bermuda sometime tomorrow.'

I saw Rob smile. 'How long d'you think it'll take you to get here?'

The radio hissed. 'It'll be another couple of weeks at least.'

Rob's smile broadened at the news. 'How's everyone doing?'

'It's a bit crowded and we're having to ration the food and water, but we're holding up.' The signal faded out for a moment before coming back. '—ow are things at your end?'

Rob sank down onto the nearest seat before he replied. 'Much better now we know you're safe, and that you're on your way.'

That evening was calm and warm, and after we'd eaten our evening meal, we sat around an open fire we'd built just in front of the hut. What with the success of the shark hunt, and the re-establishment of contact with Jack, we were in a celebratory mood. Much to everyone's surprise,

Ben had rowed out to his boat and returned with a case of beer. After he'd set it down, Rob leaned forward and pulled out a bottle. 'Where on earth did you dig this up from?'

Ben shrugged nonchalantly. 'It was on the boat when I first got it.'

Daz frowned at him. 'An' you're only sharin' this information with the rest of us now?'

'I was saving it for a special occasion.' Ben held out a bottle-opener to Rob. 'And the way I see it, if today doesn't qualify as a special occasion, then nothing does.'

Once everyone had a bottle, including, much against my better judgement, Sophie, Jimmy and Jeff, Rob pulled himself to his feet and raised his. 'To being re-united with absent friends!'

We all took a mouthful of beer, and then Daz stood up. 'An' to huntin' sharks!'

We drank to that, too, and then to everything else we could think of, taking it in turns to propose toasts that grew ever-more ludicrous with every gulp of beer consumed. None of us had had a drink in a very long time, and soon we were all drunk and sleepy. Not long after that, Sophie dozed off, her head resting on Daz's shoulder, while both Jimmy and Jeff's heads were nodding as they fought to stay awake. Out of nowhere, someone started singing a song:

'Show me the way to go home,

'I'm tired and I want to go to bed,'

Despite our very different backgrounds, we all seemed to know the words and the tune, and as one, those of us who were still awake joined in.

'I had a little drink about an hour a go,

'And it's gone straight to my head.'

We sang the song over and over, each time faster than the time before, Daz and Rob drumming along on the now-empty case of beer. Eventually, it got so fast, we could no longer keep time with each other and the singing descended into drunken laughter. My head swimming from the beer, I looked round at the others, and realised that for the first time in a very long time, I felt, at least for that moment, happy.

Chapter Ten

By the time we woke the next morning, the sense of gloom which had hung over us since we'd lost touch with Jack and the rest of the Hope Town community had completely evaporated, and we all moved around with an added spring in our step. I even heard Rob absentmindedly humming the song from the night before to himself as he gutted some fish and prepared them for our lunch. While we were all pleased that Jack and the others would soon be here, there was one thing that concerned us: where they would all stay once they arrived? They couldn't remain crammed into Jack's boat, but although we now had the walls of two cottages rebuilt, we still had to find something we could use to finish them off and make them inhabitable.

As we ate our midday meal, we discussed the matter. 'We can use turf or thatch for the roofing, that's how it would've been done traditionally, and we can get that here on the island,' Rob took a mouthful of food, 'but we'd still need wood for rafters to hold it up, and something to stop the wind and rain getting in through the windows.'

'Are you talkin' about havin' to chop down trees an' stuff like that?' Daz lifted another bit of fish from the pan that lay in the middle of the table in the hut, and set it down on his plate, before attacking it with a fork. 'Would that no' be dangerous? I mean, if we do that, it's goin' to make an awful lot of noise. Would it no' attract infected?'

Mike grunted, possibly in agreement, or possibly as a request for more food. Like Jeff, Jimmy and Sophie, he had awoken much the worse for wear. Although they'd drunk less beer than the rest of us, their relative inexperience meant that they were feeling the after effects far more. Mike, in particular, looked very much like he had at the height of the seasickness which had downed him as we'd crossed the Atlantic. I couldn't help thinking that it was just as well we were safe on the island because if the infected struck any time soon, the four youngsters would've had little chance of reacting fast enough to escape.

Thinking back, I realised it would've been the same for all of us the night before, and this sent an unexpected shudder through my body. Last night, we'd all been concentrating on having fun, celebrating our victories against the world and letting our hair down. Yet, if, somehow, an infected had reached the island during that time, or while we were sleeping it off afterwards, the results would've almost certainly been fatal. We knew the island was very safe, but we also knew it wasn't one hundred per cent impregnable, and it was still possible for drifters to make it ashore. It might just be the odd one or two, but if there were more vessels like the Russian training ship we'd encountered on our first voyage from Soay to Mingulay, it could be an entire boatful all at once. Even on Mingulay, could we really afford to relax, and drop our guard, even for the occasional celebratory evening?

I was drawn back to the conversation by Mitch. 'What d'you think, CJ?'

'Huh?' Lost in my own ruminations, I hadn't been paying attention to anything the others had been saying.

'I was just saying maybe we don't need to worry about roofing the buildings quite yet. Maybe we could just gather together some boats that the others could live on until we work out how we're going to finish off the cottages. We can anchor them in the bay. It's nice and sheltered, and there's plenty of room for another five or six

185

boats. Once they're here, they can also help us with rebuilding more cottages.'

I nodded absent-mindedly, my thoughts still on what we'd done the night before, trying to work out just how much of a potential risk it had been to our survival. Was Mingulay really safe enough for us to ever let our guard down, even if it was only for a few hours at a time? I did my best to push them away, and concentrate, instead, on remembering how much fun it had been to relax, truly relax, for the first time in many, many months. Yet, still it niggled away at me, even as I responded to Mitch's question. 'Yeah, that sounds like a good idea.'

***

'What's that?' Sophie pointed off towards the nearby shore.

I followed her gaze and saw something move. At first I thought it was just an infected, but then I realised something more was going on. 'I don't know. Shall we take a closer look?'

Sophie nodded. When it came to the infected, we always investigated anything that seemed unusual, as long as it was safe to do so, in case it was an early indication that something about them was changing. We lived with an ever-present, low-level fear that there might still be things we didn't know about the infected, about how they behaved, about how this might change over time as the virus continued to dig itself ever further into every possible recess of their bodies, and their brains. All we knew for certain was that this lack of knowledge could have deadly consequences. Already, we'd seen that some infected seemed to be able to remain relatively well-fed even as those around them starved, and none of us could say for sure exactly why this was happening or what it meant for the long-term survival of the infected, and so, for our own survival in a world where they were king. With this in mind, I turned the wheel and adjusted the sails until we were heading towards the land.

We'd spent the last five days locating suitable boats and moving them back to Mingulay so they'd be ready for Jack and the others when they eventually arrived. We were now returning, Sophie, Daz, Ben, Jeff and me, on the catamaran, Rob and Mitch, along with Mike and Jimmy, on the last of the boats we needed. Only Sophie and I were out on deck, the rest were dozing in the cabin.

The hand-held radio clipped to my waist buzzed with static, then Mitch's voice emerged from it. 'You're going a little off course there, aren't you, CJ?'

I pulled the radio off my belt and spoke into it. 'Just checking something out.'

'It's a cow!' Sophie had the binoculars trained on the shore. 'And it's got a little calf with it. Oh god, and there's an infected trying to attack it.'

I turned the wheel until we were pointing away from the shore again. 'There's not much we can do about that.'

'But we can't just leave it there,' Sophie pleaded with me. 'Is there nothing we can do to help it get away?'

I considered this for a moment. 'I suppose we could try to distract the infected; that would give it a chance to escape.'

Sophie lifted up the binoculars again. 'Let's do that then.'

I steered the boat back towards the shore. Once we were closer, I could see more of what was happening.

There seemed to be a stand-off between the infected and the cow. The infected prowled round, clearly wary of the cow, but intent on getting to where the calf lay. Judging by the wet sheen on its skin, the calf had only just been born, and I wondered if this was the reason the infected had managed to sneak up on the pair. All the cattle we'd seen since we'd arrived in Scotland had been very skittish, dashing off the moment they spotted anything which looked even vaguely human. Now I understood why: while the infected's main driving force was to attack humans in an attempt to pass the virus on, some at least, if not all, still retained the instinct to feed, in order to keep their bodies alive, and this drove them, every now and then, to seek out other sources of food to sustain themselves. They clearly preferred the flesh of humans, but it seemed that when they really needed it, any flesh would do.

This made me wonder: in places where other animals were available, would the infected ever, as we'd so often hoped, starve to death? Watching the events now unfolding on the shore, it seemed like this would be unlikely to happen. Instead, the infected would persist, maybe not in the same numbers as before, but nonetheless they'd remain an ever-present threat for decades to come. Humans no longer held the position of ultimate predator at the top of the food chain which they'd occupied for so long. Now, we'd been replaced by the infected and been pushed into the role of prey, and this, it was becoming increasingly clear, was unlikely to change any time soon.

It was a depressing realisation, but one that didn't shock me. When it came to the infected, almost nothing surprised me anymore. Suddenly, I felt the need to help the cow and her newborn calf. It wasn't out of any maternal instinct, but rather because it would allow me one little victory in the ongoing battle with the infected, which we were almost continuously losing.

I cast my eyes around to get my bearings. We were about eighty feet from the shore and, as yet, neither the cow nor the infected had realised we were there. Suddenly, the infected made another lunge towards the calf as it, in turn, struggled once more to get to its feet, but its mother cut the infected off. The infected seemed wary of the threat posed by the cow and it backed off again. I wondered if this was the difference between when they hunted for food rather than when they were driven by the far greater desire to infect humans. If so, I hoped to use this difference to help save the cow and her calf. 'Sophie, go wake the others, and bring the hand-held foghorn with you.'

Sophie disappeared and reappeared a moment later, shortly followed by a bleary-eyed Ben and then, one by one, the others.

Ben looked round and stretched. 'What's going on?'

I glanced at him and smiled. 'Oh, just tormenting an infected while we have the opportunity.'

I took the hand-held foghorn as Sophie held it out to me and blew it hard. It had the effect I was hoping it would and immediately the infected lost interest in the calf. It turned, focussing all its energy and attention on finding the source of the new sound that now assailed its senses. I blew the foghorn again and the infected raced towards the beach, only stopping at the water's edge, where it paced back and forth, trying to work out how to get to us. I blew the foghorn a third time and in response the infected snarled and roared, our presence so near and yet so unattainable, sending it apoplectic with anger and rage.

'How's it no' running away? The cow I mean.' Daz sounded puzzled.

We'd given the cow the opportunity to flee, and I hoped she'd take it, but she didn't. Instead, she turned and nudged her calf in an attempt to force it to its feet, but although the calf tried, it was still too young and too weak. Now we were close enough, I could see the cow was of a nondescript breed that I didn't recognise, dark and small in size, but feisty in defence of her calf. She lowed desperately and walked a few feet away before calling again, hoping that this would drive the calf to follow, but it still hadn't made it onto its feet. For a moment, I thought the cow would leave the calf there, but she returned to where it lay, nuzzling and licking it affectionately.

'She doesn't want to leave her calf behind. We've got to do something.' Sophie looked round at me and Ben. 'Can't we rescue them? Can't we take them back to Mingulay with us? They'd be safe there, just like we are.'

Ben looked thoughtful for a moment before he responded. 'You know, it would be good to have a supply of milk, especially with the baby on the way.' He pointed towards the infected. 'But how do we get rid of *that*?'

Daz frowned at me. 'Can we no' shoot it with the rifle you've got on board?'

I shook my head. 'We don't have bullets for it.'

A puzzled look spread across Daz's face. 'But when you first picked us up on Soay, you had it out in the cockpit. Why'd you have it out if you'd no' got any bullets?'

'That was just for show.'

'It was a bluff?' Daz sounded incredulous.

I nodded. 'Basically.'

'Oh.' Daz had obviously fallen for it, and was now

feeling a little sheepish.

I looked round the cockpit. 'Anyone have any other ideas?'

Ben stepped forward. 'If we could get a rope round the infected, we could drag it into the sea and drown it.'

Daz's eyes lit up. 'Hey, that'd work.'

'I don't know.' I craned my neck, trying to get a better view of exactly what we'd be up against. 'It might be a bit dangerous. You'd have to get pretty close to get a rope round it.'

Ben stared at the infected as it paced back and forth, letting out the occasional frustrated roar, its eyes focussed on the boat. 'All we'd need to do is lasso it, and we should be able to do that from a safe distance away.'

Jeff frowned. 'You think you can do that?'

Ben leant on the side of the boat and watched the infected closely for a few seconds before straightening up again. 'Only one way to find out.'

I glanced round nervously. 'This is about as close as I dare go.'

Ben and I sat in the dinghy about ten feet from the shore. Looking over the side, I could see the water was deep enough here that the infected wouldn't dare venture this far out, but any closer and it might just take the risk. It knew exactly where we were, and it was stalking angrily along the water's edge, contorting its gaunt features into grotesque caricatures of the human face it had once been. Its skin was drawn tight across its cheek bones, and I could see its ribs through its skin as its tattered clothes flapped in the gentle breeze. It was clearly close to death, and this was presumably what had driven it to take on the cow in order to try to sustain itself, but now it knew we were there, its hunger for food had vanished, forced out by a much more powerful instinct: to attack and pass on the virus. Rage still burned deep in its eyes and I knew it would do anything within its power to reach us — except venture into water more than a few inches deep.

I'd often wondered about this: what exactly was it about water that they feared so much? Why was it the one thing that could halt their otherwise inexorable progress? It was almost as if the virus which inhabited them knew that water meant death for its host, and so death for itself, and it instilled this fear to prevent that happening. Yet a virus wasn't conscious; it didn't have a brain; it couldn't possibly know anything, not in the traditional sense of knowing at any rate. In many ways, it seemed so strange, yet it was probably the only thing that had allowed us to survive for as long as we had, and if, for any reason, this ever changed, I couldn't help thinking that it would mean the end for all of us.

Knowing these ruminations weren't getting us any closer to dealing with the infected on the nearby shore, I returned my focus to the matter at hand. I manoeuvred the dinghy so the stern was facing the shore as Ben tied one end of a length of rope to the small metal hoop on the back. Taking the other end, he fashioned it into a loop and stood up. He whirled it round above his head and then threw it towards the infected, but it landed short. He pulled the rope back in and tried again. This time he hit the infected, but it glanced off its shoulder; the infected's attention was so concentrated on us that it didn't even notice. On the third attempt, the rope landed around the infected's neck and Ben yanked it tight. 'Go!'

I gunned the engine, looking back just in time to see the infected being jerked from its feet and flying through the air before landing with a loud splash in the water and disappearing from sight. Halfway between the shore and the catamaran, I stopped. The rope sank down until it hung vertically from the stern, vibrating rapidly. The infected on the other end was clearly still alive and thrashing around in the water. I peered into the depths, trying to see if I could spot it, but the water was too dark. 'How long do you think it'll take to drown?'

Ben peered into the water, too. 'I don't know. Might as well just cut the rope and be done with it. Have you got a knife?'

That was when I realised we hadn't thought our plan through thoroughly enough before we'd put it into action. 'No.'

'I guess I'll just need to untie it then.' Ben leant forward, his fingers wrestling with the knot just inches from the water.

Suddenly, a hand shot through the surface and fastened itself onto one of Ben's wrists. Instantly, the blood drained from his face. 'It must have pulled itself up the rope!'

Another hand appeared: this one grasping the top of the engine and the infected started to lever itself upwards. Its head emerged next, lips pulled back, teeth bared, inching towards Ben as he fought frantically to unfasten the infected's vice-like grip on his wrist. I looked around, desperate to find something I could use as a weapon, but there was nothing.

'CJ, do something!' The terror was clear in Ben's voice. The infected was almost close enough to sink its teeth into Ben's face and with his wrist trapped by one of its arms, he couldn't get away.

Then it came to me: I slammed the engine into reverse

and turned the throttle; the dinghy shot backwards and the razor sharp propeller tore into the infected's chest, turning the sea red with blood. Its head disappeared, followed by one of its arms.

'Stop!' Ben yelled out, and instantly I saw why. The infected still had a tight grip on his arm and as it was being pulled under the boat, it was threatening to take Ben with it. I slammed the engine into forward and twisted the throttle again. More blood spread across the water as the propeller bit into the infected once again, and pieces of flesh floated to the surface.

Ben cried out again and fell backwards, landing heavily on the bottom of the dinghy. The second pass must have hit the infected's shoulder because while its hand remained firmly wrapped around Ben's wrist, the arm ended in a ragged wound which oozed blood. Ben leapt to his feet before peeling the arm free and casting it over the side. He stared at his wrist, turning it backwards and forwards as he inspected it closely.

I gawked at him, petrified, knowing what it would mean if the infected had broken his skin. Even the smallest wound from an infected was enough to let the disease in. I tried to say something, but I couldn't find the words. If he'd been infected, there'd be little any of us could do about it. The terror Ben would feel, knowing what was inevitably going to happen to him, would be unimaginable. Finally, I found my voice. 'Are ... Are you okay?'

Ben rubbed his arm with his other hand, the sleeve of his jacket pulled over it for protection, and then examined his wrist again, this time more closely than before. Finally, he looked up. I could tell by the relief on his face that he was uninjured. 'Yeah, I'll be fine. The skin's not broken: there's no chance I'm infected.'

Ben returned to the stern and, with his hands shaking, undid the rope. Together, we watched the remains of the infected disappear from sight into the depths of the sea. I shook my head disbelievingly, wondering how we could've been so stupid. It had seemed such a simple, straightforward plan, but it had almost gone so horribly wrong. That was the trouble with dealing with the infected, one small slip, one slight misjudgement and an encounter could turn deadly in an instant. I let out a long, loud breath, and then turned to Ben. 'That was close.'

Ben scowled back at me. 'No kidding!'

With the infected finally gone, we could start on the task of trying to persuade the cow to clamber onto the catamaran so we could transport it back to Mingulay. I backed the catamaran up as close as I could to the beach, and as Jeff kept a lookout from its roof, Daz, Sophie, Ben and me stood on the shore discussing what to do next. All the time the cow stared at us warily, ready to run at a moment's notice if she really had to, but not wanting to leave the calf which was still trying to struggle to its feet.

Daz ran a critical eye over the situation. 'Can we no' just herd her on board?'

Ben looked from the cow to the catamaran and back again. 'By the looks of it, it's not going to be that easy; she's pretty scared. We can give it a go, though. CJ, Sophie, you go round that way, Daz and I'll go round this way.'

The cow, however, was having none of it. She stamped and snorted, and made brief charges whenever any of us came near, her tail swishing angrily through the air behind her. After ten minutes, we'd got nowhere: the cow resolutely refused to be herded anywhere and I was starting to worry that if we carried on much longer, we'd end up attracting the attention of more infected.

I looked up. 'Jeff, is everything still clear?'

'Yeah. Nothing moving. Wait.' Jeff lifted the binoculars and pointed them towards the shore. After a few seconds, he lowered them again. 'Infected. About ten of them.'

Ben shielded his eyes with his hand as he glanced towards Jeff. 'How far?'

Jeff scanned the shore with the binoculars again. 'About half a mile.' He lowered the binoculars and pointed. 'They're just coming out of the trees of that wood over there.'

I turned to the others. 'We need to go.'

Sophie remained where she was. 'We can't leave her here. They'll kill her and the calf, and they don't deserve that.'

Ben stood on his tip-toes craning his neck as he tried to spot the infected for himself. 'If she doesn't want to come with us, we can't make her.'

Sophie was adamant. 'But we can't leave them here.' She walked slowly forward. The cow huffed and stamped, but stood her ground. When Sophie was close enough, she reached out and patted the cow on the side of the neck before stoking her nose. Their eyes were level, and Sophie looked deep into the cow's in an attempt to communicate that she meant her no harm. The cow huffed again and flicked her tail, but didn't shy away. Sophie turned back to the rest of us. 'I think she just doesn't want to get separated from the calf. Daz, can you pick it up?'

'Guys, they're getting close.' Jeff was tracking the infected with the binoculars and he was starting to sound worried. Following Sophie's request, Daz stepped forward and lifted up the calf. He staggered slightly under its weight. 'Bloody hell, this thing's heavy.'

Sophie ignored him. 'Now walk towards the boat.'

Daz did as he was told, walking slowly and unsteadily. The cow remained where she was for a second and then followed, calling gently. I went ahead and undid the guard rail on the stern of the left-hand hull. Daz entered the water and waded the short distance to the back of the catamaran, shuffling his feet as he tried to make sure he didn't trip on any rocks hidden beneath the surface. The calf struggled to get away, but its movements were weak, and he managed to keep it from slipping from his grasp. Finally, with the water just over his knees, he reached the back of the boat and climbed on board before setting the calf down gently on the deck. All the time, the cow remained on the shore, unwilling, or unable, to follow. Sophie spoke to her gently, whispering in her ear and urging her forward, but she stubbornly refused to follow Daz.

Ben scratched his head. 'Maybe the water's too deep; maybe it can't get to the boat.'

I was just about to answer when Jeff called out. 'They're getting real close.'

I bit the inside of my lip. Even though we'd been on Mingulay almost six months, being on the land still made me nervous. 'We're just going to have to leave her.'

Sophie was shocked. 'We can't.'

Ben put an arm round her shoulder. 'Sophie, we don't have a choice.'

'We can't. I won't let you.' Sophie's face had a level of intensity on it that I'd never seen before. 'We can't just leave her here.' She shook Ben off and glared at him. 'I won't let you do that again.'

I could tell there was something deeper going on here, but there wasn't time to ask. 'We've got to go.'

Daz was stroking the calf gently, trying to keep it calm. 'What do we do with this?'

I knew that if we took it with us, we'd have nothing to feed it and it would almost certainly die. If we left it here, with its mother, there was a chance it might survive: a slim one, given the number of infected now racing towards us, but a chance nonetheless. 'Take it back onto the shore.'

'No!' Sophie's voice was firm, and her eyes burned with determination. She whispered to the cow again, and then the calf let out a high-pitched sound. The cow must've heard it because she finally started forward, splashing through the shallow water. She reached the back of the boat and paused, momentarily unsure what to do next. Then the calf called again, and the cow seemed to understand what she had to do. She lifted her front legs onto the steps at the back of the catamaran, and with Sophie, me and Ben pushing from behind, she somehow managed to scramble up and into the cockpit.

Sophie smiled as Ben wiped his hands on the waterproof jacket he was wearing. He glanced at me; then over his shoulder: we could see the infected now, running as fast as they could over the rough ground. Ben turned back to the boat. 'Let's get the hell out of here.'

As Sophie climbed on board, Ben and I pushed at the catamaran, trying to get it moving away from the shore, but it refused to budge. We tried again, still nothing. Panic flashed across Ben's face. 'Tide must've dropped; the boat's grounded.'

'Shit!' Terror shot through me: once before, we'd found ourselves grounded and with a horde of infected racing towards us; while we'd eventually got away, it was only by the skin of our teeth, and it came at a heavy cost: the loss of Bill's life, and his leadership. I tried to think of a solution, and remembered that last time, Bill had ordered us to shift as much weight away from the point where the hull was grounded. That was when a thought occurred to me: maybe it was just the extra weight of the cow at the back of the boat that was stopping us getting away. I looked up. 'Daz, see if you can get the cow to move forward.'

'They're almost here!' There was urgency and fear in Jeff's voice. Mixed with this, I heard the cow moo as its hooves skittered on the cockpit's deck.

I glanced round: the infected were rapidly closing in on us. 'Jeff, get down from the roof and get ready to start the engine the moment I say so. Daz, where's the cow?'

Daz's voice was slightly muffled when he answered. 'She's right up front in the cabin.'

I muttered a pray to a god I hadn't believed I since I was a child, knowing that this might be our last chance to try something, anything, before the infected reached us and we'd have to stand and fight. If we were forced to do that, there was little chance of any of us surviving. After all, with the infected, escape was always preferable to combat. I looked at Ben. 'Ready to try again?'

He nodded and we put our shoulders to the back of the boat. This time it moved. I grinned at Ben. 'That's it!'

Together, we pushed the boat until it was clear of the shore, then we pulled ourselves onto it and I shouted to Jeff. 'Start the engine!'

I heard it splutter into life and then clunk into gear. Back on the shore, the infected had reached the water's edge, and I knew we'd escaped only by the slimmest of margins. I looked skyward: I didn't believe in heaven, or spirits, or anything like that, but even from beyond the grave, Bill's memory was still helping to keep us safe, just as he'd done when he was alive.

'Hope Town calling Mingulay. Come in, Mingulay.'

Darkness had fallen as we made our way back to the island. The cow now had a loose rope halter around her neck and this had been secured to a cleat at the back of the boat. A few minutes after leaving the shore, the calf had finally managed to find its feet and, standing unsteadily on trembling legs, it had started suckling for the first time. This had calmed the cow, and she called softly and contentedly to herself and her calf. Sophie had already christened the cow Betsy and was now arguing with Jeff and Daz over what they should call the calf.

I picked up the microphone. 'Hope Town, this is Mingulay. How're you doing, Jack?'

'We're doing good. A bit hungry and seasick, but we're doing good. I got a good look at the sun at noon. You want to know our latest position?'

Like us, Jack had a sextant on board, but unlike us, he was highly skilled at using it. I moved over to the chart as he reeled off the numbers and plotted them. I returned to the radio. 'That's close, Jack.' I could hear the excitement in my own voice.

'I know.' Jack didn't sound as excited. In fact, he sounded strained.'

I pressed the transmit button again. 'Is everything okay?'

There was a few seconds silence before he answered, just long enough for me to worry that there was something he wasn't telling me. 'Everything's fine.' There was another gap, this time slightly longer. 'If we can keep up our current speed, we should be with you in about a week.'

I smiled at the thought, but there was still something in Jack's voice that left me feeling unsettled.

***

Jeff stretched and yawned as he came into the cockpit. 'There's someone calling you on the radio.'

It was early morning; the sun had yet to rise and we were still a few miles short of Mingulay. Considering the time of year, the weather was gentle and I was alone at the wheel while the others slept inside.

'Is it Rob?' I figured he might be calling on the VHF radio to find out where we were.

'No.' Jeff's forehead wrinkled. 'I think it's Andrew.'

'Andrew?' I echoed Jeff's last word, wondering why Andrew would be trying to reach us this early in the day. Then panic gripped me: there was only one reason Andrew would be calling us while it was still dark. 'Jeff, take the wheel.'

I didn't usually trust Jeff to be at the helm on his own in the dark, but something was clearly wrong, and I felt that, at that moment, I had no other choice. I could feel beads of sweat starting to form on my brow as I raced inside and heard Andrew's voice coming out of the shortwave radio. 'Hope Town calling Mingulay. Rob, CJ, are you there?'

I grabbed the mike. 'Andrew, what's wrong? What's happened?'

'Nothing.' There was a pause. 'Not yet at any rate.'

Andrew's voice had the same strained tone as Jack's. There was clearly something going on, but I couldn't work out what. 'Why're you calling at this time in the morning then?'

'It's ...' Andrew's voice faded into a silence that hung heavily in the air for what seemed like an age before he spoke again. 'I ... I didn't want Jack to know what I was doing.'

My heart started to race: what could be going on that Andrew wanted to keep secret from Jack. 'Why?'

'Jack's concerned. So am I, but Jack didn't want to worry you. After all, we might have enough to get us there.'

I could feel a knot starting to form in my stomach. 'Enough what?'

'Diesel.'

That one word sent a tremor of fear down my spine. If they ran out of fuel before they got to us, they'd be in real trouble. Unlike the catamaran, Jack's sport-fishing boat didn't have sails it could use as an alternative to its engines, and without them they'd be at the mercy of the wind and the waves. I did my best to calm myself. After all, maybe I'd misunderstood what Andrew was talking about. 'But I thought the tanks were full when you left?'

'They were, but it was always going to be close.' The radio crackled with static for a second before Andrew's voice came through once more. 'The thing is, we used up a lot of fuel getting away when we were attacked, and then with all the extra people on board, we're carrying much more weight than we'd planned. We've used up a lot more than we thought we would've by this point.'

Andrew's words did nothing to quell the anxiety that was building inside me. I swallowed. 'How much have you got left?'

'As long as we don't run into any trouble, just about enough for us to get to, you, but we'll be running on fumes by then.'

Part of me was relieved that they might still be able to make it; another part was even more worried that if they encountered even the slightest of difficulties, it could mean they'd fail to reach us in time. 'Bloody hell, Andrew.'

'I know.' There was a pause before Andrew spoke again. 'Jack didn't want you worrying, but I thought you should know. How much diesel d'you guys have there?'

'Not much.' I tried to work out where he was going with this. 'Why?'

'Because if we don't make it, we're going to need you to come get us and, if that happens, the best thing would be for you to bring us out enough diesel to make it back to shore.'

I thought about how much diesel we had, and even with the shark oil, it was only about twenty gallons. While this was enough to last us for several weeks, maybe even longer if we used it sparingly, the much larger engines on Jack's sport-fishing boat would probably burn through it in a couple of hours. 'We don't have that much, but I'm sure we can scrounge up some more from somewhere.' In my heart, I doubted this was true, but I wanted to say something to reassure Andrew, to reduce his worry, at least for the time being. 'How long've we got?'

'As I said, it's going to be close, so we're probably not going to start having problems for at least another five or six days. We should be real close to you by then, maybe only fifty or a hundred miles out. You never know; we might even make it without your help. Jack's been trying to lighten the load. He's been getting rid of pretty much everything that isn't nailed down.' There was a momentary pause. 'And some of the things which are, too.' Andrew was trying to sound light-hearted, but he was failing. Instead, he just sounded tired and desperate.

'We need to get our hands on as much diesel as possible, then.' Rob paced back and forth as he spoke.

We were back on Mingulay, where the cow and her calf had been unloaded, and together they were now standing at the top of the beach, the cow munching nonchalantly on the lush grass that grew there, looking as if nothing remotely interesting had ever happened to her in her entire life. All of us, with the exception of Jimmy and Jeff who'd gone ahead up to the hut with Dougie, were gathered on the sand, discussing the conversation I'd had with Andrew earlier in the day.

'But we've pretty much used up all the supplies we can access safely.' Ben scuffed the toe of one shoe along the ground, leaving behind a shallow furrow. 'All that's left is the fuel in the fishing boats or ...' Ben's voice faded out.

This piqued my interest. 'Or what?'

Ben glanced uneasily at Sophie and I wondered why. Daz shifted uncomfortably, as did Mitch: there was something going on here, but I couldn't tell what. The longer the silence went on, the more tense it became, until it was palpable, hanging over us like a thunder cloud on a humid summer's day. Finally, Ben carried on, avoiding eye contact with Sophie as he spoke. 'Or we could try Rhum.'

'No.' Sophie glared at him. 'You promised we'd never go back there.'

Ben moved to comfort her, but she ducked out of his reach. Not knowing what else to do, Ben crossed his arms. 'Sophie, it's the only place left where there's a reasonable amount of diesel and it's already all in barrels.'

Daz took a step towards Sophie. 'It's an emergency, Soph. We've got no choice.'

I'd never heard Daz call her 'Soph' before, only ever Sophie, and it seemed to strike a nerve deep inside her. She narrowed her eyes and stared at Daz ferociously; the look was so intense it stopped him dead in his tracks, and he stood there, not knowing quite what to do next. When Sophie finally spoke, her voice was filled with hurt and rage, mixed with other emotions I couldn't quite place. 'You promised.' She whirled round to Ben and Mitch and then back to Daz. 'You all promised: we're never going back there; none of us are, ever. And that's final.'

With that Sophie stormed angrily off up the beach.

Mike stared after her. 'What was that all about?'

Again there was an uncomfortable silence as Ben, Daz and Mitch exchanged looks. Finally, Daz broke the silence. 'That's where Claire … where Sophie's mum is.'

I frowned. 'You mean that's where she was killed.'

'No.' Daz looked down distractedly at his hands. 'That's where she got infected.'

'She's infected?' Mike was shocked. 'I thought she'd died?'

Ben cleared his throat. 'No. She was infected when we were trying to get away from Rhum. It was pandemonium: people were running everywhere; we couldn't tell who was infected, and who was just running scared. One of them grabbed Sophie and Claire fought it off. She saved Sophie's life, but she got bitten. She insisted that we leave her there.' Ben glanced round at the others. 'Sophie made us promise we'd never go back there, no matter what. She wants to remember her mum as she was while she was alive, not what she'll have become.'

I found Sophie sitting by the unnamed man's grave, staring out to sea. Her eyes were red and puffy, as if she'd been crying. When she saw me coming, she wiped them and sniffed, but remained silent. I sat down beside her and put my arm around her. She responded by leaning her head against my shoulder.

After a minute or so, I felt it was time to start speaking. 'Did I ever tell you about how Jon died?'

I felt her head shake. I'd told her who Jon was, about how much I'd hated him at first and how much I'd loved him by the end. She knew he'd died, but I'd never told her how. 'They were out on a boat we'd found, Rob, Jon and Andrew; there was an accident and it sank. They were forced to go ashore to try to get back to the bay where we were all anchored. They almost made it too, only some infected spotted them, and started chasing them. They ran into an old lighthouse, but the infected followed them right up to the top.'

I swallowed, remembering what it had been like to watch them fleeing for their lives, not knowing if they'd survive or not. 'They made it into the light itself, but they couldn't get the doors closed, not at first. It was Jon who managed it in the end, but he got infected ...' My voice faded away, leaving nothing but silence.

It was a few seconds before Sophie spoke, 'How?' There was a slight quiver in her voice, as if she was afraid to hear the answer to her question.

I took a deep breath before I replied. 'He was scratched on the arm by one of *them*.' I spat the last word out, unaware until that moment, quite how much I hated each and every one of the infected: for what they were; for what they stood for; for everything they'd done to the world. But deep down, I knew it wasn't their fault: they hadn't done any of it on purpose. Instead, they were just doing what the virus made them do. 'It wasn't much, the scratch, but it was enough. Rob says that what Jon did saved his and Andrew's life, and I know it's petty, but I wish he hadn't been so brave.' I looked out towards the distant horizon, remembering Jon's final moments as he raged around the top of the lighthouse, infected and angry that Rob and Andrew had somehow escaped his grasp. I remembered Rob lining up the rifle and pulling the trigger, hearing the shot; burying my head in Jack's embrace, not wanting to look, but being unable to resist. Seeing Jon fall, tumbling against the blue sky and then he was gone.

Sophie sniffed again, and wiped her nose with her sleeve. 'My mum was infected, too. It happened when she saved my life. It was all my fault.'

I smoothed her hair. 'No it wasn't. Ben told me what happened. You're not to blame; no one is.'

'But, it was; it was my fault.' There was a moment's hesitation. 'And now you want to go back to Rhum just to get the fuel to save your friends. I don't want them to die, but I don't want anyone to go back there. There must be another way to get them diesel.'

'I understand, but there isn't. We've talked about it; it's really the only option. The fishing boats in the harbour on the mainland are too heavily infested with infected, and there's not enough diesel left on any of the smaller boats which are anchored away from the shore, not in any of the ports we've visited. We've used most of it up already.'

Sophie pulled away from me. 'What about killing more sharks?'

'Daz suggested that, too, but we'd need to kill an awful lot of them. Jack's boat isn't a sailboat. It's a sport-fishing boat; it needs a lot more fuel than our boats do.'

'But why didn't they use a sailboat in the first place?' Sophie sounded both angry and confused.

I sighed and rubbed my forehead; I understood where Sophie was coming from, but I still found it frustrating. 'Because Jack's boat was the only one that was ready to go when they were attacked, and it was the only one that was fast enough to get away.'

'Couldn't you just go out and pick them up?' Sophie was watching me closely as she spoke.

I shook my head. 'There are twenty-two of them. We'd never be able to fit that many people safely on the catamaran.'

Sophie pulled up her legs and wrapped her arms around them in an attempt to comfort herself. 'So take Ben's boat, too.'

I shook my head again. 'It's not set up for going that far offshore. It'd be too dangerous.'

Sophie swallowed. 'So the only way to save them is to go back to Rhum?'

I nodded. 'Unfortunately, yes.'

Tears welled up in Sophie's eyes. 'But I don't want to see what happened to her; what she's become. I want to remember her the way she was before she got infected. I've seen others with the disease, and they look horrible, like living skeletons, especially when they've had the disease for a long time. I don't want to see my mum like that.'

I knew how she felt: to see the effect the disease had on Jon had been terrible, but he'd only been infected for a few hours. Sophie's mum would have been infected for more than nine months, and I had no doubt that, by now, she'd be barely recognisable as the woman she'd once been. Yet, enough might remain that Sophie would be able to recognise her. 'You wouldn't have to come; you wouldn't have to see her.'

'But to get the diesel, you're going to have to go ashore, aren't you?' Sophie picked distractedly at the skin around her fingernails as she spoke.

I suddenly felt very uncomfortable, knowing where Sophie's thought processes were taking her. 'Yes.'

'That means ...' Sophie looked away. 'That means you'll need to kill all the infected on the island first, doesn't it?'

I turned and stared out to sea. 'Yes.'

'That means you'd have to kill my mum?' Sophie's voice was starting to tremble.

'Yes. But she's not your mum any more, not really.' I remembered when Rob had explained this to me just before he shot Jon. It hadn't made it any easier at the time, but it had made it easier afterwards.

'I know.' Sophie sniffed and then stood up. 'But if she's going to die, I want to be there when it happens.' She sniffed again. 'I owe her that.'

I stood up, too, and hugged her tightly, wondering how she could manage to be so strong. If all this had happened to me when I'd been her age, I'd have fallen apart. I'd very nearly fallen apart when I'd first found out what had happened, and I was five years older than her. Then I thought about what I'd told Rob when he'd asked me about how I'd learned to cope with everything and I'd told him I'd had no choice, but to grow up fast. I guess the same was true for Sophie. She coped with everything this cruel world threw at her simply because she had no other choice: it was either cope or die, and she was too much of a fighter to let that happen.

Chapter Eleven

'So how exactly are we goin' to do this?' Daz scratched distractedly at his patchy beard as he ran his eyes nervously over the nearby island. Beside him stood Jeff, Jimmy and Mike, looks of trepidation, worry and excitement mixed on their faces.

We were anchored in the same long, narrow bay on the east side of Rhum where we'd anchored when we'd visited it shortly after arriving in Scotland. The bay looked exactly the same: the large stone mansion, built to resemble a castle; the barbed wire strung out along the grass in front of it; the piles of equipment on the ground between the wire and the water's edge; the infected loitering amongst the debris of what had become of it all, looking lost and lonely as they waited for something to happen.

Rob swept the shore with the binoculars and then passed them to me. I took them and pointed them towards the island; I could see about forty or fifty infected, and knew there'd be more hidden from sight amongst the trees or sheltering in the shadow of the building. This was more than I'd expected and I had no idea how we'd be able to cope with so many.

'The diesel's over there in those barrels.' Ben pointed to the far corner of the building where they stood neatly stacked in three rows that were two barrels high, each containing fifty-five gallons of fuel.

Rob took the binoculars back and examined the barrels closely for a minute before he spoke. 'That should be more than enough.' He lowered the binoculars and returned his gaze to the infected. 'But what are we going to do about them?'

Mitch looked towards the shore. 'Could we herd them out of the way somehow?'

Mike leant on the guard rail nearest the shore. 'What if we took the dinghy and then drove close to the shore. We could make a noise and get them to follow us. That way, we could lead them away.'

Daz nodded. 'It'd be worth a go, wouldn't it?'

'I can't see her.' Sophie had picked up the binoculars and was now scanning the shore.

Jimmy frowned. 'Can't see who?'

Sophie kept the binoculars trained on the nearby island. 'My mum.'

Jimmy and Jeff exchanged looks. I thought maybe she might've talked to them about it at some point, but clearly she hadn't.

Jeff took a step forward. 'Your mum's here? She's infected?'

Sophie nodded, her lips pursed tightly shut.

He put a hand on her shoulder. 'Sorry.'

Sophie lowered the binoculars. 'She must be here somewhere, but I can't see her anywhere.'

Despite all Sophie had told me about not wanting to see her mother as she now was, she sounded disappointed. Maybe *disappointed* wasn't the right word; it was more that she'd been preparing herself for this moment and now it was here, she wanted to get it over and done with as soon as possible. Yet it was not playing out the way she'd expected.

Sensing how she was feeling, Daz came up behind her and put his arms round her. 'She'll be there somewhere.'

Two hours later and we were back in the same position as when we'd started. At first, it looked like trying to lure the infected away might work, but while we managed to move them along the beach, the rocks at either end were too high and they couldn't get over them, no matter how hard they tried. This meant that the furthest we could get the infected to move was only a couple of hundred yards away from where the barrels were stored, and that wasn't nearly far enough. I knew how fast the infected could move once they locked onto a target, and they could cover that sort of distance in a matter of seconds. That meant there was no way we could risk going ashore unless we could find a way of killing them, and not just some of them, but all of them; every last one.

'So what now?' We were all gathered in the cockpit once more, and I was staring back to where the infected milled, moaning and snarling, still riled up by our final attempt to lead them away from the diesel we so desperately needed.

Daz leaned on the back of the boat. 'What about shootin' them?'

I turned to him. 'We don't have any bullets, do we?'

'I was no' talkin' about usin' your gun. I meant with one of those.' Daz pointed to where the remains of two large ridged-hulled inflatable boats lay tipped onto their sides. The inflatable pontoons were flaccid and cracked, but the fibreglass hulls were still in good shape. I hadn't noticed it before, but up near the bow of each one was a large machine gun that I was certain would make short work of any infected it was fired at.

Rob leant on the side of the catamaran. 'But how would we get one of them?'

There was silence as we all contemplated the problem, then Ben spoke. 'If we can keep the infected occupied at the other end of the beach, we could see about getting

212

a rope tied to one of them and then we could pull it into the water. I think the hull would still float, at least for long enough for us to get the gun on board.'

Rob glanced round. 'Anyone got any better ideas?'

Again there was silence, but this time no one came up with an alternative, viable or otherwise.

After a minute, Rob clapped his hands together. 'Okay. Let's give it a go.'

He was trying to sound confident, but there was an undertone to his voice that betrayed his true feelings. Like me, he realised this was going to be a dangerous plan to implement. Yet, what other choice did we have?

I glanced round one last time: Daz and Ben were in the dinghy at the far end of the bay, floating near the shore, but at all times making sure they didn't drift too close. I could hear them blowing on the hand-held foghorn and banging on the side of the boat. The infected were building themselves into a frenzy in their efforts to reach the source of the noise. They knew it meant there were people near, but as always, they wouldn't venture into the water to get to them. Instead, they just stalked the water's edge, snarling and howling with anger and rage. There were about seventy of them now, all crowded together, pushing and shoving each other, jostling to be the ones closest to the dinghy. Others were still coming out of their hiding places: drawn by the noise and the commotion, they'd race out from the nearby woods and building, and down the beach to join the assembled throng. At first, a lot had appeared, but now it was just the odd one or two that, for some reason, had taken longer to reach the shore. Maybe they'd been shut in rooms in the house and had to break their way out, or maybe they'd been further away, having wandered off in the many months since Rhum had been overrun.

Figuring it was now as safe as it was ever going to be, I secured one end of a long rope to the back of the catamaran before taking the other end and slipping over the side. The water was cold, but I barely noticed as I swam steadily towards the shore, trying not to splash, or make any other noise, the rope snaking out behind. After a couple of minutes, I felt the ground beneath my feet and slowly straightened up. Water poured from me, splashing down loudly onto the sea that still came up to my waist. Worried that the sound might attract any nearby infected, I paused and looked round, but they remained focussed on the distant dinghy. Once I was certain they hadn't heard me, I waded forward and soon found myself standing on the soft, muddy sand about three feet from the remains of the ribs. Picking one, I crept forward and inspected it: the pontoons had been slashed and the remains of a man dressed in what looked like it had once been a black military uniform lay half in, half out of it, his head and left leg missing. Much of the rest of him had been reduced to bare bones, either by the elements or, more likely, by the scavenging of the infected as they tried to satiate their hunger for human flesh.

Trying not to think too much about what I was doing, I moved the body to one side. The bones rattled against each other as it landed on the beach, and even though the noise was nothing in comparison to that being made by Daz and Ben, I was concerned that it might attract the attention of any infected which hadn't yet been drawn to where they were. I glanced round, but saw nothing moving closer to me. Relieved, I returned my attention to the task at hand. Now the body was out of the way, I could see a metal towing loop at the front of the rib, and I crouched down until I was level with it. My hands were cold and wet after the swim ashore, but it didn't take long to loop the rope through it and start tying the knot. When I'd first come aboard the catamaran, Bill had shown me the best one for such tasks, one that when completed wouldn't slip loose, or tighten so much that it was impossible to ever get it untied again. I thought back to his words: round twice, then over and under, over and under, and then once more for luck. The knot was officially called a round turn and two half-hitches, but Bill always did three. Bill had always been like that: overcautious, always playing it safe, but still he'd been the first of us to die at the hands of the infected. Jon had been more carefree, and would've said the standard two were quite enough, but although he'd survived longer, he'd still died in the end.

I was halfway through the knot, lost in my thoughts about Bill and Jon, when a noise behind me brought me back to the present. With fear coursing through my body, I twisted round and found an infected standing only a few feet away, its attention continually shifting from me to the dinghy at the other end of the beach and back again. It stood, momentarily frozen by indecision, dressed in all that was left of mismatched clothing, its long hair and slim features suggesting it had once been a woman.

Instantly, I felt myself break into a cold sweat, the sudden moisture making my fingers slippery. My hands shaking, I fumbled with the rope, trying my best to finish the knot while making as little movement as possible, but knowing I had to try to complete the task I'd set out to do. At first, I thought I'd got away with it, but then the free end of the rope slipped from my grasp and before I could grab it again, it swung against the fibreglass hull of the rib, hitting it with a loud *thunk*. This was enough to break the spell and suddenly the infected knew which target it wanted more. As it leapt towards me, I turned and ran, diving into the safety of the water as soon as I reached it. Behind me, the infected threw back its head and roared. Other infected heard this and, knowing what it meant, raced towards the remains of the ribs. Soon, almost all the infected had congregated there, and only a few remained by the dinghy.

I swam slowly back to the boat, no longer caring whether I made any noise or not. I thought about how close I'd just come to being caught, and felt the bile rise in my throat: I'd been careless; I'd let myself get distracted when I should have been paying more attention to what was going on around me. I cursed my stupidity, knowing in my heart that if I'd taken even a split second longer to notice the infected, it would've been too late. What would the others have done then? Would they have carried on with the plan? Or would they have given up on getting the diesel from Rhum? If they had, would that've meant they'd also have had to give up any hope of rescuing Jack and the others if they ran into trouble? Would my carelessness have resulted not just in my own death, but in the death of many others as well?

Not wanting to dwell on the possibilities, I, instead, turned my thoughts to the infected that had suddenly appeared beside me. I wondered where it had come from, and why it had taken so long to respond to the noise Rob and Ben were making in the dinghy. I'd never find out, not for sure, but it made me think: we'd need to make very sure we'd got every single one of the infected on the island before we dared to venture ashore to get the diesel.

I pulled myself out of the water and on to the boat just as the dinghy arrived back.

Daz clambered out and up on to the catamaran, 'What the hell happened there? One minute, we were all they were interested in; the next, they all shot off along the beach.'

I started to dry myself off. 'I was surprised by one of them. I didn't see it creep up on me.' I shuddered at the memory of turning and seeing it so close to me. 'Luckily it was more interested in you guys than me, at least until I was dumb enough to drop the rope.'

'But you got away!' Jeff's voice was half-relieved, half-impressed that I'd been so close to an infected and still escaped unscathed. Mike and Jimmy were beside him, looking similarly impressed by the narrowness of my escape.

I felt the need to admonish them. 'Yeah, but I shouldn't have got myself into a position like that in the first place. I should've been more careful, I let myself get distracted.'

'By *what?*' Sophie sounded incredulous, as if there was nothing she could think of that could have distracted her if she'd been the one on such a critical mission.

'It's not important.' I snapped back, instantly sorry for losing my temper. After all, I wasn't angry at her, I was angry at myself, but there was no time to apologise. Rob had already untied the rope from the back of the catamaran and wrapped it around one of the winches for the main sail. He was now pulling it tight before slipping the winch handle into place and starting to crank it in. Our conversation cut short, all of us looked shoreward. Together, we watched the rope tighten further and further, to the point where I thought it was going to break and then suddenly the rib moved; just an inch, but still it was movement. The infected that were now gathered round it sprang backwards, snarling and growling as they tried to work out what was going on.

Inch by inch, the remains of the rib crept towards the water's edge, but as it did, I noticed my knot was slowly coming undone. Three would have been better, but two would have done the job. Unfortunately, I'd only completed one half-hitch, the rope slipping from my hand before I could complete the second, let alone a third. I called out. 'Stop! The knot's coming loose. I didn't have time to finish tying it properly before the infected went for me.'

Rob straightened up. 'Well, you can't go back and tie it again, can you?' He looked towards the shore, a worried expression on his face. 'It's held this far, we'll just have to hope it holds long enough to get the boat into the water.'

With that, Rob stooped and cranked the winch handle once more. The rib moved slowly again, but then it seemed to get caught on something. Rob cranked the winch even harder, increasing the tension on the rope. Then the knot gave out and, with all the pent-up energy suddenly released, the rope zipped through the air. Safely on the other side of the cockpit, Mitch, Jimmy, Jeff, Mike and Sophie were in no danger, but the rest of us weren't so fortunate. As the rope flew towards us, Rob, Ben and I threw ourselves to the deck to get out of its way, but Daz, who had been standing next to us, didn't see what was happening until it was too late. The rope caught him squarely in the face, sending him stumbling backwards as he cried out in pain, and causing the infected on the shore to roar with anticipation.

'Daz!' Sophie shot across the cockpit and was down beside him in an instant, gently helping him to sit up. 'Did you bang your head when you fell?'

Daz shook his head and winced. 'No, it's just my face. How's it lookin'?'

Sophie tilted his head backwards and examined him closely. One eye was already starting to turn black and there was a cut across the bridge of his nose where the end of the rope had caught him. He'd been exceedingly lucky: an inch either way and he would've lost an eye. Sophie sat back, clearly relieved that his injuries weren't worse. 'You'll survive.'

Once Daz had been patched up to Sophie's satisfaction, and she'd made sure there was no lasting damage, Ben and Daz set out in the dinghy again, this time taking Mike with them, to try to draw the infected away so we could get the line attached to the rib's hull again. Almost immediately, it became clear that the infected were now more interested in what was going on with the catamaran, and they refused to be led away. As they crowded the shore around the rib, I spotted the woman who'd tried to attack me forcing her way to the front, eyes searching the sea, alert to any sound or movement.

Beside me Sophie gasped and turned away. 'Sophie what's wro—?' Suddenly I realised who the woman was. Even though she was little more than skin and bone, I could see the family resemblance in the hair and the shape of the face. I looked across at Sophie. 'Are you okay?'

She closed her eyes and steadied herself before turning back to face the shore once more. 'Yes.' The word caught in her throat, telling me she was more upset than she was letting on. 'It was just a shock to suddenly see her there.'

Sophie stared at her mother, or rather the creature that had once been her mother. Now she stalked the shore, anger and rage burning in its eyes, testing the waters as she tried to work out how to get to where we were anchored. Before she'd become infected, Claire would have done anything to keep her daughter safe. Now, in her changed state, she'd do anything she could to kill her, to rip her apart, to feast on her flesh.

Jeff and Jimmy glanced at each other as they tried to work how best to respond, but Mitch didn't need to think about it. She crossed the cockpit and put a comforting hand on Sophie's arm.

'It's always hard when it's someone you know, someone you love.' There was immense sadness in Mitch's voice, and I wondered who she was thinking of. We stood silently, the three of us, not wanting to look, but unable to take our eyes off the woman prowling angrily back and forth along the edge of the sea, desperate to get to us, yet unwilling to enter the water.

The moment was only broken when Daz, Ben and Mike returned to the boat. Daz called out as they bumped alongside. 'It's no' workin' this time. They seem to be more interested in ...' Daz glanced up and saw us staring intently towards the shore. 'What're you all lookin' at?'

He turned his head to follow our gaze and almost immediately his eyes fell on Claire. 'Oh, shit!'

Daz pulled himself on board and went to Sophie. 'You okay?'

She nodded, not trusting herself to speak.

He rubbed the top of her shoulder. 'You sure?'

She shook her head, then turned and walked into the cabin. Daz crossed his arms and frowned. 'I should go after her, shouldn't I?' He looked at me. 'What do I say?'

I smiled at him sadly as I thought back to when I'd lost Jon and how I'd wanted people to treat me then. Although I was consumed with grief, I was still me, and I didn't want people treating me differently just because

I'd lost him. Yet, I didn't want them to ignore what I was going through or to pretend it hadn't happened. 'Just be there for her, Daz, and listen when she's ready to speak. That's all I wanted when I was in her shoes.'

Daz nodded and disappeared inside.

'What about trying to lasso it?' Ben pointed to where the gun was mounted. 'I think I could get a rope around that.'

Rob, Ben, Mitch and I were in the cockpit trying to work out what to do next. Now that the infected were clustering around the remains of the two ribs, there was no way to sneak ashore and re-attach the line.

'From a safe distance?' Rob looked sceptical.

Ben nodded. 'I lassoed that infected the other day from further away and it was a moving target.'

I grimaced at the memory of what had happened next. 'Yes, and look how that almost turned out.'

'But I won't be trying to lasso an infected this time, will I?' Ben shivered as he spoke, rubbing his arm as if he could still feel the infected's grip on his wrist. 'I'd just need to get a rope over the gun.'

Mitch looked round, her hands on her hips. 'It's the only solution any of us have come up with.'

Rob nodded. 'Good point. We can at least give it a go. Even if it doesn't work, I can't see it making things worse.'

'Damn! Missed again.' Ben pulled on the rope, dragging it through the water and back towards the dinghy. While the gun Ben was aiming for wasn't a moving target, the infected were making it difficult to get the lasso over it. As they felt the rope flying towards them, they'd reach out, trying to grasp it, causing Ben to miss his mark every time he threw it.

While the rest of us watched from the nearby catamaran, Mike was once again in the dinghy with Ben. 'Are you going to try again?'

Ben lifted the end of the rope from the water and did his best to shake it dry. 'I'll give it one more go.'

He adjusted the loop and raised the rope over his head, spinning it first slowly and then faster. Finally, he let go: the loop sailed through the air towards the shore and once more the infected reached up as it approached. This time it hit its mark and dropped over the gun, but as it did so, it also encircled one of the infected. Ben swore loudly.

Mike stood up beside Ben in the dinghy. 'Is that going to be a problem?'

Ben turned and called back to the catamaran. 'What d'you think? Will that do?'

Rob picked up the binoculars and focussed them on the gun, and then lowered them again before replying. 'It'll have to.'

Mike and Ben motored back to the boat, and handed the other end of the rope to Rob. Rob attached it to the winch once more and pulled it tight, causing the infected it also encircled to be jammed against the gun. It struggled and thrashed, but with the rope running across its shoulder and chest like a sash, it was held firmly in place. Rob inserted the winch handle and then paused. 'Everyone ready to duck if the rope comes loose again?'

Jimmy, Mike and Jeff nodded, but Daz was more vocal. 'Damn right! I'm no' gettin' smacked in the face twice in one day.' He grinned, and then winced with pain.

Daz and Sophie had emerged from the cabin after about twenty minutes, and Sophie now stood beside him in the cockpit, silent and stone-faced, looking everywhere, but at her mother.

Rob glanced at her. 'Are you ready, just in case?'

Her forehead creased. 'In case of what?'

Daz put an arm round her 'Don't worry, I'll make sure she's safe.'

She shrugged it off. 'I can look after myself.'

Daz looked hurt, but he was prevented from saying anything by Rob. 'Right, let's get started.'

Rob cranked the winch and the rope grew tighter and tighter. I could hear it stretch and strain, but the rib didn't move. The infected which was now tied to the gun was still fighting to free itself, but the rope was cutting deep into its flesh. Rob turned the winch again: the rib still didn't move, but the rope tightened further, slowly slicing the infected in two and causing its head and upper body to tumble over the side of the rib and onto the ground. The rest of the body remained standing, held in place by the rope.

Suddenly, whatever had been preventing the rib from moving gave out and it shot forward, propelled by the tension which had built up in the rope. As it raced towards the water, the rib slammed into the infected which crowded in front of it. Some were crushed beneath it or were dragged into the water, where they struggled briefly before disappearing below the surface. Others were scooped up and thrown into the hull itself. A second later, it was afloat, and the momentum of the rib sent it shooting straight towards us. The infected that had landed inside it, sensing they were finally closing in on us, scrambled to their feet and I saw, to my horror, that one of them was Claire.

Mike was the first to react. 'It's going to hit us. We need

to stop it.'

Jimmy's jaw dropped and his eyes widened as the meaning of his brother's words swept over him, while Jeff, standing beside him, let out an involuntary yelp of fear.

Ben stared disbelievingly at the rapidly approaching rib. 'We can't.'

Mitch glanced around desperately. 'There must be something we can do.'

The damaged rib was now only a few feet away and within seconds it would collide with the back of the boat. When that happened, it would be easy for the infected to scramble on board and then they'd be on us in an instant. There was only one way we were going to survive. I cried out, 'everyone inside!'

As one, we turned and ran, but before we'd even made it as far as the cabin door, there was a screech behind us. I looked over my shoulder to see Claire pulling herself over the guard rail, closely followed by two others. They raced across the cockpit, reaching the door just as the last of us threw ourselves inside and I slammed it shut. I flicked the latch to lock it and then I glanced at Rob, trying to control the terror that was rising inside me. 'Are any of the hatches open?'

Fear shot across his face. 'All of them!'

He raced off and I heard a hatch slam shut. This caught the attention of one of the infected and it disappeared towards the front of the boat. I heard the second hatch close and the sound of Rob rushing round to the third. Then there was a shout. 'It's trying to get in!'

Looking round, I saw the flare gun lying in the draw beneath the chart table. Rob had used it before on an infected and I knew it could prove an effective weapon. I grabbed it and ran forward, shouting over my shoulder,

'Bang on the glass. Keep those two there.'

As I reached Rob in one of the forward cabins, I heard the sound of fists pounding on glass coming from the main cabin and I knew that would keep the other infected distracted while we dealt with the third one. Rob was hanging on desperately to the underside of the hatch, but the withered, skeleton-like arm that snaked through from above meant he couldn't close it. I opened the flare gun and slid in a cartridge before snapping it shut and pointing it upwards. I readied myself. 'Let it go.'

Rob stared at me like he thought I was crazy. 'Let it go?'

I didn't take my eye off the hatch for a second. 'Yes.'

Rob heard the steeliness in my voice and did what I was asking. A second later the hatch flew open and the infected glared down at us. For a moment it hung there, framed by the opening, lips drawn back, teeth bared, then I pulled the trigger. The flare shot from the gun and streaked upwards through the hatch. It hit the infected square in the face, burying itself into its flesh and sending it spinning out of sight. As Rob leapt up and pulled the hatch shut, I heard a splash, telling me the injured infected had fallen into the water. With the hull finally secure, Rob sat down, breathing heavily. 'That was close.' He looked up at me. 'Now what?'

'I don't know.' I ran back into the main cabin. There, the two remaining infected clawed at the glass, trying their best to get in. I could now see Sophie's mother up close: her skin weathered and worn from being out in the elements for so long; her hair hung limp and lifeless, caked in mud and salt; her face was drawn, her cheeks sallow, but despite the anger that burned deep in her eyes, she was still recognisable to those who'd known her before she'd become infected. The clothes she was wearing had survived better than most, but still they were stained and ragged, and where her skin was exposed, it was burned and blistered by the sun and wind, and was peeling off in long strips.

I glanced round the room. Sophie had her head buried in Daz's chest; Daz looked terrified, as did Mike, Jimmy and Jeff; Mitch and Ben were terrified, too, but at least they were trying to work out a way out of our predicament.

Mitch was speaking when I came back into the cabin. '... but there are three of them. That's too many for that to work.'

I coughed. 'There are only two now.'

'How the hell did you manage that?' Ben sounded both relieved and surprised.

I laid the flare gun down on the table. 'An old trick Rob learned early on. Flare guns can be a remarkably effective weapon at close range.'

Ben considered it. 'Could we use it on the others?'

'No.' Sophie's voice was firm, but calm.

Ben looked at her disconsolately, 'I know that's your mum, but we've got to do something.'

'I know.' She swallowed, 'but not that. It'd hurt too much.'

Mitch turned to her. 'Sophie, your mum's gone. Those creatures out there: they can't feel pain; they can't be hurt; they don't feel anything.'

Sophie's eyes narrowed. 'How d'you know that?'

Mitch opened her mouth and then closed it again. How did any of us know what the infected felt? How did we know they didn't feel pain? We knew being injured didn't necessarily slow them down, but that didn't necessarily mean they didn't feel it, did it? How much pain would someone be in as a flare burned its way through their flesh? Now I'd thought about it, could I knowingly cause that sort of pain to someone, even if they'd like nothing better than to kill me? I came to a conclusion. 'We need to do something, and at the moment the flare gun's the only option we've got.'

Daz let go of Sophie and stepped forward. 'Hang on. I've got an idea.'

An hour later and everyone was in position. Claire and the other infected hadn't paused once in their assault on the cabin door. At first, I'd worried it might not hold, but after the first few minutes, it became clear it would, yet we were still trapped inside. In the beginning, I was sceptical about Daz's plan, but the more he explained it, the more I could see it might just work, and besides, we had few other options.

Rob and Mitch set to work jamming a wooden batten ripped from one of the fittings in the galley into the runner of the cabin door so that, no matter how hard the infected tried, it couldn't be slid open more than a couple of inches. Meanwhile, Daz had taken an old broom and snapped off the brush head. In its place, using lengths of duct tape, he'd secured a large knife from the galley. Once he was finished, he inspected his handiwork and nodded approvingly. 'This'll do the job nicely.'

Jimmy and Jeff had watched him intently as he'd worked and now Jimmy couldn't resist asking. 'How d'you think of that?'

Daz smiled a sad sort of smile as he ran his thumb along the edge of the knife, checking its sharpness. 'Where I grew up, people were always lookin' for ways to make things more dangerous. For them, anythin' could be made into a weapon; you just had to use your imagination.' He was trying to sound confident, but the hesitancy in his actions and the slight tremble in his hands gave away his true emotions. 'Everyone ready?'

We all nodded. Daz had assured us his plan was foolproof, but given how badly wrong our attempt at pulling the rib's hull off the shore had gone, I remained nervous.

Rob and Ben stood by the door, preparing to slide it open the few inches it would now go, while the rest of us were gathered on the other side of the cabin, as far from the door as possible, armed with anything we could find which could be used as a weapon, just in case the plan went wrong. Between us stood Daz, his homemade lance held at shoulder height, ready to be used as soon as the door was opened. He took one last look round, checking everything and everyone was where they should be, before turning back to the door, 'On the count of three. One ... Two ...' He adjusted his grip on the broom handle and breathed out heavily. 'Three!'

The door moved about two and a half inches along its runner, and then stopped abruptly: it seemed the first part of the plan was working. While Claire continued to hammer on the glass, the other infected found the gap and peered through it before reaching a hand inside. This was the moment Daz had been waiting for and he thrust the broom handle forward as hard as he could, the knife disappearing up to the hilt into one of the infected's eyes. As Daz twisted his makeshift weapon and pulled it backwards, the infected dropped like a stone. Drawn by the movement, Claire stepped to her right, and curled her blackened, blood-stained fingers round the edge of the door. With all the strength left in her withered body, she tried to wrench the door open. When it didn't move, she

228

changed tactics and tried instead to force her way through the gap. Daz lifted the broom handle again, but before he could ram it home, there was a shout.

'Wait!' Sophie darted forward and grabbed his arm.

Daz turned to look at her, confused. 'What?'

'I think … If anyone's …' Sophie swallowed. 'I should be the one to do it.'

Jimmy and Jeff stared at her, while Mike muttered something I didn't quite catch. Rob and Mitch exchanged a look, then Rob's eyes narrowed. 'Have you ever done anything like this before?'

Sophie let go Daz's arm and glared at Rob, almost challenging him to stop her. 'Who hasn't?'

Seeing the determined look on her face, Rob backed off. 'Are you really sure you want do to this?'

'Sophie,' Mitch moved towards her. 'Let Daz do it. You don't want that to be your last memory of Claire.'

'And is this memory any better?' Sophie's voice was loud, almost shouting, yet it wasn't with anger, it was with pain. 'Seeing her like this, knowing that she'd like nothing more than to kill me?'

I reached out and touched her gently on the arm, 'Sophie,' I thought for a moment she'd squirm away from me, but she didn't. I knew what I wanted to say, but I had to compose myself for a few seconds to give myself the time to find just the right words. 'You need to do what's right for you. None of us can tell you what that is, but you have to make sure that whatever you do is the right thing. This isn't one of those things you can go back and change later if you find you've made the wrong decision. Whatever you do next is going to live with you for the rest of your life, so you need to make damn sure that it's right for you.'

Sophie stood there, silent and still, her brain working overtime as she tried desperately to decide what she should do. In that instant, I hated the world more than I ever had before: for forcing her to have to make such a choice; for putting her in this situation in the first place; just for existing. This was a situation no one should ever have to face, and certainly not a fourteen year old. I felt for Sophie; felt her pain; felt the weight of the impossible decision she was being forced to make.

As we waited for Sophie to come to a conclusion, Claire reached as far as she could through the gap in the door, her hand clawing the air as she tried desperately to reach us, any of us, her harsh, guttural cries echoing round the cabin. The door shuddered and shook, and I could see the wooden batten, which was holding it in place, starting to bend alarmingly each time Claire tried to force her way further inside. Out of the corner of my eye, I saw Mike adjust his grip on the large wrench in his hand. Then he spoke. 'Whoever's going to do it, needs to do it fast. The door isn't going to hold out much longer.'

That seemed to snap Sophie from her ruminations and in that moment she knew what she needed to do. 'You're right.' Slowly but firmly, she took the homemade lance from Daz before stepping forward. She stared at her mother, staying just beyond the reach of her grasping hand, causing Claire to howl with anticipation, and frustration. Tears welled up in Sophie's eyes as she readied herself. She looked deep into Claire's, searching for anything that might be left of her mother, but found nothing. Sophie wiped her eyes and steadied herself; then, with a cry of anger and pain, she thrust the weapon forward and into Claire's left eye. As the blade pierced it, blood spurted out and ran down the side of her face, but Claire didn't stop: she didn't even seem to notice. She bared her teeth and gnashed them together, a low groan emanating from her throat, her skeleton-like hand still reaching forward, trying to grab hold of Sophie so she could tear her apart. We watched, horrified by the scene unfolding in front of us, then Sophie spoke, the words coming out so quietly I could barely hear them. 'I'm sorry, Mum.'

With that, she twisted the weapon, just as Daz had done. Claire stood frozen for a moment, her face no longer contorted with rage, then she slowly slipped down the glass door before coming to rest on the deck alongside the other infected, leaving behind a blood-smeared trail. Sophie pulled the knife from her mother's head and handed the lance back to Daz before going below, her face filled with both horror at what she'd done, and relief that it was finally over; that her mother was finally at peace.

We peered nervously through the cabin door, trying to see if there were any more infected outside. While they still stalked the shoreline, all seemed quiet on the catamaran. Ben moved his head back and forth. 'You think it's safe?'

'I hope so.' With that Rob released the cabin door, slid it open and stepped gingerly over Claire's body, before moving out into the cockpit. He looked this way and that, Daz's makeshift weapon gripped in one hand and alert to any possible signs of danger. After a minute, he called back, relieved. 'All clear.'

Ben was the next to leave the cabin, followed by myself, Mitch and then the boys. We gathered at the back of the boat and looked down at the remains of the rib, which now floated a few feet from our stern.

Jeff stared, transfixed, at the lower half of the infected

that was held tight against the machine gun by the rope we'd used to pull the rib from the shore. 'What're we going to do with that?'

Rob set his weapon down on one of the seats in the cockpit. 'Get it untied and throw it over the side. Then we can think about getting the gun on board.'

Mike leant forward. 'How're we going to do that?'

Rob crossed his arms. 'I'm not too sure, but we'll manage it somehow.'

Rob looked round the assembled group. 'Any one got any idea how to work one of these?'

Between us, Rob, Mike, me and Ben had removed the bolts which had fixed the machine gun to the rib and then manhandled it onto the catamaran. We'd then bolted it on to the right-hand side of the deck near the stern so it pointed backwards towards the shore. While we'd been doing this, Jimmy and Jeff had gone through all the different compartments of the rib and had found several handguns, two small machine guns and enough bullets to last us for the foreseeable future. These were now stacked on the opposite side of the cockpit. Above them, on one of the seats, Claire's body lay wrapped in some old sailcloth. While the other infected had been unceremoniously dumped into the sea, Sophie had insisted we keep her mother's body. She wanted to bury her properly, and after all she'd been through, I couldn't blame her.

Ben shook the machine gun to make sure it was firmly secured to the boat and sat back on his heels. 'I thought you knew about guns?'

Rob shook his head. 'Hunting rifles yes, but nothing like this.'

Ben looked at me. 'What about you, CJ?'

I nodded towards the other guns we'd recovered from the rib. 'Those, I can handle, but something this big? No.'

Ben levered himself to his feet. 'Maybe Daz knows.' He turned and called out. 'Daz?'

Daz's head appeared in the cabin's doorway. 'What?'

Ben pointed to the machine gun. 'You know anything about how to use one of these?'

Daz strode over and examined it, then, after a few seconds, he straightened up. 'All guns work on the same basic principles. We'll need to strip it down an' check that it's no' blocked or anythin', but that should no' take too long.'

He sounded confident and I eyed him curiously, wondering where a teenager from Glasgow could've gained the knowledge to do what he was proposing. 'You've done this sort of thing before, Daz?'

'No, no' exactly,' Daz was flustered by the question, and he now sounded less confident than he had before. 'but it can't be *that* difficult, can it?'

It turned out that stripping down, cleaning and rebuilding the machine gun was much more complicated than Daz had anticipated, but to give him credit, he eventually got it not only re-assembled, but working. He loaded in the first cartridge of bullets and, with a satisfied look on his face, sent a short volley across the bay. The infected on the shore howled and roared, enlivened once more by the new noise coming from the catamaran.

He turned and smiled. 'Shall we get started then?'

We gathered at the stern and watched the infected milling on the nearby land, the bodies of the ones which had been crushed by the hull of the rib being trampled underfoot by those who were still alive. We looked at each other and nodded.

Daz steadied himself, took aim and pulled the trigger. The sound was ear-shattering and I had to duck out of the way as spent bullet-casings were sent spinning through the air. Daz fired in short, controlled bursts, targeting small groups of infected each time he pulled the trigger. The bullets blasted into them, tearing their flesh and ripping holes in their bodies. When one infected went down, the others didn't try to run. Instead, they whipped themselves into an ever-greater frenzy as they tried to work out how to get to the source of the noise.

After about half of the assembled infected were dead or dying. Daz stopped and leaned on the back of the gun. 'Anyone else want a go?'

Mike, Jimmy and Jeff rushed forward.

I wasn't too sure about this and frowned, 'Is it safe?'

Daz grinned. 'No' for the infected!'

The others laughed.

I glared at him. 'I'm serious, Daz. Will Jimmy and Jeff be able to handle it?' I'd been around guns enough to know they could do a lot of damage if the people using them didn't know what they were doing.

Daz waited just long enough to let me know he'd considered the matter properly before giving his answer. 'They'll be okay, CJ. Because it's mounted on this,' He kicked the stand where it was bolted to the deck. 'It's no' goin' anywhere. All they need to do is make sure they keep it pointin' in the right direction.'

'Hmm.' I remained sceptical. 'Okay, but you need to keep an eye on them.'

Daz gave me a thumbs-up and moved to his right to let Mike replace him behind the gun. Soon it was firing again, and on the shore more infected were dying. I watched, wondering whether our life would've been any easier in Hope Town if we'd had something like this to defend ourselves, but I figured we'd still have run out of bullets eventually, and we'd still have been left with the problem of drifters. I looked away from the killing zone on the beach and let my eyes roam around the rest of the bay. New infected were still appearing in ones and twos, drawn by the sound of the gunfire; it would only be safe to go ashore once we'd got all of them, and I wondered how we'd know when that had happened.

Leaving the boys to it, I went inside. Sophie was sitting by the table in the main cabin, hands together, staring off into space. I walked across to her. 'Are you okay?'

She didn't respond.

I tried again, this time a little louder. 'Sophie?'

She looked up. 'Huh?'

I smiled at her. 'How're you doing?'

She glanced down and picked at her nails. 'I don't know. I never thought I'd ever have to do something like that.' She paused and looked up again. 'But there's a part of me that's glad I did it; that I was the one who finally managed to give her some peace. There was nothing else I could do for her once she got infected ... except that.' She paused again and gazed out of the window. 'I needed to do it for me, too. It was eating away at me, thinking of her here, wandering around all on her own, being out in the open all the time.' She shuddered and wiped a tear from her eye. 'I think I'll be able to start moving on now.'

Outside the machine gun finally fell silent. The last of the infected that had gathered on the beach were now dead.

Chapter Twelve

'How's the eye?' I'd woken early and had gone out into the cockpit only to find Daz was already there. His right eye was a vivid shade of purply black that faded into yellow across the bridge of his nose and onto the other side of his face. The dressing Sophie had put across the cut on his nose must have come off in the night and I could see the wound was crusted with dried blood. 'I bet it looks worse than it feels.'

Daz reached up and touched it tenderly, before wincing and withdrawing his hand. 'In that case, it must really look like shit, because it's hurtin' like hell. It's been keepin' me up all night.'

Saying nothing, I let my gaze wander across the calm waters that surrounded us and up on to the nearby shore. Seagulls had gathered by the carcasses of the dead infected, yet they seemed to know there was something wrong with them. Instead of falling on the scraps of flesh and bone, they walked round, eyeing the bodies suspiciously. I wondered if there was a smell they could sense; some sort of odour given off by infected flesh. Was this how the infected themselves knew who had the disease and who didn't? Was this how they knew who to attack, for they rarely, if ever, attacked each other? Trying to find an answer, I went over to where Claire's body lay wrapped in the sailcloth and sniffed, but I could smell nothing beyond the slight smell of death and decay. While officially it was spring, the nights were still chilly and there was a touch of frost on the grass in front of the large sandstone house, so her body remained relatively fresh.

There was a noise behind me and I turned to find Mitch and then Rob coming out into the cockpit. Mitch spoke first. 'Any more infected turn up in the night?'

'No,' I looked back to the shore, 'But then again, we haven't been making much noise so we wouldn't be drawing them in.'

Rob rubbed his face, trying to wake himself up after what had clearly been a restless night. 'That's a point.' He turned to Mitch. 'How many people d'you think were here when ...?' He hesitated, not knowing how to finish the sentence.

'When it was overrun?' As Mitch considered the question, she leant forward on the guard rail. 'A couple of hundred. A fair few must have been killed outright, though.'

Daz ran his eyes over the bodies on the beach. 'We must've killed about eighty yesterday.'

I pondered the numbers. 'So there could be another twenty or thirty of them left, maybe even a few more than that.'

Mitch nodded. 'That about sums it up.'

Daz frowned. 'So where are they?'

Together, we looked silently towards the island, trying to work out where they might be hiding, ready to attack us the instant we set foot on the land.

***

We spent the day firing the machine gun in short bursts at regular intervals to draw out the last of the infected, and by the time we were due to have our evening check-in with Jack, we hadn't seen any new infected in over six hours. Rob explained what we were up to and why, but Jack was concerned by our actions. 'Andrew shouldn't have told you. I'm sure we'll make it. I don't want you

237

risking your lives just to get us diesel when we might not even need it.'

Rob pressed the transmission key on the microphone. 'Jack, we're not taking any risks, and we need to be prepared in case the worst happens and you do run out.'

'Okay.' There was a buzz of static before Jack spoke again. 'Thanks, Rob.'

Even though Jack couldn't see him, Rob smiled. 'You'd do the same if the tables were turned.'

There was another burst of static and then Jack's voice. 'Still, thanks.'

After we said goodnight to Jack, we sat around talking: the boys still excited about having fired the machine gun; Sophie still mulling over the events of the previous day; the rest of us making plans for the morning. We decided the best thing would be to wait until noon, as that would mean no new infected had turned up for more than twenty-four hours.

***

At twelve o'clock the following day, we gathered on the deck and discussed exactly what we'd do once we landed.

As captain, Rob took charge. 'The priority's the diesel and that's what we need to deal with first. Anything else can wait until we've got enough of it on board.'

Sophie scowled, clearly not happy with Rob's priorities, but unwilling to challenge him directly. 'But after that, we can bury Mum?'

Initially, Sophie had wanted to take Claire back to Mingulay and bury her there, but Ben and Rob were against the idea from the start. Even though she was dead, her body was still riddled with the virus, and they were adamant that it was too great a risk to take her back to the so far disease-free island. I had to admit, I felt the same way, and it was clear that Mitch and Daz, as well as the other teenagers, also shared the same opinion. Eventually, Sophie relented and settled for being able to bury Claire on Rhum, with Rob and Ben promising her that she could come back and visit whenever she wanted to, as long as Rhum remained free of infected.

Assuming that was all the arrangements we needed to make, we started to disperse and ready ourselves for the day ahead, but then Ben cleared his throat. 'If we're going to bury Claire, I'd like to see if I can bury Tom, too.'

Ben's voice sounded flat. He'd never really explained what had happened to Tom, but I knew from the few details he'd shared that it had to have been bad.

I looked at Ben. 'Will you be able to find him? It's been a long time.'

'I know exactly where he'll be.' There was a bitterness in Ben's voice that I hadn't heard before. 'It's just a question of whether I'll be able to get to him.' I waited for him to say more, but instead he just walked away.

'Right. Let's check our weapons one last time.' Daz glanced at me and Ben. 'Everythin' loaded an' safeties off?'

While the others remained by the beach to dig Claire's grave, Ben was heading off in search of Tom's body, and Daz and I were going along to provide some added protection, since we were the only ones who had any sort of experience with handling the types of weapons we'd recovered from the rib. Daz had been shown how to use the small machine guns by the marines, when they were all on better terms, and I was familiar with something similar from my days of trailing my dad around gun shows during summer holidays. Ben had taken a handgun, but he didn't look comfortable handling it and I wondered if he'd be able to use it effectively if we ran into any trouble.

We'd spent the early afternoon loading the barrels of diesel on to the catamaran, looking round nervously, ready to drop everything and run at a moment's notice, but no more infected appeared. Each barrel had to be tipped onto its side, rolled down to the beach, avoiding the human remains that lay scattered across the ground, before being floated out to the catamaran and winched on board. It was slow, dirty work, but by the time we'd finished, we had so much diesel on board that it rode low in the water.

So far, everything had gone to plan, with the exception of Jimmy, who'd managed, at one point, to back into one of the tangled runs of barbed wire. He'd tried to struggle free, but this only made matters worse and eventually he just lay there, spread-eagled and motionless, looking like an abandoned puppet, his clothing hooked onto the metal barbs. After we'd finished laughing, we disentangled him, and Sophie insisted on cleaning up the scratches he'd received in the process to ensure they didn't become infected. I thought she was being overly cautious, but we were gradually starting to rely on her whenever we had any sort of medical issues, so I was happy for her to do what she thought was right.

Now Ben, Daz and I were ready to set out in search of Tom's body. With our eyes darting left and right, constantly searching for any signs of trouble, we headed off, Ben leading the way, towards a path which snaked up through the woods behind the large house.

At the edge of the trees, we stopped and looked at

each other uneasily. Despite the spring sunshine, the forest was dark and forbidding, capable of hiding all manner of shadowy creatures, real or imagined. Daz shifted back and forth, contemplating what lay ahead. He glanced at Ben. 'You sure this is what you want to do?'

'He was my closest friend, Daz. I'd never have survived this long without him. I couldn't be there for him when he really needed me.' Ben's voice was starting to tremble. 'The least I can do is try to give him a proper burial.'

Daz patted him on the back. 'Let's go then.'

With that, he stepped forward and into the gloom between the trees, his finger moving closer to the trigger of his machine gun as he did so. Without another word, Ben followed and I brought up the rear. Amongst the trees, there was silence: not a bird sang or a squirrel scuttled. I wondered where they were. I'd always thought that such places would be crawling with all sorts of small creatures, but this wood was empty, devoid of life. Still in their winter torpor, even the trees seemed lifeless. Was it because of the infected? Had their merest presence been enough to send every other living thing fleeing before them? Was this what the infected did? Did they clear the land of everything, forcing all other life to go into hiding, just as it had forced us to do? Ben had told me that red deer roamed Rhum in high numbers, stags brandishing long, branching antlers, hinds trailed by calves; loose aggregations that would move in slow processions across the hillsides and along the beaches, but so far we'd seen no sign of them. Had the infected hunted them down and consumed them in order to be able to stay alive? Or had they just melted away in the face of an enemy they could never hope to evade?

Feeling the oppressive and empty silence pressing down on us, we walked as quietly as possible, placing each foot carefully, one in front of the other. When we did accidently step on a stick or scuffle some leaves, the sound seemed deafening and we froze, searching the gloaming for any hint of danger, our ability to detect anything limited by the dim light filtering through the closely packed trees.

We didn't say a word to each other until we emerged into a small clearing encircled by the remains of portable lights on rusting metal stands. Most of these had fallen over, no doubt brought down by harsh winter winds, but enough remained standing to be able to tell that they'd once all been pointed towards an opening in the ground. Ben stopped, his eyes blank as he relived everything that had happened the last time he had been here. Daz pointed towards the hole with his machine gun and whispered, 'In there?'

Ben nodded, but while Daz crept off, slowly circling the clearing, he remained rooted to the spot by his memories of past events that still seemed fresh in his mind. Daz finished his perimeter search and readjusted his grip on his gun. 'By the looks of it, there's no' been any infected around here in a long time.' He glanced at Ben. 'You want to check the pit?'

Ben shook his head. 'Can you do it?'

'No' a problem, pal.' Daz edged forward until he was close enough to the hole to peer down into it. He craned his neck, moving his head left and right before turning back to where Ben and I stood. 'They're all dead.'

Curious to know what Daz was talking about, I walked softly towards him and looked down into the pit myself. Inside, emaciated corpses lay piled on top of each other, while the near skeletal remains of what had once been a human being lay curled up in one corner, most of its flesh picked clean by grasping hands, or torn off by bites so deep I could see the imprints the teeth had left on the now-exposed bone. Around the edge of the hole were scratch marks, as if those inside had tried desperately to pull themselves out, but the crumbling earth meant they couldn't get the purchase they needed to escape.

I swallowed. 'What was this place?'

'They kept infected in it.' Hearing Ben's voice unexpectedly close behind me, I jumped, almost dropping my gun.

'Bloody hell, Ben, don't creep up on people like that.' Then it struck me what he'd just said. 'Why were they keeping infected in a pit? Wasn't that dangerous?'

Ben cleared his throat. 'At first, they wanted to study them, learn more about them, and what the disease did to people, but eventually it became a play thing which they'd threaten people with so they'd do what they were told. They used it to torture anyone who stood up to them.'

Horrified, I wondered what sort of people could've done such a thing. I'd always thought that in the world of the infected, they were what we had to fear the most. Yet, here, there had been people who were much worse than any infected: the infected did what they did, not out of malice, but because they were running on instincts controlled by the virus which had taken over their bodies and their brains. What had happened here was done through choice; deliberate acts by rational, thinking human beings, done for no other reason than to instil fear and terror in others.

'That's Tom there.' Daz pointed towards the body in the corner. 'I recognise the hair.'

The body had long hair that clung in clumps to fragments of skin which had dried taught across the skull.

'But …' Ben sounded both confused and disbelieving. 'Look at the way he's lying. I thought he was dead when I left, but he can't've been. He must've crawled over and curled up in the corner, trying to protect himself. Shit!' There were tears running down his face now. 'I can't believe I left when he was still alive.' He shook his head. 'I was so sure he was dead; I was sure no one could've survived in there for long.'

Daz tried to change the subject. 'How're we goin' to get him out?'

Ben looked confused. 'What?'

Daz tried again. 'How're we goin' to get him out so we can bury him properly?'

Ben thought for a moment before replying. 'I'll go in and pass him up to you guys.'

He made to slide over the edge of the pit, but Daz stopped him and pointed at the pile of infected. 'Should we no' make sure they're definitely dead first? After all, you'd no' want to get in there an' find any of them are still alive, would you?. You'd've no chance.'

I nodded. 'He's got a point there, Ben, but how do we do that?'

Daz grinned. 'Easy!'

With that he fired into the pit, raking the emaciated corpses with bullets that tore them to shreds.

I turned to him. 'What the hell did you do that for?'

Daz shrugged. 'It was the quickest way to make sure.'

'But if there are any infected left in these woods, you've just let them know exactly where we are,' I hissed back.

A worried look raced across Daz's face. 'I'd no' thought of that.'

He jumped down into the pit and gently lifted Tom's

body before passing it up to me and Ben. For a grown man, the body was surprisingly light, but then again there was little flesh left on it, and what remained was dried and desiccated. There was no smell of rot or decay, just a distinctive mustiness that I knew would stay with me for the rest of my life. Hidden deep in the woods and sheltered from the elements by the sides of the pit, Tom's body had become mummified, locking it in the same position it had been in when he'd finally died: arms flung up, trying to protect his face. It'd made little difference; most of the flesh had been stripped from his head, teeth marks visible where the infected had gnawed it away. I only hoped that Tom had been long dead by the time that had happened, but given what Ben had said, I doubted this was the case. As carefully as possible, we laid Tom on the ground so we could pull Daz out of the pit, and then, with Ben carrying Tom's remains, we headed back through the forest and down to the bay, half-walking, half-running, worried about what might be pursuing us in the dimly lit forest.

The journey up through the woods to get to Tom's body had felt long, yet we were back out in the sunlight in what seemed like no time at all. Once there, we saw the others gathered by the dinghy, ready to leave at a moment's notice. As we neared, Mitch called out. 'We heard shots. Were there infected in there?'

I slowed to a more sedate pace and looked back over my shoulder. 'No, nothing like that; Daz just got a bit overzealous.'

'Is that him?' Sophie was staring at Ben, and the desiccated remains in his arms.

Ben nodded.

Looking solemn, but determined, Sophie beckoned him over.

She led us to where two graves had been hastily dug. They weren't as deep as normal graves, but they would do. Claire's body already lay in one of them and Ben carefully laid Tom's remains in the other. We stood around them in silence, each saying our own prayers to the universe, and then we set to work covering them up before marking each one with a large stone. I hadn't known Tom or Claire, but I cared about those who had, and I felt both the pain of their loss, and the closure of finally being able to lay them to rest.

I surveyed our surroundings, trying my best to ignore the disarticulated human remains that lay all around us, and the pile of dead infected further away on the shore. I concentrated on the scenery beyond these reminders of the world as it now was. The waters of the sheltered bay lay smooth and unruffled, reflecting the surrounding land. Behind me, a mountain, clad in green, loomed over us. Up on a distant crest, silhouetted against the skyline was the form of a single stag: an indication that there was, in fact, still life here; that the infected hadn't, after all, eliminated every living creature from the island. Shifted my focus back to the graves which lay in front of me. As final resting places, they were basic, but they were better than most got these days.

Chapter Thirteen

'I don't see why we can't just stay on Rhum. Look at all the equipment that's already there, and that big house. We could have a much better life there than on Mingulay.' Jeff looked imploringly at each of us in turn.

We'd departed from the island a few hours before and were now well on our way back to Mingulay. I crossed my arms, annoyed at Jeff's inability to grasp the dangers that life on Rhum would contain. 'It's too big and there're just too many places for infected to land. On Mingulay, the cliffs make it much safer. There're only a few places where they can wash up, and the land's more open. If any infected ever do turn up, we'd be able to spot them easily. On Rhum, there are just too many places where they can hide undetected or creep up on us from.'

Rob was at the helm. 'It's also too close to other islands.' He turned the wheel slightly to the left before straightening it up again. 'There's too much of a risk of drifters reaching it.'

None of our arguments seemed to be convincing Jeff and it wasn't until Sophie spoke that he finally relented. 'And it's got too many bad memories.'

Given past events, Jeff could relate to that and this caused him to change tack. 'Are we just going to leave all that equipment there? There are solar panels and wind generators, and loads of other really useful stuff.'

The previous inhabitants of Rhum had clearly worked hard, scavenging things from far and wide, and bringing them back to their settlement. It was just unfortunate that they'd been overrun before they could make use of most of it, and it now lay, abandoned, in piles on the grass between the big house and the water's edge.

Rob looked across at Jeff. 'We can go back for it once we're sure Jack and the others are safe.'

I got up. 'Speaking of Jack, he'll be calling us soon.'

I went inside and turned on the shortwave radio. 'Mingulay calling Hope Town. Come in, Hope Town.' I released the transmit button and waited. For a few seconds there was silence and just as I was beginning to worry where they were, Jack's voice burst out of the loud speaker. 'Mingulay, this is Hope Town. How're you doing?'

'We're doing good, Jack. We've managed to get plenty of diesel, so if it looks like you're going to run into trouble, just let us know and we can sail out and meet you.'

'That's great news, CJ.' There was a brief moment of static, then Jack's voice again. 'I've just been updating my calculations, and as long as the weather holds, I think we'll just make it, but it's good to know that there's another option if we need it. We'll all sleep easier in our bunks knowing that.'

I smiled as I pressed the transmission key. 'Us too, Jack. Us, too.'

***

'CJ, get up.' I woke to find Jeff standing over my bed, shaking me vigorously.

I sat up, in the dim light of the cabin I could only just make out Jeff's face, but I could tell he was concerned. My first worry was that there was a problem with the boat. I remained still for a second and listened, but everything seemed normal. We'd been about halfway back to Mingulay when Rob and Mitch had relieved me at the helm and I'd come below for a rest. Jeff had remained on watch with them, being there to act as an extra pair of hands if they needed it. I glanced at my watch. I'd been asleep for just under an hour. 'What's wrong?'

'Come quick!' Jeff was already leaving my cabin. 'I tried to wake Jimmy up so he could go on watch and I could get some sleep, but he won't wake up. I think there's something wrong with him.'

I leapt out of my bunk and followed after him, not knowing what I'd find when I reached the cabin that Mike and Jimmy shared. As I entered, I saw Mike shaking Jimmy violently, trying desperately to rouse him, but his body remained limp. I strode over to Jimmy and put my hand against his forehead, finding it hot and clammy. 'Feels like he's got a fever.'

I stepped back and crossed my arms, unsure about what to do next. If it was a fever, then we'd have little to treat it with, and it could quickly turn fatal, but maybe I was getting ahead of myself, after all, I still didn't know what the true situation was. Without taking my eyes off Jimmy, I spoke to Jeff. 'Go and get Sophie. She might have a better idea of what's going on.'

Sophie's eyes narrowed. 'We need to go back to Rhum right away.'

I looked at her, concerned. 'Why?'

She put her hand against Jimmy's forehead, checking his temperature, and then removed it. 'Because he's got an infection. He must've picked something up when he fell into the barbed wire. Dirt must have got into some of the scratches: I thought I'd got them cleaned up properly, but I must've missed something, or not been quick enough.' She pulled back Jimmy's t-shirt. 'Look.'

Sure enough what had previously been just scratches

were now angry red lines snaking across Jimmy's well-tanned skin.

Mike glanced at her. 'Why Rhum?'

Sophie pulled Jimmy's shirt down again. 'Because there are antibiotics there. They'd been setting up a clinic for Mum to work in, and they'd filled it with loads of medical supplies. If we don't get Jimmy on antibiotics soon, he'll die.'

That was all I needed to hear. After having lost so many, I was determined that we weren't going to lose Jimmy, too, not because of something as simple as an infected scratch, and not when it could be so easily avoided. I rushed up to inform Rob and Mitch, and seconds later we were heading back the way we'd just come.

I stared up at the sandstone mansion which towered over us in the early morning light. 'Where exactly is the clinic?'

'One floor up and then it's about halfway down the corridor to the left, so ...' Sophie counted along the windows before stopping. 'It would be that room there.'

It had taken us until daybreak to get back to Rhum, and with every passing hour, Jimmy's condition worsened. By the time we went ashore, his breathing had become shallow and erratic, and his whole body was soaked with sweat. While Mike stayed with him, too worried to leave his brother's side, Mitch and Jeff took up the position of lookouts on the roof of the catamaran. Rob manned the machine gun we'd bolted to the boat's stern, just in case any infected turned up. He hadn't used it before, but he was a good shot and he seemed confident enough he'd be able to follow the hurried instructions Daz had given him if he had to. That left me, Daz, Ben and Sophie to go ashore to get the antibiotics. We'd all argued that Sophie should stay behind, but she refused, telling us in no uncertain words that not only was she the only one who knew exactly where the different medicines were kept in the clinic, but that she was also the only one who knew which one did what. It might've taken a while for her to convince us, but eventually all of us, even Daz, accepted she was right.

Just as when we'd gone in search of Tom's body, Daz and I carried machine guns, while Ben and Sophie carried handguns. Sophie being armed was something else I'd not been keen on at first, but again she wore me down with her unwavering logic. Instead, I settled for teaching her how to use the gun she'd be carrying. It turned out that with a little training, she wasn't half bad and I was confident enough that if we did get into trouble, she wouldn't do more harm with it than good.

Now we stood before the door, plucking up the courage to go inside. Daz glanced round at the rest of us. 'Weapons check.'

We each gave our weapons a quick once over. The front door lay open, and we assumed that any infected which had been inside would've been drawn out by all the noise we'd made on the day we'd arrived at Rhum to get the diesel, but we were taking no chances. Everyone nodded as Daz looked at them, indicating they, and their weapons, were ready. He stared into the building's poorly lit interior, clearly wondering, like I was, what it might hold. He closed his eyes and shook his head, as if trying to rid himself of any such thoughts, before opening them again. 'Let's do this!'

He strode forward, self-assured, but not overly confident, and the rest of us followed in single file. Inside, we found ourselves in a large entrance hall, with a staircase leading up to the next floor. The walls alongside the stairs were filled with all sorts of strange items: stags heads, traditional Scottish swords and shields, and old photographs in dusty frames showing people who'd been dead long before the world we'd once known had come to an end. With the door being left open, the weather had got inside the once-grand building. There were large pools of water on the floor, and objects ripped from the walls by strong winds were interspersed with dead bodies that had been picked clean by infected.

Out of the corner of my eye I caught a movement. I froze as I tried to work out what it was, then I saw it: a robin, its beak full of nesting material. The local wildlife, it seemed, wasn't wasting any time now that the infected had been cleared out before they were moving in and taking over places that had once been rightfully theirs.

Sophie saw me staring. 'What is it?'

I pointed. 'A robin; it looks like it's building a nest somewhere.'

Sophie smiled and we watched as it disappeared into a gap behind an old bookcase.

The spell finally broken, we pushed on up the stairs and were soon standing in a long, dark corridor, the door to the clinic straight in front of us. Unlike almost every other door we'd past, this one was shut and this made me fearful. 'Any chance there could be infected inside?'

Sophie scuffed a shoe nervously along the carpeted floor. 'I guess so, but there was no one in the clinic when we were overrun so I don't see why there would be.'

That wasn't quite the re-assurance I'd been looking for. 'Are you sure?'

'It wasn't even fully operational at the time. No one really used it, but me and Mum.' For once Sophie didn't flinch at the thought of her mother and what had happened to her. Finally being able to bury Claire seemed to have done her the power of good.

I stepped forward and lowered my gun to give me a free hand to open the door. I grabbed the knob, then hesitated. Was there really nothing on the other side beyond the medication we'd come to retrieve? There was only one way to find out. I twisted the door handle, threw it open and leapt backwards, raising my gun as I did so. The door banged as it hit its doorstop, making us all jump, and then bounced back; inside, nothing moved.

I heaved a sigh of relief and lowered my gun again. I glanced at Sophie. 'Looks like you were right.'

I turned back to the door and was about to walk through it when something hit me like a freight train. I flew backwards, slamming into the floor a fraction of a second before something heavy landed on my chest. My eyes shot wide open as I realised what it was. I struggled, but there was nothing I could do: the infected had me pinned. I could feel its bony legs straddling my waist and its skeleton-like hands holding my forearms in its vice-like grip. The infected had once been a man, and judging by the remnants of his clothes, he'd been in the military. Ben had told me there had been marines on the island and I figured he'd once been one of them. The infected leant forward, readying itself to tear into the tender flesh of my neck. I could feel his fetid breath on my skin, and see every crack and fissure in the yellowing, waxy skin that was pulled tight across the front of its skull. I knew I should scream, but I was frozen with fear: inside I knew I only had moments left to live.

Suddenly and without warning, the infected's face exploded and instantly it went limp. Not understanding quite what had just happened, I rolled out from under it and scrambled to my feet. While both Ben and Daz stood staring, Sophie was holding the pistol she'd been carrying in one hand while she wiggled a finger from the other in her right ear. She nodded to the gun. 'Jesus, it's a hell of a lot louder when you fire it inside, isn't it?'

I could feel myself shaking from the adrenaline coursing through my body. 'Thanks, Sophie.'

Sophie looked concerned. 'Did he ... Did he get you?'

'No. You were to quick for him.'

At first Sophie looked relieved, then her face hardened as she stared down at the infected. For a moment she was still, then she stepped forward and kicked the dead infected. 'It's nothing more than he deserved.'

She kicked it again, this time hard enough to detach what was left of its head and send it skittering out of sight down the darkened corridor. With a satisfied look on her face, she stuffed the pistol into the waistband of her trousers and strode into the now-empty clinic. Once inside, she started ransacking the cupboards for antibiotics and other medicines, stuffing the bag she'd brought with her to carry them back to the boat. Once she was finished, she moved across to shelf filled with medical textbooks and grabbed as many as she could carry. Sophie's actions finally stirred Daz into life, and he followed her into the clinic, taking great care to stamp as hard as possible on the infected's lifeless body as he passed. I looked questioningly at Ben. 'What was that about?'

He bent down and examined the body for a moment before straightening up again. 'That's Nick. I'd recognise the uniform anywhere.' He glanced down at the remains of the infected again. 'Or, rather, that's what's left of Nick.' Ben's voice dripped with a level of hatred I found frightening. 'It was because of him that Tom died and Claire got infected. He was the one in charge of this place; he's the one that destroyed everything we'd achieved around here.' Ben drew back his right leg as if he was about to kick the body which lay between us, but then he stopped himself. 'He's not worth wasting the energy on.'

Ben looked across at me, and it was as if he was suddenly seeing me for the first time. 'CJ, you're covered in …' He paused as he struggled to find the words, then gave up. 'I don't even know what half that stuff is. Are you sure you're okay?'

I wiped the congealing blood and flecks of brain matter from my face, and then set about picking fragments of skull from my clothes. 'I'll be fine once I get cleaned up.'

Sophie shook her head, her lips pulled tight and her brow furrowed with worry. 'He's not responding.'

We were now back on the boat, and were crowded into Jimmy's cabin; those who weren't able to fit in entirely loitered by the door, craning their necks as they tried to see what was going on inside. Sophie had given Jimmy the first round of antibiotics just over three hours ago, and according to her, if they were going to work, they'd have started having an effect by now. She pressed her hand to his temple and withdrew it almost immediately, deeply concerned. 'I've never felt someone get so hot before.'

'I have.' Ben sounded nervous. 'I've seen someone sick just like this before.' Sophie turned to him, confused. He carried on. 'You have, too. And Daz.'

Suddenly, Sophie realised what he was getting at and her face dropped as her eyes shot wide open. She sprang backwards, landing some two feet from Jimmy's side. 'You mean Jake? You mean, you think he's not just infected with some disease; he's infected with *the* disease? How could he have caught it? He hasn't been attacked.'

Ben swallowed. 'No, but what if there was blood from an infected on the wire where he injured himself? It would have acted like a syringe, injecting it into his body.'

Mike looked from Sophie to Ben and back again. 'You think he could pick it up just by scratching himself on something that had infected blood on it?'

'Yes.' Ben avoided looking at either of the two brothers. 'There are diseases you can pick up that easily, aren't there, Sophie?'

Sophie nodded, and then turned and ran from the room, pushing people out of the way as she went past. I was about to go after her when she returned. She sat down on the bed beside Jimmy and lifted up one of his hands, examining it carefully. She seemed to find what she was looking for because she set it down again and then pulled two objects from her pocket. One was a syringe and the other was a small vial containing a clear liquid. She set them on the bed sheets, and keeping her eyes on Jimmy, she spoke. 'Ben's right. He's just like Jake was at the end. There's no other disease that makes people like this, not that you could catch out here at any rate.'

Mike began to protest, but Sophie touched his arm. 'Deep down, you know it's true, don't you?'

Mike opened and closed his mouth a few times and then slumped down on Jimmy's bed. 'Yes.' He stared hard at the floor for a moment, and then spoke again. 'I've seen it, too. It's just how Sam was before he turned.'

While Ben, Daz, Mitch and Sophie were curious, the rest of us knew the story. Sam was Mike and Jimmy's older brother and they'd survived almost a week after the outbreak in Miami had started before he was attacked. He'd escaped, though, and made it back to the airboat they were travelling on at the time, but he'd been infected and later he'd turned. Mike had had to push him over the side in order to save his life and Jimmy's.

Sophie picked up the vial and filled the syringe from it. She held it out to Mike. 'This is morphine; enough to put him out of his misery.'

Mike was horrified. 'I can't do that. I can't kill Jimmy. He's the only family I've got left.'

Sophie said nothing, she just kept the syringe held out in front of her.

'What if you're wrong? What if it's something else? What if you try different antibiotics?' Mike was clutching at straws.

Sophie glanced down and shook her head slowly, then she looked up at Mike. 'I've done everything I can. I'm certain, and I think you know Ben's right, too.'

Mike stared at the syringe as if it was something so alien he didn't even know how to touch it, but after what seemed like an age, he finally reached out and took it.

Sophie guided him. 'If you pick up his right hand in your left, then try to find a vein, like that one there.' She pointed at Jimmy's hand. 'Now hold the syringe with your fingers looped under there and your thumb on the plunger.' She paused to allow Mike to follow her instructions. 'That's it. Now slip the needle into the vein. Don't worry, it won't hurt him; he's already too far gone. Now push the plunger down.'

Mike did as he was told and almost immediately Jimmy started breathing slower and more evenly. Sophie leaned forward and removed the syringe, carefully replacing the protective cap on a tip that was now coated with infected blood. She got up and ushered the rest of us from the room, leaving Mike to be alone with Jimmy until the end finally came. A few minutes later, we heard an anguished cry, telling us Jimmy was gone.

Jimmy was the first person we'd lost from our group since we'd arrived in Mingulay some six months before, and we were all devastated by his death. Mike carried him ashore and dug a grave for him beside that of Tom and Claire. For so long we'd been unable to bury anyone, but now we'd had our third funeral in a little under twenty-four hours. Jimmy's was different from the previous two, though; he'd been lost so suddenly and unexpectedly, and he was one of us.

His death also raised some worrying questions. How long could the virus survive outside the human body, sitting on some sharp object just waiting to catch us unawares? Was it hours, or days? Or perhaps even years? If we could become infected in this manner, how could we possibly defend ourselves against it? All of a sudden, we no longer felt safe and this unnerved us. The only answer seemed to be to restrict our movements as much as possible to Mingulay, where we knew the virus had never been, and ensure we wore heavy protective clothes if we ever had to visit anywhere there was even a chance there had once been infected. The only trouble was, where would we get such clothes? There might be some on Rhum, brought there along with the other equipment, but how could we be certain it wasn't already contaminated in some way? The same went for everything else which had been accumulated there before the island had been overrun. While much of it might be uncontaminated, we'd never know with any certainty that anything was safe. We'd been lucky so far that no one else had cut themselves on any of it, and now we knew the danger that anything which had been in contact with infected blood could pose, there was no way we could risk taking any of it to Mingulay.

This danger must've always been present, and it was probably just blind luck that none of us had been infected this way before. Suddenly, the realisation dawned on me that the changed world was much more dangerous than I'd ever thought it was. Even if the infected were ever wiped out, through starvation or by being killed, the contamination they'd leave behind would mean that the risk of a resurgence of the disease would be ever-present wherever they'd once been. Even after the infected had gone, the disease itself would remain, waiting to catch out the unwary and the careless. The land which had fallen to the infected might never again be suitable for human habitation.

Mutterings drifting into the cabin from the cockpit roused me from my depressing musings. Daz and Sophie were talking to Rob, Ben and Mitch in concerned tones. I glanced up and looked outside to see Rob shaking his head, but whatever the discussion, he seemed to be losing. Over on the other side of the cabin, Jeff sat with Mike, trying to console him. I decided to give them some privacy and headed outside. Almost immediately, the others stopped talking and, as one, turned to face me. Sophie glanced at Rob and then nodded in my direction, as if trying to urge him to say something, but he remained silent. I frowned, 'What's going on?'

Daz avoided making eye contact, as did Mitch, Rob and Sophie. Only Ben seemed to be able to look at me. He took a deep breath. 'CJ, we're concerned you might've got infected when Sophie killed Nick. His blood, and god knows what other stuff, was all over you. If Jimmy could get infected just by scratching himself on a bit of barbed wire, then you could be infected, too, and just not know it yet.'

I felt my eyes widen as I stood there, unable to take in what I was hearing. 'But he didn't hurt me; he didn't break my skin. How could I be infected?'

Sophie put a hand on my arm. 'It's not likely, CJ, but it *is* possible. If some of his blood got into your mouth, or your eyes, or you breathed it in, then you could be infected.'

'But I don't feel anything; I don't feel like I'm burning up. Rob, you told me that when Jon was infected, he could feel it almost straightaway.' I was now the one clutching at straws, trying to find something, anything, that would give me hope. 'You told me that, didn't you, Rob?'

Rob still couldn't bring himself to look at me. 'But he was scratched by one of them. This is different, CJ. It might take longer for you to feel it if you're infected this way. After all, we really don't know anything about this disease. Until Jimmy, we didn't know you could catch it just by cutting yourself on something that had been contaminated with infected blood. Without knowing for sure if you're infected or not, we can't really take the risk of assuming that you're not.'

'But, Rob, the same thing happened to you, with the man in the life raft, and you weren't infected, were you? Remember?' The incident had been our first close encounter with infected, and it had so nearly been our last. We had been anchored up when a life raft with two of them on board drifted into us. Rob had killed one with the flare gun, but the other had got on to the catamaran and Rob had only just managed to club it to death before it could attack him. Afterwards, he'd been spattered with blood, and Mike, worried that he'd been infected, came close to shooting him there and then, just to be on the safe side. This was soon after we'd picked up Jimmy and Mike, and they'd yet to become part of our group, so he had only been thinking about their own safety. It didn't help that they'd had more experience with the infected than we'd had back then, and it was only the fact that I'd tackled Mike to the deck which had stopped him from doing it.

Rob crossed him arms defensively, 'Maybe I just got lucky. Did you ever think of that? Maybe I didn't get enough on me. You were soaked in the stuff, CJ, a lot worse than I was. It was all over you, all over your face. The more that gets on you, the greater the chance of infection, isn't there, Sophie?'

Sophie grimaced and nodded noncommittally, not happy at being drawn into what was becoming a stand-off between myself and Rob, but not wanting to lie about what she thought.

I stared at Rob, not believing his lack of loyalty after all we'd been through together, but wondering if he was right; wondering if I really could be infected, and if so, how long it would take for me to know for sure. Was the virus, even now, coursing through my body, replicating itself and worming its way into my brain? If it was, when would I finally feel it? How long would it take to overwhelm me? And if that happened, would the others be able to do what they'd need to do in order to ensure their own survival? All these thoughts racing through my brain were starting to cause my head to spin. Or was this the first sign that I was, indeed, infected? Not knowing which was the truth, I slumped down on to a seat and looked up dejectedly at those who now stood over me. 'So, what do we do now?'

'CJ, I'm going to take your temperature next.' Sophie was speaking to me softly and calmly. She'd already taken my pulse and examined my eyes, now she put her hand on my forehead. By then, I knew the routine; she'd been doing the same thing every fifteen minutes for the last two hours and so far she'd detected no change.

The catamaran was still anchored in the bay on Rhum, but the two of us were alone in the cockpit. Taking charge of the situation, Sophie had ordered the others inside, but at first they'd refused to go. Yet, she'd insisted, telling them that medical issues were her area of expertise, and that they had to listen to her. Reluctantly, they obeyed, but not until Daz had stalked into the cabin and returned, forcing the pistol Sophie had used to kill Nick into her hand before disappearing inside again. His reasoning was clear, and I could see him now, out of the corner of my eye, armed with one of the small machine guns, standing by the door, ready to react at a moment's notice.

I looked up at Sophie. 'How long are we going to keep doing this?'

I was tired, drained of all energy, by worry, by the sheer terror of the very thought that I might be infected and what would happen if I was, but I'd yet to feel anything which suggested that this was the case. Sophie took her hand away and sat back, business-like in her manner, although her eyes betrayed the fear that she was really feeling. 'For as long as it takes.'

I stared at her, and at the gun which was now pushed into the waistband of her trousers, trying to work out how things had gone so wrong so fast. 'But how long's that going to be?'

For a while, Sophie said nothing, but then she stood up. 'Jimmy took about nine hours to start showing symptoms, at least as far as we know. With Jake it was sooner; it was less than an hour.'

I remembered Sophie saying this name when she was in the cabin with Jimmy, but other than that, I'd never heard her mention it before. 'Who's Jake?'

Sophie's face was vacant and she spoke quietly, her voice flat. 'He was my little brother; he was only six. We'd been getting tickets for a concert and had just got back to the car when we were attacked ...' She faded out and it was several minutes before she spoke again. All the time I sat there silently, unsure of what to do or say. Until that moment, I'd never even known she'd had a brother, and now I knew why she'd never talked about him before. The memory was just too painful to recall unless she was forced into it.

'Ben, Daz and Tom rescued us, but by then it was too late; Jake had already been infected. It was just a scratch, no more than that, but that was all it took. In the end Mum had to put him out of his misery, just the same way that I made Mike do for Jimmy. That's how I knew what had to be done.' Sophie looked upwards and blinked rapidly, as if trying to stop the memories overwhelming her as she relived past events. 'I hated her so much when I realised what she'd done. I didn't understand; I didn't realise what we were up against; what the disease did to people. I was so naive back then.' Sophie shook her head dismissively and sat down next to me. She put her head on my shoulder and I put my arm around her. She carried on. 'Now I understand. I wish she was still here so I could tell her that, but she's not; she's gone and I'm all alone.'

I squeezed her. 'You're not alone, Sophie. You've got us; you have me, and Daz, and all of us.'

She sniffed again. 'But what if I lose you, too, CJ? I don't think I can go on without you.'

I squeezed her again. 'I'm not going anywhere, Sophie, I promise.'

She smiled at me, grateful for what I was saying, but still not allowing herself to believe it was true, and I didn't blame her. I still didn't yet know what to believe myself.

Chapter Fourteen

We left Rhum late in the afternoon, despondent about Jimmy's death. No one spoke unless they had to, and Mike and Jeff spent the hours until darkness, sitting together on the foredeck, staring off into the distance. They only came inside when Mitch went forward and insisted, and even then they both went straight to their cabins.

Sophie sat, stone-faced, her head leaning against Daz's chest, his arm draped round her. Rob and Mitch sat together, too, leaving me feeling oddly alone. It didn't help that it was still unclear whether I'd been infected or not, although with every passing hour it seemed less and less likely. Yet, the others kept their distance, even as they watched me, eagle-eyed, for any indications that I might be starting to succumb to the disease. After eight hours with no change in my condition, this was the decision we'd come to as a group: rather than delay the return to Mingulay with our precious cargo of diesel any longer, my quarantine was over. Instead, I'd be accompanied at all times by someone who could monitor me and make sure I wasn't becoming unwell. No one had said what would happen if I did become ill, but no one needed to. If that was the eventual outcome, there'd only be two options: the quick and painless route that Sophie had chosen for Jimmy; or the even faster, but potentially much more painful route offered by a bullet in the head.

Not wanting to dwell on it any longer, I got up and went out into the cockpit, where Ben had taken charge and was guiding us back to Mingulay.

I sat down and looked up at the skies. Unlike Hope Town, where you almost always had clear skies, meaning you were pretty much guaranteed to be able to see the stars on any given night, in Scotland, cloud was common, especially in spring. Tonight, the stars being obscured was a better match for my mood.

I'm not too sure how long I sat there before Ben spoke. 'It's been a hell of a few days, hasn't it?'

Not knowing what to say, I just nodded.

Ben stared out into the darkness. 'How're you holding up?'

'I just watched a fourteen year old show a sixteen year old how to kill his little brother, and I might be next. How d'you think I'm holding up?' I snapped angrily. I knew none of it was Ben's fault, but he was the one who was there, so he was the one I took it out on.

He seemed to understand what was going on and didn't take it personally. 'Yeah, it's one fucked-up world we find ourselves in, but look on the bright side, at least it doesn't seem like you're infected. It's been almost twelve hours; if you had been, I think you'd know it by now.'

'That's the bright side?' I slumped down on the seat. 'Every time things seem to be getting better, something like this happens.' I paused as I tried to organise the thoughts which were racing through my head. 'I'm really not too sure how much more of this I can take.'

I didn't know why I was telling Ben this. It was a feeling that had been with me ever since we'd first found out what had happened to the world. Most of the time, it just hung around somewhere in the background, gnawing away at me, but then we'd lose someone, or we'd realise life was going to be more difficult than we'd originally thought, and it would push its way to the fore, taking over my thoughts so completely that I could think of little else.

Ben smiled at me with a sad sort of knowing smile.

'Yeah, I get that way too from time to time, especially when we lose someone.'

This admission surprised me. Ben wasn't like Rob, who tended to wear his heart on his sleeve, especially when the pressure was getting to him, and the way Ben acted, it always seemed like he took everything in his stride. The feelings I'd had for Ben the night we'd watched the northern lights together once again reared up inside me, and as before, I did my best to quash them, yet still they threatened to overwhelm me. I didn't understand what was going on or why I was feeling this way. I knew I'd grown to like Ben a lot, but was I betraying Jon's memory by feeling this way about him? Or was this allowed? I just wished I had someone I could talk to, to ask about this, but there was no one. Mitch was Ben's friend, so hers was hardly an independent point of view, and Sophie wasn't old enough to provide the advice I needed. Rob was a possibility, but he'd known Jon and now had a relationship with Mitch. Given that, could he really provide an objective opinion on the situation? Not knowing what to do, I chose the default option and did my best to ignore how I was feeling. Instead, I turned my attention to what Ben had just said. 'D'you still miss him? Tom, I mean.'

'Every day.' Ben sighed. 'The worst thing is knowing that he made it through the hard bit, surviving the initial outbreak and getting to safety. If it hadn't been for Nick and his bloody plans to set up his own little empire, Tom would still be here. So would Claire and a lot of other people: it wasn't the disease that got him; it was Nick.'

'Yeah,' I nodded, knowing exactly where he was coming from, 'it was the same with Jon.'

We both sat in silence, thinking about the world we now found ourselves in and how there was as much danger from the way others acted as there was from the disease itself.

Ben was the first to speak again. 'How d'you think Sophie's coping with all this?'

I shook my head. 'I don't know. She seems to be fine, but she tends to keep everything bottled up.' I thought back to the conversation I'd had with her high on the hill above the hut, the morning after Mitch had told us she was pregnant, when I'd realised for the first time just how lost she really felt. 'She doesn't like showing when she's upset. I think she thinks it makes her look weak and she knows she has to be strong. I guess she's doing okay though. I think finally getting to bury her mum has made a big difference to her. It's allowed her to find some closure, and I think she feels like she can finally start grieving properly.'

'I guess there's a lot of truth in that.' Ben made a slight adjustment to the wheel, causing the sails to droop slightly before refilling. 'You and her seem to be getting on well. She really looks up to you, you know; she trusts you, values your opinions on things.'

I blushed and was glad it was dark enough that Ben couldn't see. 'That's only 'cos she doesn't know how much of a mess I actually am.'

'Isn't that always the way?' Ben stared out across the water. 'Aren't we all scared that one day someone will pull back the curtain and see the scared little child we feel like inside, rather than the tough act we put on for the benefit of others?'

I shifted uncomfortably. The way Ben described it, it was as if he could see right into my soul. 'Is that really how you feel?'

He nodded. 'Most of the time: like a little kid playing at being a grown-up, all scared in case anyone else finds out the truth.'

I sat back, starting to feel a little better. This was exactly how I felt, and it was nice to know I wasn't the only one.

There were a few minutes of silence before Ben spoke again. 'What did you do before all this happened?'

I was startled by the question. It seemed like it had become an unspoken rule never to ask each other about our lives before everything went wrong. There were many reasons to avoid it, but mostly it was because of the memories such topics might bring back.

I shrugged. 'I was a schoolgirl.'

'A schoolgirl?' Ben sounded incredulous.

'Pretty much. I'd just left, but it wasn't like I'd done anything else, other than travel for a few months.'

Ben adjusted the wheel again. 'I always forget how young you are, CJ.'

I glared at him for a second, then realised he meant it as a compliment. Now he'd raised the subject, I was curious about his background. 'What about you?'

Ben told me about his life before: about how he'd studied marine biology at university and then ended up working as a juggler with Tom. He told me about working on whale-watching boats and about setting up his own business. It was fun to hear him talk about it, and about some of the things he'd got up to over the years. For once, with just the two of us alone in the cockpit, it almost felt like it was the way things used be; as if things were normal again. Alone in the dark, we could pretend that everything was back the way it had been before the virus, and for a few brief hours I was able to forget all that had happened since the world had been turned upside down.

***

'D'you want to see something amazing?' I woke to the sound of Ben's voice, wondering why my bed felt so cold.

My first thought was that it was a symptom of the disease, that this was the beginning of the end, then I realised I was still in the cockpit and that there was a blanket wrapped round me that I didn't remember bringing outside. I concentrated on my body, and was relieved to realise I felt no different than before. It seemed I'd been lucky and after almost twenty-four hours, it was now almost certain that I'd not, after all, been infected. I stared at Ben through bleary eyes, 'See what?'

Ben nodded to the east. 'That.'

I looked where he was indicating: the sun was just coming over the horizon and it was ablaze with fire; yet, the day hadn't fully started, and to the west, the sky was still dark and stars twinkled. Between these two horizons the sky blended through the full spectrum of midnight blues, yellows, oranges and reds. The wind had dropped, meaning we were barely moving, and the sea's surface was an oily mirror that undulated gently, creating a kaleidoscope of colours as it reflected the cloudless sky above. Off in the distance, a whale surfaced, its sleek back emerging from the water before disappearing again a couple of seconds later, leaving nothing but ripples and a cloud of exhaled air.

Despite everything, I smiled, glad that Ben had woken me. It reminded me that even though the world was tough, indiscriminate and dangerous, there was still beauty in it, too, and maybe that made all the difference.

Ben turned the wheel a few inches to the left and then tightened the main sail. As he did, he started to sing, his voice deep and smooth in the stillness of the newly born morning:

'Heel y'ho boys, let her go, boys,
'Bring her head round now all together,
'Heel y'ho boys, let her go boys,
'Sailing homeward to Mingulay.'

I'd never heard the song before, but it had a poignant, lilting melody that moved me unexpectedly as I watched the sun continue to rise. Then I realised why: I was starting to think of Mingulay as home.

When we arrived back at the island, Dougie was, as always, on the beach waiting for us. He never liked it when we left, but neither did he like being on any of the boats, so he remained on shore, guarding the island whenever we went on a foraging or scavenging expedition. He was well used to fending for himself and was happy to snuffle through the seaweed on the beach, searching out crabs to chase before crunching them up and swallowing the remains. I guess that was how he'd survived for so long all on his own before we'd rescued him. We'd been gone much longer than usual this time, and he bounced around ecstatically as we dropped anchor and Rob began ferrying people ashore in the dinghy.

As soon as we set foot on the sand, Dougie ran between us, sniffing and wagging his tail as he weaved between our legs, but by the time all of us had landed, Dougie had realised someone was missing. He kept looking out towards the catamaran, wondering when Jimmy was coming ashore. As we walked up the beach, Jeff called to him, but Dougie remained at the water's edge, staring out to sea. He was no longer jubilant at our return; instead, he was confused. We watched as Jeff went back to him and tried to make him follow us, but

Dougie refused, choosing to wait resolutely at the water's edge for his friend and companion to come home. Yet, there was a sadness to the way he sat, ears down, head drooping, as if he knew that his was a futile vigil and that Jimmy would never again return.

'I'm coming with you.' Mike was on his feet, a determined look on his face.

Jeff was standing next to him. 'If he's going, I'm going, too.'

A call had come through from Jack a few minutes before and the news wasn't good. As they'd neared the end of their crossing, the weather had worsened and the heavily laden boat was struggling to make headway through the growing waves. From Jack's latest calculations, they were about fifty miles to our south-west, but it was becoming increasingly clear that they'd run out of fuel before they reached us. As soon as he'd heard this, Rob told Jack that he'd head out immediately, bringing them the fuel they needed to complete the crossing. Now, we were arguing over who would go with him and who would stay behind.

Rob was happy for Ben, Daz and me to come along, but he was less keen on the others joining us.

'Jeff, you're too young, and anyway, it's just the four of us that will be going.'

Mitch cleared her throat, 'Five, Rob.'

Rob looked at her. 'I'm not taking you with me, not in your condition.'

Mitch glared at him. 'I'm pregnant, Rob, not ill. Pregnancy isn't a disease. You might not realise it, but women have been getting pregnant for thousands of years and still doing their fair share of the work.'

Rob spluttered. 'But ...'

'No, Rob. You're going to need all the help you can get out there, and there's no way I'm letting you go without me. I love you, Rob; I'd never forgive myself if something happened to you and I wasn't there to do all I could to stop it.'

Rob shifted defensively, but knew better than to try to persuade her to change her mind. 'Okay, just the five of us.'

Mike folded his arms. 'Daz isn't much older than I am. Why's he allowed to go and not me?'

'Because ...' Rob struggled to come up with a good reason.

Jeff stood up. 'If Mike's going, then so am I!'

Sophie got up, too. 'I'm not being the only one who's left behind!'

Rob glanced at his watch. He was keen to get going as soon as possible and he knew that arguing about who was coming and who was staying was just wasting precious time. He raised his hands in surrender. 'Okay, okay; we'll all go. Let's just get the anchor up and get out of here.'

As we sailed south-west towards the last position Jack had given us, the weather began to change. The sky had been blue and clear over Mingulay, but now it was shrouded in thick, angry looking clouds. The wind was picking up too, coming with ever-increasing strength from the west. With all the diesel on board, we were close to being overloaded and the catamaran was making slow progress as it tried to cut through the growing swell.

Rob examined the chart which was laid out on one of the seats in the cockpit. 'At the rate we're going, it'll be nightfall before we get there.'

Ben leant back. 'That'll make finding them all the more difficult.'

Jeff looked troubled. 'But we'll find them, won't we?'

From behind, I put my arms around his neck. 'Don't worry, we'll find them.' I tried to sound confident, but inside I was really starting to worry. In the last conversation with Jack, he'd sounded not just concerned, but down right scared. It was the first time I'd ever heard fear in his voice. He'd always seemed so confident before, no matter what was happening, but now he was terrified. The storm was growing in intensity and he knew that if they ran out of fuel before we got to them, they'd be at the mercy of the wind and the waves, and that wouldn't be good.

Ben examined the chart. 'They're going to be running on fumes by the time we reach them. It's going to be really close.' He glanced across at Rob. 'You think we can get this thing to go any faster?'

'We're at latitude—' Before Jack could finish, there was a crash in the background and the radio fell silent.

I grabbed the microphone. 'Jack?'

After a second, his voice came back. 'I'm still here, CJ.'

I felt my brow furrow. 'What was that?'

I heard Jack clear his throat before he replied. 'Just one of the cupboards in the galley emptying itself.'

I heaved a sigh of relief. 'How's everyone doing?'

'They're pretty scared.' I heard Jack release the transmission button and then press it again a second later. 'And I can't say I blame them.'

Night was starting to fall, and as far as we could tell, we were only five kilometres short of Jack's location. The only problem was that we were still struggling to work out our own position, and therefore, which direction to head to make the rendezvous. Jack had finally run out of fuel twenty minutes earlier and with the engines no longer running, they were now being tossed around like a cork on swells that were a good ten feet high. With each wave, the boat rolled steeply onto its side as it was swept up its face, then as it tipped over the top, it would roll across onto its other side before the same action would begin again when it reached the bottom of the next trough.

'But are you all right?' I heard the urgency in my own voice. 'Can you hold on until we get there?'

It was several seconds before Jack replied. 'To be honest, CJ, I don't know. Maybe if you're quick, but if the weather gets any worse, there's a real risk that we'll either get swamped, or be rolled all the way over.' He fell silent. I picked up the mic, but didn't press the transmit button. I had no idea what to say.

The radio crackled into life again. 'Sorry, CJ, I shouldn't have told you that. We'll make it. Just get here as fast as you can.' With that, Jack reeled off his latest position and I took it out to the cockpit. It was just an estimate, made by dead-reckoning based on his last midday measurement with the sextant. It would make finding them all the more difficult, but with no GPS, it was the best he could do.

Daz pointed into the night. 'Is that them?'

I craned my neck. 'Where?'

'I thought I saw somethin', but I can't see it anymore.' Daz shrugged. 'Maybe it was just wishful thinkin'.'

We'd reached the area where we thought Jack was, and we were starting to search, moving back and forth along a series of parallel transects. Jack had been firing off flares once every half hour to try to help us find him, but either we weren't close enough or the weather was just too bad to be able to see them. He was now down to his final two; after that there'd be little chance of us finding them before daybreak and by then it might be too late. We were all on deck, scanning the darkness, searching for the latest flare which we knew from his radio transmission Jack had just fired.

The storm was now roaring around us, the wind pulling at our clothes and the rain rattling off our faces. This made spotting anything that was more than a few yards beyond the side of the boat difficult, if not impossible. With increasing frequency waves were sweeping across the deck as we rode low in the water, weighed down as we were with the extra diesel. The youngsters were struggling to stay on their feet and Daz had had to grab Jeff on two different occasions to stop him being thrown to the deck. Yet, knowing that we needed to find Jack as soon as possible, he refused to go inside.

At one time, we'd had safety harnesses to wear under such conditions, but in the intervening months, these had been adapted for other, more urgent purposes, or cannibalised for parts that were needed to make repairs elsewhere. These had seemed like logical decisions at the time, but now I was regretting that we no longer had them to keep us safe. We'd also once had a powerful hand-held spotlight that would've proved very useful after we located Jack and had to manoeuvre alongside in the darkness, but the bulb had eventually blown, rendering it useless, and we had no hope of finding a replacement. This was a problem we faced constantly: the loss of equipment which would've otherwise made our lives easier, through damage, destruction or just plain old wear and tear. With the way the world was, unless we were very lucky, once this happened, it meant we'd lost them, and the functionality they provided, forever.

A wave crashed over the bow and washed across the deck, bringing me back to the present. I glanced at the nearest barrels. 'Rob, do we really need all this diesel?'

Rob was hunched over the wheel, gripping it so tightly that his fingers had turned white. 'Why?'

I wiped the rain water from my face. 'Because we need to lighten our load or we're going to risk being swamped.'

Ben shielded his eyes, trying to protect them from the wind and rain. 'She's right. If this weather gets any worse, there'll be a real chance of us sinking if we don't.'

Another wave crashed over the bow and swept along the side of the boat. Rob fought the wheel, and it took all his strength to keep us pointed in the right direction. He was reluctant, but in his heart he knew that Ben and I were right. 'Okay, do it.'

It took us twenty minutes, but by the time we'd finished untying half the barrels and tipping them over the side, we were riding much higher in the water and fewer waves were crashing across the decks. The lighter load also allowed us to pick up speed and we were moving faster through the water. This, I hoped, meant we'd have a greater chance of reaching Jack before it was too late.

I pulled nervously at the frayed cuff of the waterproof I as wearing as Rob raised the radio's microphone. 'Jack?'

'I'm still here.' Jack sounded petrified. 'But we almost went over there. We got lucky this time, but I don't know how much longer our luck's going to hold out. This is the last flare, Rob. This is our last hope.'

Rob pressed the transmission key. 'Roger that, Jack. Give me to the count of thirty and then fire it.'

There was a burst of static before Jack finally replied. 'Fingers crossed.'

Rob put the mic down and I saw his lips move as he counted slowly under his breath and strode back out to the cockpit. I followed, and together we joined the others peering out into the darkness. Rob glanced round. 'Now.'

'There!' Sophie yelled and pointed. 'I see it!'

Ben spun the wheel to the left, 'I see it, too,' He glanced at the compass. 'Bearing of 265 degrees.'

Together, we watched the flare reach the top of its arc and started to drop towards the sea again before finally vanishing from sight. I glanced at Rob. 'How far away d'you think they are?'

'A couple of miles, maybe three at the most.' Rob sounded both relieved and excited. He cast an experienced eye over the sails. 'We should be there in about twenty minutes; half an hour at the most.'

'I see them!' Rob turned the wheel as he called out. 'Over there. Ben, tighten the jib up. CJ, pull in the mainsail.'

As we'd neared Jack's location, Rob had taken over the helm from Ben and was now the one in charge. Ben and I leapt into action, while the others searched the darkness. A second later Mitch cried out. 'There! I see them too.'

I glanced up, and sure enough, there was Jack's boat, lights shining from its windows, on the crest of a wave. It was side on to the swell and rolling violently, but it was definitely there. Unable to stop myself, I whooped with delight. A second later, Jack's boat dropped into a trough and disappeared from sight, and it was almost a minute before it appeared again. With Rob shouting orders from the behind the wheel, we were closing rapidly, and it looked like we'd have Jack alongside in a matter of minutes. Transferring the diesel over in the storm would be difficult, but it was by no means impossible. I raced into the cabin and scooped up the microphone for the radio. 'Jack, we can see you! We'll be there in a couple of minutes. Five at the most.'

I released the transmit button and waited, but there was only static.

I tried again. 'Jack, are you there?'

I waited for a few second before pressing the transmission key a third time, panic starting sweep through me. 'Jack?'

Finally, the radio burst into life. 'CJ, we can see you, too.' The relief in Jack's voice was clear. 'I'm going out on deck to get things ready.'

'Roger that, Jack.' I felt a surge of euphoria rush through me as I put down the microphone and went back into the cockpit. I could hardly believe it: we'd found them, one small speck in the tumultuous expanse that was the North Atlantic, and we'd get to them before it was too late. I stared across the hundred or so yards of water that was all that now separated the two boats, wondering how long it would take to get there. As I did so, Jack, lit by light streaming from the doorway, emerged from his cabin, shortly followed by another figure I didn't recognise. They looked round, searching the darkness, and then waved when they saw us. I whooped again and waved back.

'What the fuck's that?' I turned to see that Daz wasn't looking at Jack's boat, but rather he was staring at something behind us, and it took me a couple of seconds to realise what it was. Out of nowhere, a wall of water had risen out of the sea, many times larger than any other wave we'd encountered in the storm so far. Its crest frothed and foamed, but below this was a solid mass of inky blackness. I turned back to the others: everyone else except Daz was concentrating on Jack's boat, and none of them had seen the rogue wave. I cried out. 'Rob! Look out!'

Rob glanced round and as he saw the wave, a look of disbelief shot across his face, quickly followed by one of sheer terror. The massive wave was coming in on our starboard quarter and if it hit us at that angle, it would almost certainly sink us. Rob turned the wheel as quickly as he could and yelled out instructions. 'Ben, get the jib across; Daz, do the same with the main sail. Everyone else, inside. Now!'

Ben and Daz leapt into action, but the rest of us remained rooted to the spot by the sight of the ever-nearing wall of water. Even though it was still fifty yards away, it already towered over us, taller than the mast, blocking everything else from sight. Beneath me, I felt the boat turn until we were facing it head on, then I heard Rob scream. 'Everyone, hold on!'

A second later, the wave was on us, first lifting us up, higher and higher. As we rose, the face of the wave steepened, tipping us backwards until it seemed like we were going to flip over. Yet, before that happened, we reached the top. For a moment, we hung there and I got a brief glimpse of Jack's boat. Jack was still on deck, preparing for our arrival, unaware of the approaching wave. Then we dropped down the far side. For what seemed like an age, we were in free-fall as we plummeted downwards, but finally we smashed into the sea with a crash that sounded like we'd hit a brick wall. The boat shuddered and water swirled across the deck, knocking me from my feet. I looked around desperately, and saw that I wasn't the only one who was down. Rob gripped onto the steering wheel, while Ben was holding onto the rope for the main sail and Daz had his arms wrapped tightly around the stand for the machine gun, close to where it was bolted to the deck. I yelled across to them, but they were too busy trying to hold on to hear me. Sophie was lying on her back and was being pulled towards the side of the boat by the receding water. Somehow, I managed to right myself, and I lunged, grabbing the back of her jacket just as she slipped between the lowest guard rail and the edge of the deck. This stopped her going any further, but it wasn't a good enough grip to allow me to pull her back on board. The next thing I knew, Daz was beside me, reaching through the guard rail and manhandling Sophie back onto the deck, where she lay, soaking wet and terrified.

With Sophie safe, I leapt to my feet again and whirled round, looking for the others. Ben was helping Mitch up, but Mike and Jeff were nowhere in sight. Then I spotted them: the guard rail at the side of the cockpit where they'd been sitting before the wave hit had broken and they were clinging onto the outside of the boat, being alternatively plunged into the freezing cold water and then dragged from it again.

I raced across to them. 'Rob, Ben. Help me.'

I got there just as Jeff's hands slipped and disappeared. I screamed. Ben shot past me and threw himself down onto his belly, leaning as far as he could over the side of the boat. He called back. 'It's okay. Mike's got him.'

I looked over the side. Mike was now holding on with just one hand, his other arm wrapped tightly around Jeff, but his strength was fading rapidly. I got down beside Ben. 'Mike, give me your hand.'

Mike shook his head. 'No, take Jeff first.'

Ben grabbed a handful of Jeff's jacket. 'Don't worry, I've got him.'

I yelled at him. 'Mike, your hand.'

Again, he shook his head. 'Not until I know Jeff is safe.'

I shimmied over to Ben and together we dragged Jeff on board. I turned back to Mike, but he'd vanished. 'Ben!' I could hear the panic in my voice.

Ben leapt to his feet. 'Rob, Mike's gone over the side.'

I leapt up, too, joining the others as we searched the darkness. For a moment, there was nothing and then Mitch called out. 'There!'

Mike was bobbing up and down in the water some twenty feet behind us, struggling to keep his head above the surface. In one movement, Ben grabbed the life ring from the back of the boat and threw it towards Mike, but it landed short. As quickly as possible, he pulled it back and threw it again. By this time, Mike was thirty feet away, disappearing into the darkness and in big trouble. It was clear to me that if we kept on going the way we were heading, we'd soon be too far away to reach him. 'Rob, we need to turn around.'

Rob grimaced. 'We can't. It's too dangerous. The sea's too rough.'

'We have to.' I urged him. 'We can't lose Mike. Not now. We've got to do something.'

Ben was pulling the life ring back again. 'She's right, Rob. We've got to turn round if we're going to have any hope of saving him.'

Rob glanced up at the sails, and then at the surrounding sea. 'Okay. Everyone, keep your heads down and hold on!'

Rob spun the wheel, causing the boat to jerk and sway

violently. In the gale-force wind, the main sail crashed across to the other side, just as Rob yelled, 'Daz, release the jib.'

Daz whipped the jib's rope off its cleat and let it go.

'CJ, pull it in on the other side.'

I grabbed the rope and pulled, dragging the jib across and securing it to the winch, before cranking it tight. I looked up: we were now racing back the way we'd come, but Mike was nowhere in sight. Panic welled up inside me. We hadn't lost anyone in so long, but now it looked as if we were going to lose both Jimmy and Mike within a matter of hours.

Then I saw him; his head barely above the surface. 'There!' I grabbed the life ring from Ben and threw it; it landed a few feet short. I pulled it in as fast as I could, then searched the sea as I prepared to throw it again, but I couldn't see Mike anywhere. After what seemed like an age, he reappeared, his head breaking the surface, coughing and spluttering as he tried to draw breath before he was sucked underwater once more. I hurled the life ring towards where he'd been moments before, more in desperation than hope, and watched as it floated there amongst the white-capped waves. Suddenly a hand appeared, grasping on to its side, shortly followed by a head. I yelled out. 'I've got him!'

I pulled hard on the rope, dragging Mike back towards the boat, where Daz and Ben were waiting to help him back on board. A minute later and he was finally safe, standing in the cockpit, soaking wet and shaking with cold and fear. I ran over and hugged him, but he pushed me away. 'Where's Jack?'

Those two words ran through me like an electric shock: suddenly reminding me why we were out here in the first place. We'd been less than sixty yards from Jack's boat when the rogue wave struck us, and it had almost certainly struck them too, but with no power, they'd have had little chance of taking any sort of evasive action. Frantically, I searched the darkness, but there was no sign of the other boat. It was as if it had simply vanished from the face of the planet.

***

As the sky began to lighten, the storm continued to build around us. We'd had to jettison more of the barrels of diesel in order to further reduce the risk that we might be swamped, but still we'd failed to find any trace of Jack's boat.

We'd repeatedly criss-crossed the location where we'd last seen it, but with Jack out of flares, and in the darkness and the heavy seas, we had little chance of finding them again without some sort of clue as to exactly where they were. More worryingly was the fact that we'd had no further contact with Jack, either on the shortwave radio, or, now we were close enough, the VHF radio. We'd called repeatedly, but there was nothing but static.

With daylight, came the chance to see things better and almost immediately Mike spotted an object floating in the sea. 'I saw something. I'm sure I did. Over there.' Mike pointed. 'There it is again!'

I looked towards where Mike was indicating and saw it, too: a life raft, its orange peak clear against the white-flecked water and the grey sky. I turned to Rob. 'What're the chances it's got nothing to do with Jack's boat?'

Rob grimaced. 'Almost zero.'

I swallowed. 'So what do we do now?'

Rob moved the wheel to the left. 'Try to get it alongside and see if there's anyone in it.'

'There's another one!' Sophie had spied a second life raft, off to the left of the first and a few hundred yards beyond it.

My heat leapt. When we'd first seen the flare and then the boat itself, my spirits had soared, but the longer we went without finding any trace of Jack's boat again after the rogue wave had passed, the further, and the faster, they fell. Now, they rose again: whatever had happened, in my mind, life rafts meant survivors, and that could only be a good thing, couldn't it?

'Daz, pull in that sheet. Ben, get the jib. the rest of you, keep an eye on the life rafts. Make sure we don't hit them.' Rob was giving the orders, trying to bring the catamaran alongside the first of the life rafts. When we were within thirty feet, I blew the hand-held foghorn, but there were no signs of life. Rob manoeuvred the boat so it was upwind of the raft, meaning the raft would be on our lee side when we finally reached it. Only then could we hope to find out if there was anyone inside.

'No, Daz, Don't!' Sophie yelled just as Daz jumped.

He landed heavily on the side of the life raft and scrabbled to stop himself being thrown off as it bucked and danced on the waves.

We'd been tacking back and forth for ten minutes, trying to get close enough to the first life raft to bring it alongside, all the time not knowing what we'd find inside when we finally did. We were now within a few yards, but still there was no response from anyone on board. In the heavy weather, Rob was struggling to get the catamaran near enough to it to secure it without ramming into it.

Instead, Daz had offered to leap across, a rope tied around his waist so we could pull it alongside.

Daz steadied himself and gripped onto the side of the life raft before shouting back to where we stood watching him. The wind whipped his words away, but his meaning was clear. Rob had hove the catamaran to, and now Ben and Mike set about the task of pulling Daz, and the life raft he was clinging to, back towards the catamaran. It took a couple of minutes, but finally it was bumping against the left-hand side of the catamaran. Daz secured the rope to it and then unzipped one of the flaps in the orange canopy which covered the life raft. Inside, there was nothing.

'Shit!' Rob thumped the wheel and looked around, searching the surrounding seas until he found what he was looking for. 'There's still the other one.' I could tell he was trying to sound hopeful, but he couldn't hide the despair in his voice.

Daz climbed back onto the catamaran and stared at the empty life raft. 'What do we do with it now?'

Ben shrugged and glanced at Rob. 'Sink it?'

Rob nodded distractedly, all his attention already focussed on the second life raft.

Jeff frowned. 'Why? Shouldn't we keep it? Can't we use it for something?'

Ben turned to Jeff. 'It'll be too difficult to get on board in this wind, and even if we did, there's no way to let the air out of it quickly, it'd just get in the way.

'What about towing it behind us?' Mike was still shivering after his time in the water, but he'd refused to go inside to dry off until we found out what had happened to Jack and the others.

'It'd just slow us down.' Mitch interjected.

Jeff looked from Ben to Mitch and back again. 'But why sink it? We could always come back for it later.'

'So we don't keep seeing it and think it's a different life raft. We'll just waste our time chasing our tail otherwise.' Ben swept past him and into the cabin, returning a second later with a large knife from the galley. He lay down on the deck and leant through the guard rail before slashing at the inflatable rubber ring which formed the outside of the life raft. Almost immediately, it started deflating and then sinking. Ben untied the rope from it, and as he struggled back to his feet, it disappeared beneath the waves. Watching it go, I hoped against hope that this wasn't a bad omen of what was to come.

It took us half an hour to get close enough to the second life raft to see that it, too was empty. By this time, Rob was beside himself with worry. We were certain the life rafts had come from Jack's boat. They were too clean to have been in the water for more than a few hours, but there'd been no other signs of it, and no matter how often we tried, we couldn't raise Jack on either of the radios.

We spent the rest of the day going back and forth across the ocean in the heavy seas, fighting the wind and the rain, desperate for any indication of what might have happened to the others, but other than the two life rafts, we found nothing. As night was starting to fall, we gathered in the cockpit to decide what to do next. Rob was at the helm while the rest of us crowded round.

I watched Rob as his eyes continually darted back and forth across the ever-changing ocean. 'I know you want to keep looking, but I don't think there's much point.'

Rob remained resolute. 'If there's even a chance in a million that they're still out here, I want to keep searching.'

I looked away. 'I know you do, Rob, but I think we've got to face up to it. If they were still out here, we'd either have seen them or heard from them on the radio.' I wiped some stray hair away from the side of my face. 'I hate it as much as you do, but I think we've got to accept that they're gone.'

My voice sounded hollow, even to me. These were the lives of twenty-two people I was talking about: people I'd known and liked; people I'd struggled alongside to survive; people I'd hoped to build a future with. Now they were gone, lost somewhere in the depths of the ocean.

Rob gripped the wheel and glared at me. 'I'm the captain. If I say we keep looking, we keep looking.' An anger burned in his eyes that I'd never seen before. There was something else too, but I couldn't quite tell what: Disbelief? Desperation? Fear?

Mitch stepped forward. 'Rob, I know how much Jack and the rest of the Hope Town community meant to you, but I think you need to face up to the reality of the situation. They're gone, and there's nothing more you can do for them.'

Rob stared at her for a moment, his eyes glistening, then he flung his arms around her and buried his head in her neck, his loud sobs echoing around the cockpit. As Mitch led him away, I saw the others watch him, wondering, like I was, if Rob was going to be okay. I glared at them. 'Don't look at him like that. He'll be fine.'

I hoped I sounded more confident than I felt. Daz glanced at Ben. 'So, who's in charge?'

I glowered at Ben, almost daring him to say he was. He was, after all, the next most experienced after Rob, and possibly even more so, so he was the logical person to take over. To my surprise, however, he didn't move to stand behind the wheel. Instead, he nodded towards me. 'CJ is.'

Silently, I stepped behind the wheel and turned it until we were heading back towards Mingulay. We had to accept that we'd lost Jack and the others, and all we could do was head back to the island that was now our home.

***

The sun was creeping over the eastern horizon as we pulled into the bay on Mingulay. The storm had finally blown itself out and the sky was starting to clear. Here and there, patches of pale blue were visible in amongst the thinning clouds. The sailboats we'd gathered together for the rest of the Hope Town community to live on while we rebuilt more of the cottages swayed back and forth as they rode at their anchors, reminders of those we had lost. They'd got so close, survived so much, only to be swallowed up by the sea just a few hours short of what would've been their salvation. It seemed so cruel that they'd made it so far only to have been lost so near to the end.

Rob had yet to come back out on deck, and nor had Mitch. I hoped she'd be able to comfort him, to stop him slipping into the black pit of despair into which he'd sunk before. I'd never been able to do it, but she shared a connection with him that I didn't and I hoped that would make all the difference. Jeff and Mike sat despondent, staring out to sea, blank expressions on their faces. Jack and Andrew had been like family to them, as had many of the others, and they were having trouble processing the fact that they were no longer there.

Ben, Daz and Sophie were doing their best to keep out of our way. Other than as a voice on the other end of the radio, they hadn't known Jack, and they knew almost nothing of those who'd died alongside him. They knew it was a tragedy, but it wasn't their tragedy: it was ours. Mine, Rob's, Mike's and Jeff's. After all, we were the ones who'd known them best.

I stared across to the island, remembering how it had felt the first time we'd pulled into the bay, of creeping ashore to check that there were no infected hiding in the hut, and of finding the dead man's body. Now, more than ever, I felt his terror at being left alone in the world. Even though there were others here with me, we were still only eight. What hope did we have of surviving with so few of us? Jack and the others had been more than friends: they had been the community with which we'd hoped to be able to build some sort of future. Without them, could we still succeed? Could we still survive now it was only just us? And us alone? As far as we knew, we were the last of humanity; just eight of us: we were all that was left. How could we possibly hope to carry on for long when everyone else was gone? Would we not be whittled down, one by one, until the last of us, left all alone in the world finally went mad and did what the unnamed man had done, shortly before we'd arrived on Mingulay? By then, there'd be no one left to find the last body, no one left to bury it, to mourn their passing. With the last of us would go the last of humanity. Finally, the infected would have won.

Epilogue

We stood at the stone calendar, looking out to the west as the sun set. It was a month since we'd lost the rest of the Hope Town community, and as far as any of us could work out, it was a year, more or less, since the world we'd once known had come to an end. We'd gathered here to mark the occasion and mourn all who'd been lost: those we'd known and those we hadn't; those who'd died right at the beginning; and those who'd struggled on, only to be lost later. We each had our own memories, our own missing to mourn, the ones we'd never know what happened to, but who we still knew were gone forever.

The first few days after losing Jack, Andrew and the others had been the most difficult. Rob barely left his cabin, but Mitch stayed with him, helping to pull him through. Mike and Jeff were like ghosts, drifting around, physically present, but mentally absent, lost in their own worlds filled with anguish and pain. I tried to do things to cheer them up, to rouse them back to life, but I was as lost as they were. How could I bring them back to a place that I didn't know how to get to myself?

Then things started to change. It was gradual at first: the winds weakened, the skies became more blue, the rain lessened off. Flowers started to appear amongst the tussocks of grass. They were tiny, but they brought colour to the island and to our lives. Then the seabirds returned and the island began to echo with their calls: the puffins, with their brightly coloured beaks, waddled around before diving into their burrows, beaks filled with sparkling silver fish; the kittiwakes and the fulmars clung to the rocky cliff edges, their nests little more than rough piles of dried-out seaweed.

Then one morning, Sophie came racing into the hut. I'd been sitting alone, rereading the notes of the lone man who'd taken his own life, wondering if his past was my future, when she burst through the door, a wide grin plastered across her face. 'CJ, you've got to come and see this. It's amazing!'

I glanced at her before returning my gaze to the notebook. 'I'm busy.' Whatever it was, I figured it could wait.

Sophie wouldn't accept this as a response. 'No, you've got to come see.'

Knowing she wouldn't leave me alone until I'd gone out and looked at whatever it was she was talking about, I closed the notebook and got up. By then she was already at the door, beckoning me to follow her. Outside she raced ahead, up towards the old cemetery where we'd buried the man whose words I'd just been reading. When we got there, she turned and pointed. 'Look!'

At first I couldn't see what she was talking about, it was just the usual green, speckled here and there with the white of grazing sheep. Then I realised what she was meaning. Beside half a dozen of the sheep were tiny white bundles, some lying down, others standing unsteadily on legs they didn't quite yet know how to use: they were newborn lambs. Nearby, the rescued cow suckled her rapidly growing calf. Despite everything that had happened, the world was carrying on and at that moment, I knew that we could too. It wouldn't be easy, but I was sure we could do it, even though there were only eight of us.

As the sun dipped below the horizon, we gathered together and I surveyed our little community: Rob had his arms round Mitch, one hand resting on her ever-growing belly which contained what would be the first of the next generation. As our resident medical expert, Sophie had taken on the role of midwife, making sure Mitch ate the right things, monitoring her blood pressure and planning exactly how the birth would go. She'd read everything there was to say on the subject in the medical books she'd retrieved from the clinic on Rhum when we'd gone in search of antibiotics for Jimmy, finding it fascinating, if slightly terrifying. As usual, Mitch was taking everything in her stride and she found the fuss Sophie was making most amusing. She figured that since women had been giving birth successfully for thousands of generations before the invention of modern medicine, there was little for her to worry about, but nonetheless, she listen to what Sophie had to say.

Daz had his arm draped over Sophie's shoulder, and was whispering into her ear. By her reckoning, she'd turned fifteen the week before, but she seemed so much older. I remembered when I was fifteen and how I'd felt and acted, and I knew the fifteen-year-old me would never have been able to cope with everything that had been thrown at her as well as she had. Then again, I'd never have thought the nineteen-year-old me could have coped either, but here I was. Or was I twenty by now? I had to admit I'd completely lost track.

I wondered about Daz and Sophie's relationship, how they'd handle it. They seemed to be taking it slowly, instinctively knowing that in such a small community, they'd only have one chance to get it right. A few days before Sophie's birthday, I'd found Daz up here by the calendar, staring at it intently. He wanted to do something special for her, but he couldn't work out what. Eventually, he'd settled for arranging a trip over to Rhum, but not to land. After what happened to Jimmy: we no longer trusted anywhere where there had once been infected, even if they were no longer present. Instead, it was just to spend time anchored in the bay as near to her mum's grave as we dared go. It was hardly a happy day, but it was just what Sophie needed.

Off to the left, Jeff and Mike stood slightly apart, Dougie lying next to them. I wondered what their futures held. There'd be none of the opportunities for the usual landmarks in the lives of teenage boys, like first girlfriends, first cars and first break-ups. Yet, I was sure that, somehow, they'd cope.

Beside me, stood Ben. We'd continued to grow ever closer to each other, but despite how I felt inside, I'd resisted taking things further than friendship. Part of me was doing this because of my memories of Jon, and the fact that it would've felt like I was betraying him in some way, but another part of me was doing it to protect myself: I'd loved Jon and it had been torture to lose him. I wasn't sure I could risk putting myself through all that again. What if I did get together with Ben, and then I lost him too? It would be too much to have to do that twice in one lifetime.

I looked at Ben as he stared off into the distance and I wondered what was going through his mind. He turned and caught me watching him. I quickly glanced away, but I could feel my cheeks flush. I sneaked a look back and saw a broad smile spread across his face. In the last year, there had been so much tragedy and loss and sadness; the world had changed beyond all recognition and in a way that none of us could ever have predicted. My world had once been little more than school, and shopping, and gossiping with friends. Now, it was this island and the seven people who surrounded me.

The way the world was, there were no certainties any more, and all we could do was make the most of whatever time we had left in it. I wondered what was really stopping me taking my relationship with Ben further. Was it fear of what might happen? If that was all, I knew that I was being stupid. I didn't know what the future would hold for me, for any of us, but at that moment, I decided I couldn't let that stop me trying to be happy. I reached out and took Ben's hand in mine; I felt its warmth against my skin as I finally let the feelings I'd been trying so hard to keep locked away surface, lifting my heart and my spirit. Ben glanced down, surprised, then he looked at me and grinned. The past was gone, and I had to let it go: all of it. This was my future now, and I was going to make the most of it.

About the Author:

Colin M. Drysdale has worked as a marine biologist for almost twenty years. During this time, he has travelled extensively and spent much of his professional career on or near the sea. He is also a keen sailor and has sailed in Scotland, the Bahamas, Florida, Newfoundland and Labrador.

The Island At The End Of The World is the third book in his *For Those In Peril* series, and again he draws on his own experiences of life at sea, and of sailing between remote Scottish islands, to thread his story of post-apocalyptic survival into the local landscapes where it is set. In particular, he drew on his experiences of visiting Mingulay, an uninhabited island off Scotland's west coast, in the mid-1990s, to provide an authentic feel of the daily struggles of life on such a remote outpost.

He now lives in his native Glasgow, where he runs a small business providing mapping advice to ecologists and marine biologists. He is the author of countless academic papers and a number of technical books. This is his third novel.

If you would like to find out more about the world of *The Island At The End of The World*, and the *For those in Peril* series in general, visit:

www.ForThoseInPeril.net

Printed in Great Britain
by Amazon.co.uk, Ltd.,
Marston Gate.